MY SOUL TO KEEP

Carol was snapping her fingers and rolling her neck to the music when the cocktail waiter stopped at their table and took their food and drink orders.

She wasn't getting any invitations to dance, and this was all right with her. She wasn't particular about dancing anyway. "I'll be right back," she said, getting up and weaving between tables on her way to the ladies' room to wash her hands before her food arrived.

On her way back to the table, someone grasped her arm.

"Terrence!" Carol smiled, glad to see him.

Terrence was still dressed in the tan suit, just as she, Mavis, and Tanika had not bothered to change clothes after work, either. He smiled and gathered her to him, and without asking her, he began moving to the slow rhythm of blues as the contralto's voice lowered to a salacious mourn. As she moved to the beat, Carol had the strangest feeling that she and Terrence were supposed to be together. She did not believe in coincidences. Maybe she was meant to be happy after all, she mused, feeling a warmth travel to her heart as Terrence hugged her to him even tighter.

"Can I give you a ride home?" he asked.

"Yes," Carol said, as the cocoon that she had once wrapped her heart in slipped completely away, and any distrust she'd had seemed to vanish. She knew then that it was time for her to live an eager and passionate life. She considered her musing as she looked at him. His face seemed to have been holding a secret message for her. However, with all of her consideration to allow herself happiness, she still wanted to take her time, usually rushing into anything was the reason for her troubles.

The music was coming to an end when he touched his lips to her red mouth and brushed a feathery kiss against her. As he walked her back to the table, Carol felt as light as the kiss he had planted on her.

MY SOUL TO KEEP

Marcella Sanders

BOOKS

BET Publications, LLC
http://www.bet.com
http://www.arabesquebooks.com

ARABESQUE BOOKS are published by

BET Publications, LLC
c/o BET BOOKS
One BET Plaza
1900 W Place NE
Washington, DC 20018-1211

All Kensington Titles, Imprints, and Distributed Lines are available at special quantity discounts for bulk purchases for sales promotions, premiums, fund-raising, and educational or institutional use. Special book excerpts or customized printings can also be created to fit specific needs. For details, write or phone the office of the Kensington special sales manager: Kensington Publishing Corp., 850 Third Avenue, New York, NY 10022, attn: Special Sales Department, Phone: 1-800-221-2647.

First Printing: January 2003
10 9 8 7 6 5 4 3 2 1

Printed in the United States of America

her t
"Why
clutching
herself an
lips.

Chapter One

Glancing at the time on her wristwatch, Carol Grant stepped out of the boutique and rushed past five stores down to the post office. Realizing that she had less than eight minutes to mail the package, she quickened her steps, half running and half walking. If she had worn the flare-tail dress instead of the tight cool white linen summer dress, she could run faster. She toyed with that thought, which was followed by another worrisome recollection. If she didn't get the dress to Jay Prescott on the promised date, she would never hear the last of it.

She glanced up from her watch just in time to collide with her neighbor, attorney Terrence Johnson. She stumbled back, almost losing her balance, when she felt his strong broad hand grasp her waist, steadying her on three-inch heels.

"don't you look where you're going?" she asked, the package to her breast after she composed took a good, long hard look at his kissable

"I wasn't looking at my watch," he said, taking his eyes off her for a moment and looking at the package. "And running, trying to get to the post office before it closed." Terrence tightened his grasp, drawing her close enough for her to catch a faint scent of his cologne that had primarily worn off after a long exhausting day at work.

"I'm sorry," Carol apologized, realizing that she should have been thankful that he had stopped her from falling. She looked into his ebony eyes, then allowed her gaze to travel in admiration over his dark suit. "But I would like to mail this package today," she said, pushing at his hand to get out of his grasp.

"I think it might be too late," Terrence said, settling his eyes on her full red lips, stirring an unwanted rapture inside her that settled around her heart and was threatening to unwrap the cocoon that had kept her passionate emotions safe.

"If you let me go, maybe I can get inside before the post office closes," she said, pressing the package to her with one hand, and pushing his hand off her waist.

"I don't think that's necessary," he said, sliding his hand from her waist. Carol noticed that his fair complexion seemed a little flushed from the late-afternoon dry Georgia heat.

"I might . . ." She turned away from him in time to see the postmaster pull the lock down on the door. Carol turned back to him and shook her head slowly. Having missed mailing the package today was not the end of the world. But having run into Terrence and feeling his firm touch against her body promis melt the ice around her heart.

"Thanks for stopping me from falling," she ing unlike her usual self. It was not like he melodramatic over a man. But

Georgia and remet Terrence Johnson, her feelings were beginning to change.

"You're welcome." He tossed her another warm glance as she was turning to go back to the boutique. "Wait," he said, covering Carol's wrist with his wide hand and pulling her back to him as several people passed, and lingered, watching what Carol suspected they thought was an intimate moment between her and the counselor. "It's my fault that you didn't get a chance to mail the package."

"Maybe," Carol said, "but not entirely." Because she'd been balancing the boutique's accounts, she had waited too long to go to the post office.

"To say I'm sorry, let me buy dinner for you tonight." Terrence held her gaze, and she felt the unexpected warmth return, slowly sweeping through her. She looked away, turning her gaze to several business owners who were taking their wares inside their stores, preparing to close for the day.

"Thanks, Terrence, but it's not necessary for you to feel guilty because the post office closed before I could get there," she said, feeling a warm breeze stirring and touching her, mingling with the heat that the most handsome man in town was inspiring inside her.

"I think dinner is necessary, and you have to eat," he reminded her.

Carol silently agreed. Nevertheless, this was the last place that she thought she would get a dinner date. It had been a couple of years since she'd had time off from her job. She had chosen to take her vacation in Georgia because it seemed to have been the perfect place for her to relax for three months.

"What do you say?" Terrence asked, pushing his into his trouser pockets.

Preferably yes, she mused, but she'd had enough of going out to dinner with guys like Terrence Johnson.

Tall, handsome, and rich. The last dinner date she had accepted had turned into a steamy and heavy love affair that lasted for about six months. It was too bad that she'd been the one left to pick up the pieces of her shattered heart. "No," she said, understanding clearly that Terrence was probably different than her last lover. But when he touched her, familiar sensations swirled inside her.

"Come on, Carol," he said.

"Not tonight," Carol replied. *And probably not ever,* she pondered, remembering the first evening that she had arrived in the small town, when she had noticed him, getting out of the black Mercedes across the street from the house she was sharing with her cousin for the summer. That evening, she had almost broken her neck trying to get a better look at him before he disappeared inside a huge white house.

"Why?" he asked, as if she was inclined to give him an answer.

"My reason for not sharing dinner with you tonight is none of your business," she said politely, realizing that Terrence was probably not used to having anyone in town refuse a chance to go out with him. He was the talk of the whole town and he knew it, she mused, holding his gaze and not blinking. Just because he was in town defending, pro bono, a poverty-stricken teen-ager who had been accused of murder, was not a reason for him to imagine that she was required to give him an explanation as to why she was refusing his invitation for dinner tonight.

"When can we make that dinner date happen?" he asked, his eyes traveling away from hers and settling her lips again.

"I don't know," Carol replied, wishing that s'
forget the pain that she had finally rid herself of,
of the times that she had been in love. Not only

her trust wilted for the opposite sex, but she could not trust herself. Carol knew herself well enough to know that going out with Terrence Johnson would probably lead to more dinner dates, and she would like him more than she should. She was also old enough to know that he might have been in Georgia alone, but back in New Jersey there was probably a woman whom he loved, who was waiting for him to return to her as soon as the case was over.

"Okay, Carol," he said, and her eyes snapped to his. "But I still think that we should go out tonight." He smiled as he spoke to her, flashing a set of beautiful white teeth. "Anyway, I think we should keep dinner in mind for a later date," he said.

Carol was surprised that Terrence remembered her name, since it had been so many years after their first meeting. Maybe he had noticed her name on the return address of the package, she considered, shifting her gaze back to his handsome face. She was not certain. However, there was one thing that she was sure of and that was to keep distance between herself and the man who had the ability to race warm shudders through her.

"What're you doing in Georgia anyway?" he inquired in such a husky tone, she thought that if she did not get away from him, she would change her mind and accept his dinner invitation for this evening.

Carol opened her mouth to speak and not one word came out as she watched him remove his hands from his trouser pockets and fold his arms across his wide muscular chest. Finally she was able to look down at nothing in particular except the gray concrete. "I . . ." she started, allowing her gaze to travel up from his black wing tips, along his blue suit trousers, to his narrow waist and wide chest until her gaze stopped on his sensual lips again, and the black smooth mustache circling his mouth. "I'm on vacation," she said, not wanting to discuss her personal life with him.

"I wish I could say the same, but duty calls," Terrence said, unfolding his arms and pushing his hands inside his trouser pockets again. It had been a long time since he had seen her, he mused, and other than speaking or waving to her while they both were in town, this was his first time talking to her after many years. "You know, Carol, it's been a long time."

"Yes, it has been a few years," she said, recalling how time had a way of slipping past when she was not paying attention. She had to have been no more than nineteen, and Terrence had been at least twenty or twenty-one, that summer that she had traveled down from New Jersey with her cousin Mavis during their break from college. Mavis was visiting her mother in her new home, and she had come along to enjoy the quiet south central Georgia town.

"How have you been?" he asked, interrupting her memories.

"I've been fine," she said, remembering that Terrence had been visiting his grandfather that same summer. He had asked her out on a date and she had refused him because she was engaged.

Terrence reached out and, grasping her hand, he stroked his thumb against her fingers, drawing her out of the past, as he walked them away from a few of the merchants that were leaving their shops. "I stopped by a few nights ago to speak to you and you were out."

"I was volunteering my services," Carol said. She had gone to the church to play the piano for a choir rehearsal since the pianist was not feeling well.

"Mavis didn't tell you?" he asked.

"Yes, she told me," Carol replied, remembering that her cousin had mentioned Terrence had stopped by and had asked for her. Carol had not given the information much consideration, since most people in town often stopped by to visit their neighbors unannounced. "I'm sorry that I missed you," she said, slipping her hand out of his, wishing that she could shake the sensual feelings his touch was stirring around her heart. Carol sighed and met his soft sexy glance. "I'm surprised that you remembered me," she said.

"I usually remember the people that I like," Terrence said, moving closer to her, getting out of the way of a man who was walking past. "I was beginning to think that you're avoiding me. And since you're not accepting my invitation to dinner tonight . . . maybe you are—I don't know," he said.

"I've been busy," Carol said, and watched his amused glance. "Well, I've been helping Mavis," she clarified as she made an attempt to smother her smile. There was not much for her to do during the day while Mavis worked at the boutique for her mother. So Carol had decided to work a few days to keep herself from getting bored.

"As long as you're not avoiding me."

Terrence leaned into her, and again she inhaled the heady scent of his cologne that mingled with the late hot summer afternoon, and she wanted him to go away. "No, Terrence, I'm not avoiding you." But when she had noticed him sitting on his front porch at night while she was out snatching a cool breeze, she often had wondered if he was still a bachelor. When she could not stop wondering about him, she would get up and go inside.

"I've noticed that every time I come out to get fresh air, you get off your swing and go inside." A smile tipped the edge of his lips.

Carol looked out at the street, not intending to discuss her reason for going inside when she saw him. "Are you married, Terrence?"

"No," he said, "but the last time I talked to you, you were engaged. Did you get married?" he asked her, realizing that he had not felt a ring on her finger, but then, these days, some people did not wear bands for whatever reason.

"Yes, and now I'm divorced," she said, moving away from him. "It was nice talking to you again," she said.

"Yes." He bent his head close to her lips. "Take care, Carol," he whispered softly, brushing his lips against her cheek.

When he walked away, Carol felt as if Terrence had caressed her soul and opened that special door to her, as she considered that several months had passed since she had allowed a man to make such close contact with her. Her reasons were valid—she'd traveled too many reckless trips down the primrose path. She had taken her own sound advice and made a choice to keep a distance between herself and affairs of the heart.

Carol walked into the boutique, enjoying the cool air from the air conditioner, and admiring the new wide-brim hats that Mavis was displaying in the showcase. She dropped the package on the counter and went to help her and Tanika close the shop. "You didn't mail your package," Mavis said, straightening up from setting another hat in the glass case. "The post office was closed?"

"I bumped into Terrence Johnson, and by the time I had argued with him for a few minutes, it was too late to mail Jay's dress."

Chapter Two

Another week passed before Carol saw Terrence again. She and Mavis had finished their Chinese dinner, and as usual Carol kept to her after-dinner routine. She showered and sat on the front-porch swing, enjoying the cool night breeze and noticing the soft white light radiating from the windows of Terrence's large white house. Carol had also noticed that his car was not parked in the usual space, in front of the row of dark green hedges that separated the manicured lawn from the street.

Digging her heel into the porch floor, she gave the swing a light shove and rested her head against the green floral cushion as she slowly swung back and forth. The chatter of singing crickets and croaking frogs split the silence in the dark starry night. Except for those sounds, there was pure silence—peace and serenity were hers, and her life was wonderful.

Carol's days of worrying over dates, and love, were behind her. She had accepted her fate. Unlike most women she knew, who had been hurt by affairs of the heart and had immediately hurtled themselves back into the game of love, she had chosen to stand still and stay free of those special emotions. She had come to terms with reality, understanding clearly that the feelings that made her heart sing and her body warm no longer belonged to her.

She closed her eyes and allowed those thoughts to toy with her, and mingle with the robust sound of a neighbor's truck, and the soft thrum of a car slowly easing up the street, and the dull thump of a car door closing, while the aftermath of delicious aromas of Southern home cooking filled the air.

Carol relaxed, remembering plainly everything she had always wanted in her life and had never received. It wasn't because she had not tried. She had wanted more than anything to stay married to Boris because she had loved him. However, Boris's love for her was different than what she had expected, or even dreamed about. She shut the memories out, pushing them to the farthest crevices of her mind. She had come to Georgia to rest, not to remind herself of her past, an earlier passionless time that was filled with so much pain and had left her with bitter memories.

"Can I sit with you?" The husky familiar voice floated out to her, and she did not have to open her eyes. Recognizing the fragrance of his heady cologne mingling with the scent of soap, and the sound of his voice, she knew that Terrence had stopped by to visit her.

"Yes," she said, opening her eyes and noticing the loose-fitting faded jeans, his sleeveless white T-shirt that unmasked a set of healthy biceps, and the worn-out tennis shoes he was wearing. She patted the cushion beside her, offering him a seat. She could not affirm that she did not want him to visit her; it was nice having him to talk to at the end of the day, distracting her from thinking of her embittered past. Spending an evening with Terrence was probably what she needed, she mused. He was a man whom she could talk to and spend a few comfortable hours with. Carol believed that he would not do or say anything that would make her change her mind about the choices she had made for her social and personal life.

"So, how have you been?" Terrence broke the silence between them.

"I've been fine," Carol said. "I'm resting," she added, taking into consideration that helping Mavis with the account records at the boutique and with other minor chores was nothing compared to her work at the office back home. "And yourself?" she asked, giving him a side glance.

"I'm good," he replied. "I would be better if you ate dinner with me every evening." He chuckled softly, and the sound of his laughter mingled with the din of crickets and other water creatures that played in the nearby creek at night.

"Terrence I'm sure that any woman in this town will have dinner with you." She smiled, but she was serious.

"Maybe," he agreed, crossing his leg over his thigh and studying her. "You didn't have dinner with me last week," he said, and without looking at him, she felt as if his eyes were burning into her. "So, why would you think that the other women in town will want to go out with me?"

Carol laughed and turned to him. "Terrence, how long have you been in Georgia working on your case?"

"Several months," he admitted in a husky tone, and smiled at her.

"Are you saying that not one woman in this town will go out with you?" Carol asked in a teasing tone. She suspected that he was not serious.

"You're the only woman I've asked." His joviality

shifted, casting a serious expression on his attractive face.

"Are you serious?" Carol smiled, and in the dim light she stole a glance at him. She could not believe that Terrence Johnson, the powerhouse lawyer, had not been out with at least one woman since he had been in town.

"I am serious," he said, leaning closer to her. "And why aren't you on a cruise or vacationing somewhere other than this town?" He leaned away and looked at her.

Carol had no intention of telling him all of her reasons for not indulging herself with a luxurious vacation. The serenity that she found in the small town had the ability to calm all of her senses. "I like the peace and harmony," she said, feeling in control of herself and not feeling the familiar warmth she had encountered the day Terrence had kept her from falling. However, the sensual emotions that Terrence had ignited in her that afternoon had lingered with her until late that evening before fading and returning to the safe place in her heart, and had been replaced by her good sense.

"How long have you been divorced?" he asked, stretching his long legs and bringing the slow sway of the swing to a halt before he charged her with another sensual glance. His dark gaze seemed to have been warming her, and Carol felt the need to release the unwanted desire that reminded her how long it had been since she had been attracted to a man as handsome as Terrence. She had frozen her true emotion in the deep crannies of her soul. So why was Terrence's gaze having an effect on her? "I have been divorced for fourteen years," she said quietly, blaming her imagination for her heart, body, and soul's reaction to him.

"You didn't stay married long," he replied, giving the swing another push with the weight of his body.

Carol studied his face, and the shadow that was cast on his face by the dim streetlight made him appear even more handsome.

"I married too young and I made a mistake," she confessed, hoping that he would not continue on the subject of her broken marriage, because any subject concerning her ex-husband was not up for discussion.

Terrence didn't know if he was sorry or not that Carol had not stayed married, but she was calm, as if his asking hadn't disturbed her at all. He wanted to ask the reason for her divorce, but decided to drop the subject. She was probably involved in a serious relationship by now. He let that thought wing its way across his mind. "So, who's the lucky guy?" he asked, and held his breath.

"If you're asking if I have a boyfriend"—she paused—"I don't." The conversation was not going in the direction that Carol wanted. Terrence was asking too many personal questions, as if her life meant something to him. "But I'm happy with things as they are," she expressed quietly, forcing herself to smile.

"I can't say that I'm sorry that you're divorced," he replied, and then he was quiet as he permitted his thoughts to wander back to the past summers.

The first day that he had seen her, he had wanted to take her out. It had taken him all week to build up his nerve to ask her to the dance that was being held at the only club in town. She had refused him, waving her ring finger in his face, telling him that she was engaged and that her wedding was taking place as soon as she returned to New Jersey. His dreams of dating Carol Grant disappeared and he almost hated the man who was going to be her husband. But Terrence had to admire Carol for her honesty, and her loyalty to the man whom she ultimately would spend her life with, or so he had thought.

"I'm happy with the decision that I made to end the

marriage," she said in an even quieter voice. "Boris and I have moved on with our lives." The marriage was over, but the scars on her heart and her soul had remained, crippling her emotions, and she did not think she would ever trust herself to love again.

"Will you ever marry again?" Terrence knew from the sound of her voice he should have dropped the subject, but he was curious.

"No, I'm never going to marry again." She leaned slightly toward him and smiled at him. "I thought you would've been married by now and the father of four or five children."

"No, I haven't found anyone that wants to marry me," he replied, knowing that he had not been searching for a wife for a long time. He had purposely kept himself busy, leaving himself only sparse amounts of time to date, since his last serious relationship.

"I can't tell you that marriage is not nice," Carol said. "I happened to be one of the unlucky ones."

Terrence could make no comparison to her past, but since his last relationship had not worked out, he had decided to take things slow. Coming to Georgia to work the Edmond Sampson case was what he'd needed, more than the vacation he had given up. "Choosing the right partner can be a problem sometimes," he said, letting out a sigh.

"Whenever you're ready to settle down, I can guarantee you that you will not have to look too long for a wife." Carol smiled, giving him the truest advice she knew. There were women she knew who were taking cruises just to meet a handsome and successful gentleman whom they might possibly become friends with, and with any luck, their friendship might grow into a romantic relationship and finally lead to marriage. "So, you're just making excuses," she said, and laughed. Any woman in her right mind, who did not have the problem

that she suffered from, would love the status, and qualities, and gentleness that Terrence Johnson possessed.

"When I'm ready to get married, I'll let you know,"
he said, settling his fingers on her hand and squeezing
her lightly.

"I'm expecting an invitation to your wedding," she
teased, enjoying Terrence's playful attitude, and
attempting to ignore the warm shudder that was waffling
its way to her heart.

He smiled. "Not too long ago I was planning to get
married," he said, and shrugged his broad shoulders.
"Things didn't work out—and I'm still a bachelor. And
after that I made myself unavailable to anything except
casual dating," he assured her.

Carol wondered what had happened, and within seconds her inquisitive nature had gotten the best of her.
"What happened?" she asked, understanding how a
relationship that had gone wrong could force a person
to make decisions that were safe for their hearts.

Terrence took an unsteady breath. "She wasn't marrying me for love, but for her own personal gain," he
replied.

Carol blinked and turned away. Two years ago, she
had thought she was in love again, until she had found
her lover to be an unfaithful liar. It was then that she
decided that love and romance, and chocolates and
flowers from any man meant nothing more than a bait
to lure her into a loveless trap and leave her with the
awful pain of having given and then lost.

"I don't like being used," he said. "I'm sure one day
soon I'll find the right woman." He stretched his arm
the length of the swing's back, and touched his fingers
to the top of her shoulder. "How long are you staying
in Georgia?" He changed the subject, and stroked his
fingers softly against the firm muscle of her shoulder.

"I'll be here until the end of the summer," Carol answered.

"You have been in town over a month and you're not bored?" Terrence asked.

"No, being here is not that bad," she said, glad of the choice she had made for herself. "When do you think the trial will be over?" She changed the subject, because she was not telling Terrence her reasons for spending her summer in the town.

"Probably by the end of the summer, if not sooner," he stated, and looked at her. "It's kind of nice being here, away from all the traffic, and the people who I usually run into at nightclubs."

Carol listened to him, allowing her thoughts to wheel back to Terrence's reasons for not having been married. She was certain that he would find the right person one day—unlike herself. She could hardly allow herself to think about marriage. Sharing her life with another person again would most likely make for an unhappy union. She had grown accustomed to her free lifestyle. She answered to no one but God, her boss, and herself. She was sure that any holy nuptials she agreed to would result in her and her husband's despair. But she had no need to worry. She had carefully considered and evaluated this part of her life. So far, she had not found any man who was strong enough to change her mind.

Nevertheless, Carol could not help but think of the children she would never have, and the tears began to settle in her eyes. She blinked the tears back to the proper place inside her, and reminded herself that her biological clock was probably on the verge of coming to a halt. She let the thought taper and she continued to enjoy sitting inches away from Terrence and enjoy their conversation. "Terrence, what do you consider to be the right woman?" Carol asked seriously.

"I like honesty, strength, and a woman who knows

what she wants, Carol. I can do without the game play-ing," he said, stroking his fingers against her shoulder.

"Terrence, you'll be fine," she said, sounding the way she did when she was speaking to her brother's preteen and teenage sons. "There are plenty of nice hardworking women out there who're looking for a good man."

"Are you one of them?" he asked her in a voice that rose just above a whisper.

For a moment she played with his question. "Ter-rence, I am not the one to brag myself. But then, I'm not looking for a husband." She had given him the best answer, hopefully without sounding conceited. She knew exactly what she wanted, but she also knew that she couldn't have it. Not because she may experience the same abuse that she had been through, but because she did not trust herself to choose the right man to love. Even though she knew that she had to trust in a power higher than herself, she had done that twice, and both times had been disappointed and hurt. "And why are we talking about love and marriage anyway?" she asked, ready to change the subject at any given moment.

"Because you wanted to know why I couldn't find a woman to be my wife," Terrence answered her. "You still haven't answered my question. Are you a strong woman?"

Carol knew her strengths. She worked hard for what she wanted, she was dependable and honest, at least as much as most people she knew in regular situations. But she often made the mistake of loving too much. Because of this, she would not have a family of her own. She glanced at Terrence just as another surprising tear stung her, and she wiped her eyes with the back of hand.

"What—did I say something to upset you?" He lifted his arm from the back of the swing and touched her chin, tilting her face upward and looking into her eyes.

Carol touched his hand, carefully moving his fingers away. "I think it's time for me to go to bed," she said, rising from the swing, with him joining her at the door.

"I think we should talk again," he said, touching her wrist, and she felt another unwanted shiver.

Chapter Three

Terrence circled his arms around Carol's slender waist, pulled her to him, and leaned into her. All he had to do was kiss her, he mused, seriously considering how sweet she probably was, when he felt the pressure from her soft palms against his shoulders.

"This has been a long hot day," she said in a hushed voice, trying to sound as lighthearted as possible. But instead, her voice broke, and she felt that she would not be able to control the tears this time. But she controlled herself, and the tears that she had cried so many times for the love, the children, and the life that she wanted and had finally given up on. Beneath the warm golden glow of the porch light, she studied his face, willing herself to shut out the sensual emotions that were slowing racing through her. "Good night, Terrence," she said, giving him another light shove that didn't move him an inch this time.

Instead of speaking, he gathered her close to him again. His lips brushed hers, and Carol felt a shiver race up her spine as he explored her lips with a feathery kiss.

Carol knew that she should have screamed at him to leave her alone; she should have pushed and hammered her fists against his chest. Maybe she should have . . . Her thoughts ebbed and she slipped her arms around his neck and allowed herself to be swept into his passionate world, until finally he drew her in completely, parting her lips with the tip of his tongue. His kiss was like a balm uncovering and bringing to life the passion that lay deep inside her heart.

He raised his dark wavy-haired head and looked at her. Then without warning he touched his lips to hers again. "Good night." He smothered the words against her lips, still holding her close and wanting to kiss her again, instead of releasing her from his embrace and going home. He had not meant to kiss her. Nevertheless, she was as sweet as he'd suspected. "I'm . . ." He stopped. He wasn't sorry that he had kissed her. He was only sorry that he had no control over himself. At least he could have waited. But she felt good in his arms, and he couldn't resist the temptation to taste her full lips. This was not like him, losing his willpower. He lowered his head again, touching her lips again with his. "Carol, will you have dinner with me tomorrow night?" he asked, wishing that he could stay with her forever, instead of asking her to eat dinner with him.

As much as she wanted to accept his invitation, she couldn't because she had already made plans for tomorrow evening. Nevertheless, she knew that it would not be long before she would join him for dinner, because the domino effect had already begun. He had kissed her and she had kissed him back; he had held her tight and she had clung to him as if her life depended on him. It seemed that every promise she had made to herself, Terrence had chosen to challenge, and was unwilling to leave her to her dull, loveless life. At the moment of their passionate kiss, she knew she had chosen a mighty opponent.

"I'm busy tomorrow night," she answered. She and Mavis had chosen to have a girls' night out every Friday night since the both of them had been in town for the summer.

"You're busy Saturday night, too?" He slipped his arms from her waist and backed away slowly.

"Saturday night sounds good," she agreed, reaching back and twisting the doorknob and opening the door.

"I'll call you tomorrow," Terrence said, and she watched as he walked off the porch and crossed the street to the house that had once belonged to his grandfather.

Instead of going inside, Carol sat down on the swing, sinking her round hips against the green-and-white-floral cushion, and she continued to watch as he crossed the street. If she was going to be honest, first she had to be honest with herself. She could not deny that she did not want to date Terrence or even love him. The bondage that had held her captive for so many years seemed to have disappeared, releasing her from her fears, and moving her toward happiness, peace, and a desire to love again.

Carol wet her lips with the tip of her tongue, savoring the burning kiss that he'd left to linger on her lips, and looked out across the green yard that spread out in front of her, clustered with bunches of red, yellow, and purple blossoms sitting atop healthy green stems, many of which lined the gray-bricked driveway. As she took in the lovely sight, and enjoyed the cool summer late-night breeze, she allowed her mind to drift to the past.

She had been in her second year in college, studying

for a degree in business administration, when she met assistant professor Boris Myers. He was tall, muscular, intelligent, and ten years her senior.

At the college homecoming party she had noticed Boris watching her from across the room. He had finally pushed his way though the crowd of students and other guests to dance with her. They talked and danced for the rest of the evening, each getting to know the other. He told her that he worked at a university in New Brunswick, and that he was spending the weekend with his older brother, Professor Matthew Myers.

After that night, Boris drove up to the Atlantic City area and visited her every weekend. Carol knew that she loved him and not because he was showering her with chocolates, flowers, and jewelry. There were also times when he took her shopping, buying her clothes that she didn't particularly like. But she wore them to please him.

When her aunt Sarah, whom she and her brother had lived with while her father worked on a merchant ship, found out that she was dating the older man, she had a fit. Carol could still hear her sharp voice ringing in her ears. *"Child, that man is too old for you—have you lost your mind?"*

She had turned a deaf ear to her aunt's warning, refusing to listen anymore to anything she had to say about how she should live her life. Carol was past eighteen and a college student. Her aunt's days of bossing her around were over, and she would do what she wanted, when she wanted to do it, and with whomever she chose to do it. Sarah had made life a living hell the years that Carol and her brother, Bretton, had lived with her after their mother died.

At the age of twelve, Carol had had the responsibilities of a grown-up, cleaning, cooking, doing laundry. And when all the chores were completed, she had to find her eleven-year-old brother who usually was out with his friends. They usually were getting into some kind of trouble. She feared that her brother would become a drug addict or go to prison for riding in stolen cars. So she worried, and looked for him in the drug-infested streets at night. She always found him hanging out with the same gang of boys who flirted on the edge of forming a mean gang. With much protest from her brother, she managed to bring him home, but not without threatening to hit the first boy that touched her, using Sarah's night club which she held behind her back.

When that chore was taken care of, she'd complete her homework, and if she had enough time left in the evening, she'd sit at the baby grand her father had given her for a Christmas present the year their mother died, and she would play until her soul danced with pure joy.

The years seemed to drag past, and her only relief besides her music was the day her father arrived home from the sea and stayed with them for three or four months. He took charge of Bretton and she would spend her time doing a minimal amount of chores, playing her piano, reading, and going to the movies alone, unless she went with Mavis. Carol had no girlfriends since her mother's death—her aunt did not allow her to have friends.

The day her father left for his work, she always cried. Her aunt, who had put on a lovely pretense of being nice to her and her brother when their father was home, made certain that their father did not find out that she had forced his daughter to spend her time doing chores alone.

Once, Carol had gathered the nerve to tell her father about the mistreatment that she was receiving while he was away, and he had spoken to his sister about the problem. After that, Carol never told him again, because when her father left them, Sarah had forced Carol to work even harder.

Carol could hardly wait until she became of age. She had made her father promise her that when she turned eighteen, he would buy her and Bretton an apartment. He did, and she took her brother and moved out of Sarah's house.

Bretton was much happier, even though there were times on the weekend that she had to find him. By the time he was seventeen, he had made new friends in their new neighborhood, and with his father's permission and signature, he had enrolled in the local boys' club. But Carol was sure that he had changed because he wasn't being called names anymore by their aunt, or being told how no-good he was, and how he was going to grow up to be nothing more than a bum and a convict.

So when Carol met Boris Myers, her first boyfriend, she was satisfied that she had made the right choice. It was when he asked her to marry him that her father began protesting, reminding her of all the fun she would be missing out with her friends. Carol refused to listen to him, too, because she had no friends.

Finally she convinced her father that she and Boris were in love, and he reluctantly gave her his blessings. She and Boris made plans to marry shortly before school began that fall semester. In the meantime, while she waited for her wedding and her return to college, she spent her summer with Mavis and her aunt Christine in Georgia. Christine had designed and made her the perfect wedding gown, and arranged and planned every detail of her wedding.

That was the summer she met Terrence Johnson, a young man who was attending Princeton University, studying prelaw, and in Georgia visiting his grandfather, Wallace Johnson.

Terrence Johnson was a tall, lanky young man, and

when he asked her to go to the dance with him that late-summer evening, she noticed a silver retainer braced against his white teeth.

With pride she had refused his invitation and showed him her engagement ring. After that day, he never spoke to her again. And the last time she saw him, he was packing his luggage onto the back of his grandfather's truck, heading out for the airport to return to New Jersey. She had returned to New Jersey shortly afterward, and her father quietly gave her away to Boris Myers.

For the first three months, she and Boris's lives were perfect, until he began to be more demanding than her aunt. He even transferred to her college and kept a watch over her and the people she associated with— her friends and classmates. Boris was so demanding that he almost suffocated her, and she could hardly stand him anymore.

By the next spring break, she was certain that she hated her husband, and she could hardly stand for him to touch her. However, their problems began to escalate during that spring break when all of her classmates and friends had gone on their vacations, and she was stuck home going out with Boris, going to conferences and meetings with him.

One night during the spring break holidays, Boris pulled her to him and she refused the love he was offering her. It was then that he had accused her of having a lover. To Carol this was the mishap that tore the last strand of her patience with Boris. She had thrown a pillow in frustration and ran from their bedroom. Hot on her heels, Boris caught up with her, striking her across her face. Screaming and crying, she had gotten away from him and ran three blocks to Bretton, wearing nothing but her nightgown.

She never knew what her brother said or did to Boris, but when she returned to get her clothes a week later,

Boris was limping. He promised her that he would get the thugs that had dragged him into an alley late one evening and tortured him. He told her that he was not certain, but he would put all of his money on a bet that her brother had been behind the attack. She had listened to his complaint and could almost agree that her brother had not stopped visiting his rowdy friends from the other side of town. However, when she sued Boris for a divorce and a sizable amount of money, he hadn't given it to her without exchanging words.

As she recalled those days, Carol wiped the tears that had settled in her eyes. Those were the days that she had allowed herself to be robbed of her trust and the ability to find love that could one day rightfully belong to her.

She now lifted her gaze to Terrence's house as she rose from the swing and started inside. She touched her lips, no longer feeling the kiss, but the gaping hollow in her soul that he had opened like a Pandora's box, the box that once held her stockpiles of passion.

Chapter Four

Terrence Johnson lay on the bed. His bare back felt good against the cool light blue sheets as he stared out between the slightly parted drapes at the star-studded sky. He had come to Georgia to defend a teenager, to give back to the community where his grandfather had been born and raised and where his father and uncles had grown up until they were almost seven and eight years old. He had chosen to defend the young man who had been accused of murder, instead of taking his vacation and because of his choice, Terrence had found the woman that he had wanted to love many years ago.

Carol was everything he liked about a woman, with her round hips, slender waist, and long legs. He closed his eyes, visualizing the kiss that they had shared tonight, seeing her thick black long hair and her full lips that were blushing with just enough color, and complementing her beige complexion. To top that off, she was sweet and he liked everything about her.

Even in the early days, as young as she had been,

Carol had been strong, dependable, and trustworthy, and her values seemed not to have changed much.

But now Carol had changed; he understood that she was different because she had matured with age, but that was not the case. She seemed afraid, and tonight when he noticed the tears in her eyes, he wondered whether she had wanted children, too. But still her problem seemed deeper.

Terrence laced his fingers behind his head and spread his legs and continued to look at the stars sitting against the blue velvet sky as if the sparkling spheres held the answers he was searching for. He didn't want to think the worst, but he could not help but imagine what might have happened to her. Why was she afraid? What were the reasons for her distrust? He had handled many divorce cases and he knew an abused woman when he saw one. He hoped this was not one of her problems, but he could no longer ignore the horrible thoughts that tottered at the edge of his mind.

If she had been assaulted, she needed time to heal, but it had been years, and she should have had counseling by now. Maybe she had not given up on love, he speculated, and considered that Carol might have had a lover that she did not want him to know about. The thought of her having a boyfriend was not sittling right for him. The only boyfriend he wanted Carol to have was him.

At any rate, he had planned to control his actions when he was around Miss Grant, and not behave as he had tonight—kissing her. Terrence also knew that he had to convince Carol that she could trust him. He planned to take his time and keep his hands and his kisses to himself. He had waited a long time for her and without warning she had come back into his life. He would not ruin the second chance that he might have with her.

Then you must behave yourself, his quiet small voice reminded him.

Terrence played with that thought for a while and then reached for the remote control, turning on the television, preparing to watch the world news. It was not long before the low murmuring voices began lulling him to sleep. He closed his tired eyes, and visions of Carol Grant reeled across his mind, along with the memory of painful threatening tears that he had seen in her eyes before he kissed her. Terrence wet his lips with the tip of his tongue, flipped over on his stomach, and slept.

The next morning Carol showered, dabbed on her favorite perfume, slipped into a white silk robe, and headed to the kitchen. She lifted her gaze to the green plants that sat atop the cream-colored cabinets, with leaves that stopped just above the off-white wooden doors. Between those plants sat two bronze stock pots, which she doubted her aunt Christine had ever used.

Carol poured herself a cup of hot coffee that she had made earlier, before Mavis left for work, and sat at the round cream-colored kitchen table, thankful that Mavis had left instead of taking the *Augusta Chronicle* to the boutique with her.

While sprinkling a small amount of sugar into her coffee, Carol allowed her thoughts to waver to Mavis, who had gone through a terrible divorce a year ago. She, too, had taken a well-deserved vacation, which for Mavis was not a vacation at all. Christine had gone off on a gospel revival and to a few other places for the summer, and Mavis, according to Mavis, had jumped at the chance to come to Georgia and work the boutique for her mother. This way she would get a break from seeing her ex-husband on every floor of the hospital where they were both employed. Carol understood her cousin's pain and had almost cheered for Mavis when she had finally divorced him.

Carol stirred the coffee and tasted the hot black liquid for sweetness, as she flipped the newspaper over. The first photograph she saw was of Terrence, and she was unable to control the warmth that swept through her. She wished that she could have pretended that her warm feeling was the effect of the coffee. She wasn't that lucky, because pretending that Terrence's picture was not affecting her was no longer working when memories of last night were still running through her mind.

Carol lifted the cup and sipped the hot liquid while reading the article that had been written about him. *Attorney Terrence Johnson, the grandson of the late Wallace Johnson, is in town volunteering his legal services, defending Edmond Sampson, the teenager who is on trial for murder. The Johnson lawyers are known for their powerful defense . . .* Carol stopped reading and turned her attention to the open kitchen window as she overheard the next-door neighbor and her girlfriend gossiping.

"Girl, did you see that last night?" Carol overheard one of the women say.

"Yes, child. I hope he can keep his mind on his work and defend that boy, instead of spending so much time with Christine's niece."

Carol frowned as bits of the women's conversation floated through the open window, compelling her curiosity. She moved to the window to look out and hear the women's discussion clearly, and realized that she was right. The women were discussing her and Terrence's visit and intimate moments.

"While Terrence was up half the night kissing Carol, he should have been home trying to get his rest," Mrs. Benson complained, holding a pink sheet in one hand and resting the other on her broad hips. Her amber skin glistened with beads of perspiration from the morning sun. "These single women can't get a date with Terrence for her." The woman pinned one edge of the pink sheet to the clothesline while her girlfriend held the other end. "Gets on my nerves," she added, and glanced toward the window.

Carol raised her hand to cover her chuckle and knocked over a tin canister that was decorating the shelf she was standing in front of.

"Honey, don't talk too loud. I think she might be listening."

"Yeah, let's go in the house," Mrs. Benson said to her girlfriend. "I should go over there and ask her why she is eavesdropping," Carol's neighbor said, looking over her shoulder as they left the clothesline and walked toward the front of the house.

"Me, too. Down here, flouncing around, getting in everybody's way. I thought she had a husband."

"Oh, no, honey, she's divorced," Mrs. Benson said.

Carol was picking the canister off the floor when the doorbell rang. She set the canister on the shelf and moved swiftly toward the door. This was the day that she was going tell these two women off. Ever since she had been in town, all they did was talk about her and Mavis's personal business. Her aunt Christine needed to be put on punishment for telling them that she and Mavis were divorcées. Carol gave that thought serious consideration as she moved through the foyer, passing the open living room that displayed Christine's comfortable and excellent taste in furniture décor. Her aunt was definitely a tattletale. Carol smiled to herself as she glanced at the overstuffed coral chairs and matching sofa that accented the room along with plenty of green plants rising from huge colorful urns.

As she neared the front door, she wondered if Mrs. Benson had stood in the shadows of the evergreens that separated their property and spied on her and Terrence last night. And to add insult to the injury, they'd had the nerve to complain that *she* was eavesdropping.

Carol pulled open the door with a maddened force. "Good morning," she whispered, glancing into Terrence's black eyes, his tender gaze arousing a flame around her heart and drawing her even farther out of the shell where she had carefully buried her emotions. She lowered her gaze, watching as he pushed his hands into the pockets of his wide-legged khaki pants, making the sleeveless black T-shirt strain against his muscular chest.

"Hi," he said as she lifted her gaze, studying his face, except for a smooth close-cut beard circling his kissable lips.

This morning she was determined to stay in control of herself and keep her distance from him. She would not allow him to touch her and she would not stand too close to him, not because she was not attracted to him, but because she liked him *too* much.

"Can I have a cup of coffee?" Terrence moved toward her, and for the life of her she felt as if she were rooted to the floor. "Yes," she said when he set his hands against her waist and gently moved her away from the entrance so that he could enter the foyer. "I'm terrible at making coffee, unless it's pre-measured," he said. His eyes settled on her lips and the sensation that she had experienced when she saw him seconds ago was gaining strength.

"I might have another cup or two left," Carol said, wishing that he would not touch her, as his hand slipped against her waist again, sending a shivering response to her bare skin underneath the white silk robe.

"Why aren't you at work?" she asked when he'd finally moved his hand off her and she had closed the door.

"It's still early," he said. His expression was so serious,

Carol wondered what else Terrence had stopped by for, other than coffee, as she glanced at the gold-rimmed clock on the wall.

"It's nine o'clock," she said as they moved into the kitchen. Carol felt her hips pulled against the silk robe as she moved in front of him, and she wished that she had been wearing the cool large African housedress that she usually wore before she dressed.

"I don't have any appointments until later today," Terrence said, pulling back a chair and sitting, while she crossed to the counter and filled a mug with black coffee.

"I hope it's not too strong," she said, handing him the steaming mug, then sitting across from him and flipping the newspaper to another page. She looked up in time to see him taste the first sip of hot, black sugarless coffee.

"The coffee is fine," Terrence said, and shot her a sensual smile before he settled his glance on the opened vee of her robe, and she watched his gaze trail down to the imprints of her round firm breasts.

Carol felt her face grow hot along with the rest of her body as she watched his lips part slightly, and she tugged at the edges of her robe, pulling the material closer to the top of her breast, which only made her breasts raise even more. She quickly made the decision to leave well enough alone. Distracting him with small talk would be better, she mused, and began telling him about the article written about him in the morning's paper.

"Did you see it?" She turned back to the front page and pushed the paper toward him, when he reached out, and his fingers brushed against her hands.

"Yeah, but I didn't read the last part," he said, flipping the page to his client's sad photograph, looking at the young man's face for several seconds, before he gave the paper back to Carol.

"I hope Edmond didn't commit this crime," Carol said. "He's so young."

"He's a good kid." Terrence swallowed as a silent question crossed his mind. God, why had he come here this morning? Why hadn't he gone to the diner and drank coffee as he did every morning? But he could not get into his car for staring at Carol's house, and like a man with no control over himself, he had crossed the street and was standing on her porch ringing her doorbell, and now he couldn't stop staring at her. "And I think he's innocent," Terrence said, and lifted the mug to his mouth.

"I guess you would know," Carol said, having no doubt that Terrence would never pull any tricks just to let him go free. "If Edmond committed the crime he should be punished," she stated, lifting her mug and tasting the lukewarm coffee.

"I wouldn't have taken the case if I thought he was guilty." Terrence kept his gaze on the mug, fearing that he might give her more fixed glances. "I didn't come down here to lose."

So far, the small talk was working and Carol was satisfied, as the last shiver raced through her body. "Do you have an idea who killed the boy?" she asked, keeping him distracted.

"I have an idea, and I'm here to prove that my client is innocent," he replied.

"Terrence, do you think that the person who committed the crime lives in this town?" Carol asked, afraid that if Edmond was innocent, the murderer could be living in the community. Her thoughts reeled back to the past, the summer she had spent in that town. Black fear swelled inside her and quickly she tried to release the unwelcome apprehension, while she remembered the threat that had been made to her on that hot summer day.

"I don't know," he said, leaning back and studying her. "What's wrong?"

"I was thinking of the time a girl was about to be attacked down by the creek. If the young man had not seen me, he probably would've hurt her," Carol said.

Terrence ran his finger back and forth over his mustache. "Did you know the person doing the attacking?" he asked her.

"His name was Lennie," she replied. "Anyway, he told me if I told, I would be next." Carol propped her elbow on the table, resting her chin on her fist. "I was too afraid to say anything."

"I think I remember hearing something about that." Terrence leaned forward. "His name is Lennie Cass," Terrence said.

"I wish that I hadn't been too afraid to tell someone," Carol said, "but I was afraid that he would keep his promise." She wondered whether he was still an attacker or whether he had changed his criminal ways. "But I did call Aunt Christine and told her after I was home."

"Lennie could've changed—I don't know—but you were probably right not to say anything until you were home," Terrence said, and glanced around the room to keep from looking at her.

"Does Lennie still live here?" she asked, because since she had been in town, she hadn't seen the light-skinned man who had the meanest eyes she had ever seen.

"Yeah, I saw him a couple of days ago," Terrence said, keeping his gaze on the green plants sitting on the top of the cabinets.

"You know, I wouldn't put anything past that guy," Carol said, wondering if Lennie Cass had been the guilty party.

Terrence shook his head. "He didn't do it." Terrence looked at her. "I don't think so, unless I left a stone unturned." He knew that his client hadn't been the cruel young man whom everyone, except for a few people in town, thought was innocent.

Carol glanced down at Edmond's photograph again. "I hope he'll be all right," she said, thinking how she had worried years ago about her brother when he had run with the wrong crowd.

"Considering everything that he has gone through, he's depressed," Terrence said, looking past her at the huge painting of fruits and vegetables hanging on the wall, before he stole another sensual glance at her lips.

"At least he has an excellent lawyer," she said, giving him a smile. Terrence Johnson family's law firm was an icon of success, Carol mused. She was sure that Terrence would be successful defending the teenager.

"I work hard." He smiled and pushed the empty coffee mug away from him. "And when I want something bad enough, Carol, I'll go the extra mile." If only he was just as successful with getting Carol to understand his feelings for her. Last night she had returned his kiss, and that had been a start. He controlled the sensual urges inside of him that were coiling around the edges of his heart while he watched her rise from the chair and stand to full height. The silk sash lay against her flat stomach and he could not help but notice how her round hips flared out around her slender waist.

"Terrence, I'm not throwing you out, but I have to get dressed for work," she said, moving away from the table

"Thanks for the coffee," he said, pushing away from the table, and rising to his six-foot-three-inches. "Maybe I'll see you later on today," he said. Usually everyone that worked in the downtown area took their lunch

breaks at the local diner. "We can eat lunch together."
He began moving toward the door.

"I'm not sure if I'm going out for lunch today," Carol
said, expecting to be busy for the rest of the day once
she arrived at the boutique. Mavis was getting things
ready for the sale. And next month, Mavis was going to
a workshop and on a buying trip for the winter fashions,
and Christine had left word that she wanted everything
in order when she returned, unless they wanted to listen
to her complaints.

"We'll talk later," he said, and headed out of the
house.

"Sure," Carol said, not minding the least that he had
left. It seemed that all Terrence Johnson did for her
was make her realize her own needs. As much as she
wanted to ignore her feelings, she could not help but
face the truth. The sound of the front door closing
behind him brought her out of her musing, and she
went to her room to dress.

Several minutes later, Carol stood at the mirror
straightening the thin spaghetti straps on her shoulders;
she was glad she had brought the pale-pink dress with
her. She touched the space on her arm where Terrence
had pressed his fingers last night, and shook her head.
She was acting like a teenager pining over Terrence.
But she had to consider that she had not allowed herself
to be shown affection in a long time. Nevertheless, she
had to get a hold of herself; moving too fast with Terrence and thinking about him all of the time could not
be in her best interest. She also had to remember that
she was not a twenty-five-year-old woman, which was
usually the age of the women that men Terrence's age
usually liked. She was thirty-four years old and had no
energy or time to compete with the fast-and-fiery ladies.
So she shook off all the feelings for Terrence that were
rising inside her, and those swelling emotions that were

threatening to make her break all of her promises and rules to stay passion-free, and she finished dressing for work.

Once she returned to her own job, she would have no time for a boyfriend anyway, she considered, remembering exactly why she had kept her obsessions in check until last night, and she wondered whether Terrence had been honest with her.

Her last affair had been just that. Her lover had confessed his love for her, and by the time she was head over heels in love with him, she learned that he was married. She had fought her way out of the emotional and passionate battle, a struggle that had left her distrustful and almost bitter. But she had learned her lesson, or had she? Carol did not know. Terrence had a special way of touching the very core of her soul. If she could get through this summer without losing her heart to him, she would consider herself a blessed woman.

She allowed her thoughts to wander for a moment as one question after another sailed across her mind. What if Terrence was in a serious relationship? Carol picked up the comb, grabbed a handful of her long thick hair and began combing the ends as she wondered if Terrence was telling her the truth. She let the thought linger while she brushed her hair, as the curls and waves fell past her shoulders. What if he really was married and had children? Although he was not wearing a wedding band, she knew from experience that she could not trust an empty space on a ring finger. She quickly dismissed the thought and pushed the posts of her earrings through her pierced ears, stuck her feet in the white shoes with a splash of pink over the heels, and grabbed her package, hurrying out to the rented Land Rover she had driven from New Jersey.

Carol glanced across the street at Terrence's house. So far, her life was moving along just fine. She had a wonderful job working for a grant-and-loan company, she owned her home, she had money stashed away for the day she would open her own grant-and-loan business. Her work would continue to fill her life, and as much as she wished for children of her own, her three nephews filled her void with as much joy as if they were her sons.

Maybe she was worrying too much, she considered. With all thoughts of Terrence safely tucked away in the back of her mind, she slowed and turned into the street that led her downtown, when she noticed a black Mercedes turning the corner, and her heart fluttered. Even though she had seen Terrence's car parked in the usual space in front of his house, and this could not be him driving from the opposite direction so soon, she still had a sensual reaction, thinking that she had seen his car. Carol understood at that moment that forgetting about him would not be an easy task, especially when the man was making her crazy.

She drove past rows of stores, and a supermarket, and two banks, and the local barber and beauty salon where everyone in her community went to get the latest hairstyles and gossip, which sat three blocks from Christine's boutique.

Four brown-skinned mannequins, two women and two men, posed in the boutique's showcase, dressed in the latest summer fashions. Carol, Mavis, and Tanika had dressed mannequins the week before. She got out of her truck, admiring their handiwork and the red four-inch heels and matching purse that Tanika had set upon a short round post that swirled slowly enough for potential shoppers to get a perfect view. Even though Carol had not intended to work on her vacation, just as she had not intended to find Terrence in the town, she was thankful that she had something to occupy her mind, refraining her from thinking about the passion that was now unburied and inching through her body, igniting unwanted passion.

Terrence was the kindest man she had ever met, giving his precious and valuable time, helping a young man whose family was unable to pay for his defense. To Carol, his take-charge action to rescue a helpless young man made him the sexiest man alive. So why was she surprised that her spirit had been awakened from a lengthy slumber because she had made too many foolish choices in love?

Carol decided then that she would give herself one more chance to enjoy her life. What could possibly go wrong with her and Terrence dating one another? The only problem that she could think of was her need to ignore the passion that he ignited. She considered her thought carefully, because there was a problem. She did not know how to control and behave herself when he kissed her. She could not stop him when he showered her with his warm affections. Or when he spoke to her with his warm voice, his soft black eyes alone were enough to melt the ice that she had buried underneath her. She had to admit that this summer she had lost all of her control, and was now following her heart instead of her good sense and sound judgment. However, she would not worry. The summer would end, and she and Terrence would return home and probably never see or speak to one another again.

But still, a strange feeling nagged her because without warning she had found herself going starry-eyed over Terrence Johnson, in the same way she had over Boris. And because of that foolish choice, it had taken her a few years to date again.

Carol stepped onto the sidewalk in front of the boutique while dwelling on the old memories again, arriving at a frightening conclusion: maybe she wasn't meant to marry, or even to be in love. Maybe those warm affections were for other people to enjoy.

Carol dismissed her rambling thoughts and headed to the post office to mail the package to her girlfriend, before she went to work.

When she was finished at the post office, Carol entered the boutique, taking in the display of colorful dresses, suits, and silk nightgowns and robes, and the expensive jewelry stored away in the glass case beneath the counter. And then there were her favorites. Shoes, and purses, and wide-brimmed hats.

"Good morning," Carol said to two women customers who seemed undecided about which dress they should purchase for a special occasion.

"What do you think about this dress?" One of the women held up a lavender linen dress with a low, wide boat neck that promised to show lots of cleavage, and she was asking Carol for her opinion.

Carol studied the woman's small bustline for a moment. She certainly was not a fashion consultant, but she knew what she liked, and felt uneasy making a decision for her. However, with as much consideration as possible, Carol gave her suggestion. "I think that you will need one of these," she said, gesturing for the woman to follow her to the beautifully displayed silk bras and matching panties, and Carol lifted a beautiful push-up lavender bra that was designed to give a wonderful lift.

The woman laughed. "This *is* what I need. I think Christine should stay where she is and let you ladies run this place."

Carol smiled, thanking her for the compliment, but as much as she loved having the boutique to keep her busy, she had no real interest in changing her career. "Thank you," she said again, leaving the woman and going to do the job that she had promised Mavis and

Christine that she would take care of while she was in town.

While Carol sat behind the tall counter and worked on the accounts that Mavis had left for her, she allowed her thoughts to waver once more.

Life promises were fair. She had come to Georgia instead of going on a cruise or to a resort, or anywhere that handsome and wealthy men lay claim to to spend their time and money and to fall in love. She had chosen to visit the small Georgia town, knowing that she would have no worries of meeting anyone special, simply because most of the people were married, and those people who were single were already involved in relationships. And being asked out on a date was the farthest thought from her mind.

However, within two months she would return home to her familiar and safe world and surroundings. She would return to her career of fifteen years, taking her monthly trips to the museum, checking out the African art and accepting an invitation from the local art galleries to view and buy if she chose a beautiful piece of art that she just could not resist. On other weekends, she would attend one of her favorite plays, and shop, and have lunch with her girlfriend Jay.

Maybe this trip to Georgia was her divine order, or had she misunderstood the celestial arrangements? Over the years she had convinced herself that she'd had everything in her life that made her happy. Except for a hay-fever attack every once in a while, her health was almost perfect. She was thankful for the little things that made life heaven for her. She had her family and her friends, and she had her coworkers that she did not always agree with or get along with, as far as that mattered. Still, she didn't worry, and the simplest things like the rain that spilled from the sky, the snow that covered the grounds and streets, and a sunset at the end of a day, which she often watched from her office window, was peaceful. These were the things that brought her peace and joy.

Her prayers had been answered, and she had everything that she had asked for, which were all the things that she knew that she could handle. So why was God being generous, giving her what she often wished that she had, but did not dare ask for? Why was she questioning a powerful force? Because maybe she was not ready for Terrence Johnson. She answered her own question.

Besides, it was only dinner they would hopefully share and enjoy as much as the kiss they had shared and enjoyed. She gave a silent thanks, feeling like a fresh flower on a summer day, or a beautiful bird, trusting herself to spread her mental wings and soar again. She would allow her soul to guide her to a place where she would find joy.

Chapter Five

Terrence made several telephone calls, keeping his conversations quick and to the point. Earlier that week he had interviewed several people that his investigators had found. After reading their information, he was positive that their eyewitness testimonies would add more substance to the case.

Terrence sat at the desk in his study looking at the mountains of paperwork that needed filing, and he could not wait until his assistant returned. In the meantime, he began organizing the files and placing notes and letters inside of folders.

Lashaunda had returned to New Jersey to take care of her ill one-year-old son. It seemed that her husband was having problems finding someone to stay with the baby while he worked, and the day-care facilities were no longer taking care of children with the slightest sniffle and other ailments.

He finished filing the excess work, except for another folder that he needed to read. He lifted the folder and settled down behind the desk, twisting the top off a bottle of water, then tossing the cap into the wastebasket on the side of the desk. The information in the folder was not important—a few notes that he had already filed away. However, he read the information in case he had missed something important. As he neared the end, he found himself losing concentration and he gave in to his wavering trail of endless thoughts.

When he arrived in Georgia months ago, his plans were to get the case over with as soon as possible and return to New Jersey before the summer was over. But never in a million years would he have thought that in his life he would run into Carol Grant again. Seeing her again this summer after almost fifteen years was a surprise to him. They lived in the same city but he never saw her. He was certain that they had missed each other, because they ran in different circles and associated with different people.

That summer he had admired her for her straightforwardness, and for years he had often found himself looking for a woman as honest as Carol. Unfortunately he had been unlucky. Now he almost wanted to believe that fate had played a wonderful hand in his life, having her travel to the South the same time that he was in Georgia. He didn't want to get his hopes up too high, but his and Carol Grant being friends was not enough for him. As that thought eased by, he decided that he should not be greedy and accept her friendship, if friendship was all that she wanted from him. He considered that for a moment, thinking that if he and Carol were meant to be, nothing would keep them apart.

Now, this morning had been a different story. He had never learned to brew the perfect pot of coffee, at least not until major coffee companies began selling premeasured packs. Since his assistant had left, he had not found the time to stop at the supermarket. At any rate, his lack of time to shop for coffee had been the perfect excuse to get inside of Carol's house, and he was not the least bit ashamed of the action he had taken.

Every time he thought about his visit to her this morning, Terrence reminded himself that he should never have crossed the street to her house. But he had told himself that he was strong enough to sit and talk with her without touching her.

Terrence turned his attention back to the information that he had wanted to study and swung one leg over of the leather chair's arm. Resting his back against the inside corner of the chair handle, he began reading the last bit of information inside the folder, until his thoughts wavered once more, taking him back to Carol. He stared out the picture window that faced Christine's house and heaved a deep sigh. Without thinking, he had touched her waist; it was then that he realized that she was wearing only the white silk robe. He lowered his gaze from the window, and shook his head.

He could give himself some credit. At least he had not acted up as he did last night, losing his cool and kissing her. But maybe he didn't deserve too much credit. Patting himself on the back as if he had been a perfect gentleman, when every other minute he had to stop himself from staring at her round firm breasts, her full lips, and the way her black lashes framed her eyes. He had behaved like a man who was starving for affection. In a way that was true, but he did not want his intimacy from just any woman—he wanted Carol. He had broken up with his girlfriend six months ago, and the thing he had missed about her was the fact that she was not lying to him anymore. He dismissed that thought and returned to figuring out a strategy that would assure him that he would be on his best behavior Saturday night when he and Carol went to dinner.

Carol was the kind of woman that a man in his right

mind would want to spend the rest of his life loving. A strange feeling swept through him and he was feeling that she might not agree with him. His heart felt as if it had sunk in his chest. He wondered now what had happened to break the union between her and her ex-husband. He had been taught by his parents, and especially by his father, that marriage was sacred, and unless there was no other way to handle a situation after all else had failed, a divorce may have been the only problem solver. He was almost certain that Carol's vows had been special and she had probably taken her promises serious, to stay married until death. She had been so proud of her engagement, and still he had wanted her.

Terrence straightened in his chair and finished studying the file before he turned on the microcassette recorder and listened to his client's statement again. He was almost certain that his client would not have to testify in his defense. He cut the recorder and looked at the list of names of the people he was meeting with late this morning. If his meetings went as planned, he'd be filing for a motion to dismiss.

However, Terrence hoped that these people were not just strewing regular town gossip like most of the rumors he had heard since he had been working Edmond's case. He'd had a few people reporting to him that Lennie Cass, who'd once had a problem in the area when he was a teenager, may have had firsthand knowledge of the murder. After having that rumor checked out and cleared, Terrence had not found any reasons to suspect that Lennie was involved. So far, the man seemed to have changed and was now a fine upstanding citizen in the community.

Terrence lay the list aside and lifted the phone receiver, dialed the local florist and ordered a dozen red roses, requesting that the flowers be sent to the boutique. He glanced at his watch, noticing that he had an hour before his meeting, and was gathering his notes when the telephone rang.

"Yeah." He answered the call after the second ring. "No, I have not seen Wanda, Mother," he said, wondering what stunt Samantha Johnson was pulling now. "I don't need her working with me," Terrence said. He was expecting a call from Reese, who had offered to help him out if his assistant's son was still ill, since he was on vacation. "No, Mother, Wanda will be in the way," Terrence said dryly.

Wanda Mincy was a law student, and his mother's best friend's daughter, who had joined the pool of paralegals for the summer until she returned to school to work on her law degree.

It appeared to Terrence that his mother had been busy as usual taking it upon herself to find out if he had an assistant. He was more than certain that this idea of Wanda arriving in Georgia to assist him with paperwork and other clerical and legal chores was his mother's brilliant idea.

"I suggested that Wanda meet with your father and asked him if he would give her permission to assist you." Samantha Johnson's voice was clear and cheerful, as if she had fulfilled a great service for her son.

Terrence swung his head from one side to the other. He did not understand why every three to six months his mother would run an interference binge, meddling in his life. "How are you?" He rubbed his hand over his eyes while he spoke to his mother and waited for her to answer his question.

Samantha's short laughter floated out to him. "I'm feeling great," she answered. "How are you this morning?" she asked.

He'd been fine—until she called him with her ridiculous news. "I'm okay," he said, and cleared his throat.

"Why didn't you check with me before you sent Wanda to Daddy?" Terrence felt himself becoming irritated with his mother.

"It was always too late to call, Terrence, and don't use that tone of voice with me," she said.

"You could've left a message," he countered in the same irritated tone.

"Terrence, whenever I suggest an idea to you, you never return my telephone calls." Samantha sounded annoyed.

"And you know why," he replied.

"Well, anyway, I told Wanda that she could stay with you, since there wasn't any vacancy at the hotel."

"You did what?" Terrence asked her.

"Besides, it's ridiculous, paying for room and board when that house can hold and sleep several people." Terrence thought that his mother sounded even more annoyed now, but not half annoyed as he was feeling.

"No, Mother, Wanda can't live with me." He spoke quietly, but with portentous superiority. Having Wanda in town was bad enough but having her live with him was the worst idea. But he was almost convinced that this was his mother's game plan. She had been trying to unite them for the longest time and now he suspected that she thought she had the perfect alibi to get them together.

"For once you should try being nice to Wanda. She's a lovely young woman," Samantha said. "Terrence, are you there?" she asked after a rather long silence passed between them.

"Will you stop?" His voice was disapproving and laced with a slight chill. He respected his mother, but her matchmaking had gotten the best of him. She had finally given up on his brothers, Reese and Devon, after each had refused to stop dating women she had disapproved of. Terrence realized that now he was her newest target.

She was determined to choose his dates and life partner, and he was not going to allow his mother to choose the woman whom he would spend the rest of his life with.

"Terrence, get a hold of yourself," Samantha said, speaking to him as if he were a fifteen-year-old who was upset because he wouldn't listen to her reasoning.

"Get a hold of myself?" he asked, speaking in the same quiet ominous tone.

"Honey, this family has a reputation to consider, and choosing the right people to spend our time with is important." Samantha's voice was as gentle as the late-morning breeze, as she reminded him that being seen with what she thought were the wrong people was not acceptable. Terrence didn't have any idea where she was headed with the subject. Because even if Wanda worked with him, that would be the only contact they would have together. "Terrence, you must be careful about whom you're associating with down there."

"What're you talking about?" Terrence asked, as he prepared himself for the Johnsons' reputation speech again, and he gripped the receiver tighter.

"You understand that I know many of the people in that town," Samantha continued. "And I received a call from one of the ladies, telling me that you're visiting with Christine's niece. Now, Terrence—"

"Stop!" he said, losing his temper. "Where do you get off having someone spy on me?"

"Spy? Visiting that woman is bad enough, but standing underneath the porch light, kissing her, is shameless!"

"Bye, Mother." He set the receiver down and rolled away from the desk. His mother had spoken in a low voice as if Christine Hart and her daughter and niece lived in a house of sin. Now he understood clearly why Wanda was going to be in town.

The telephone rang again. "Johnson speaking."

"Don't you ever hang up on me like that again!" Samantha voice held the same fire as it always did when she was angry.

"Mother, I'm sorry, but I have a meeting," Terrence said in the mildest tone he could use with her. He would do anything for her, except allow to her ruin his chances with Carol. He didn't exactly know why his mother didn't like Carol, Mavis, and her mother, or anyone in their family. He had heard rumors but never quite took the gossips seriously.

"All right, Terrence, but make sure you tell Wanda to call me as soon as she gets into town," Samantha Johnson said to her son.

"I'll tell her, Mother," he said, and went to dress for his meeting.

While leaving the study and heading upstairs, Terrence walked past his grandfather's favorite chair. The rocking chair had been the only piece of furniture that the family had kept when they remodeled the house. This was the chair where Wallace Johnson often sat and told him the story about how he and the family survived the harsh living conditions in the small town.

Terrence remembered those summer nights. He had sat on the top step, resting his back against the huge white pillar. He had remembered the air being warm, and the crickets and frogs were singing their usual song, as the scent of honeysuckle blossoms perfumed the air. Terrence had sat quietly listening to his grandfather's true tales of how he and his wife survived and raised their three children. They were a strong lineage, willing to work hard for what they wanted, and took nothing for granted and nothing that did not belong to them. Added to that, their pride had refused them the luxury of receiving handouts.

Wallace Johnson had begun raising his three sons in the South, working the family farm while his wife,

Estella, stayed home, sewing, cooking, and taking care of the boys. To earn extra money for the Christmas holidays, she had baked cakes and sold them to people living in the area, and for miles around. For Easter, Estella made beautiful dresses for women and their daughters, and suits for their husbands and sons.

At the end of the farm year, Wallace brought clothes, shoes, coats, and toys for his children, and beautiful material for his wife. With their freezer filled with meat and jars of food that had been canned during the summer, enough food supplies were stocked for the winter as well as enough firewood to carry them through the coldest days and nights. The Johnsons were prepared for the year.

But times grew even harder when Wallace's crops were ruined one dry season when rain was scarce. He had barely enough for his family to survive, and no money to buy seeds for the crops. That was when he rented one portion of the land, and worked the other half. At the end of the year, the renter refused to pay him, and not one officer of the law forced the renter to pay. Being a poor man, it was impossible for Wallace to hire a lawyer to fight his case.

Angry because of the injustice he had had to bear, he sold the farm and earned just enough money to move his family to New Jersey and buy a small house. Wallace and his wife had taken factory jobs, working double shifts to provide for the family and to save for his sons' future.

When his sons were old enough to begin thinking about the work that they wanted to do in life, Wallace had sat with his sons and listened to them. Terrence's father and his brothers had told their father that they wanted to become lawyers. They had often heard the story of the injustice that their father had suffered.

Wallace and his wife had made certain that those

dreams came true for their three sons. They were now known as one of the finest legal services in the country, charging a heathy fee for those who could afford them, and at times they had serviced those who were wrongfully accused, or had been swindled and were unable to afford a legal service that would ultimately free them or give back to them what had been taken away. The Johnson lawyers' reputation, to look after their clients, was known nationwide. The lawyers used their defense like a fine-tooth comb, raking a case and hardly ever losing.

Terrence worked by the motto that his father had taught them. Cornell Johnson was a determined man and had made it clear to him and his two brothers that he would not accept anything less than the best from them. If they wanted to become lawyers, they would be the best. If not, they were to choose another line of employment.

Terrence knew that he wanted to be a lawyer, but he also wanted to enjoy his hobby before he studied for his law degree. He loved playing the saxophone, and if he could have just played in a couple of clubs before he enrolled in college, he would have been a happy man. He could still hear his mother's voice raised and trembling when he had made the suggestion. It was during that time that his mother set up the rules on the type of woman she wanted her sons to marry.

It was mandatory that the women were from families with money and status. Terrence had seen the agony that this rule had caused his brothers. Devon and Reese had both endured the pains of their divorces. Terrence had heard the cries of Devon's children because they did not understand the reasons that their parents had divorced. It was then that Terrence promised God and himself that he would never allow his mother or father to choose for him a woman whom he did not love, and he was not dating Wanda.

Terrence finished dressing and hurried downstairs for his attaché case, when he looked through the study's window out across the street. He noticed that Carol was getting out of the Land Rover. He drew in a deep breath and let the air slip across his lips slowly as he admired the slender pink dress that was accenting her hips and showing off her firm arms. He felt a masculine sensation gathering around him and he reminded himself again that he would take things slow with Carol. He would keep his hands off her, his lips off hers, and ask very direct questions because he wanted to know her. Already from talking to Carol, he sensed she seemed to have known what she wanted. It would make him happy if he was at the top of her want list.

His telephone rang, drawing his reflections away from Carol. "Hello," he answered, and listened to his brother's voice on the other end of the line, telling him that he was thinking about coming down in a few weeks. "Yeah, Reese, come down. I can use your help." Reese promising to join him in Georgia was like a prayer being answered. "I'll talk to you later," Terrence said, and hung up.

Chapter Six

It was almost noon when Carol arrived back at the boutique. She'd forgotten to close her bedroom window and had gone home to do so. While she was out, she had stopped at the drugstore for a bottle of sinus medicine and spent the next fifteen or more minutes talking to a woman who wanted to know when Christine was returning from her trip.

However, when she returned from her errands, she was surprised to see the roses that Terrence had sent to her. She lifted the card from the bouquet and read the message. "Remember our date. Always, Terrence."

Carol smiled, reminding herself to thank him when she saw him. With that thought in mind, she put the card in her purse and made herself busy assisting a customer, who was interested in purchasing a pair of red heels that she had seen in the showcase. It was then that she noticed Lennie Cass standing outside ogling her through the window. His yellow face looked flushed from the midday sun, and his jet-black eyes reminded her of large black olives. Carol wondered whether he had changed. That thought was followed by her wondering where the girl was that she had accidentally stopped him from attacking.

She lifted the red heels from the display in the window and went to the stockroom to see if Mavis had a pair in the woman's size. When she returned with the correct size, Lennie was still staring through the window. Ignoring him, Carol offered the shoes to the woman and directed her to the bench, where she sat to try them on.

Carol wondered why Lennie was staring at her. He had promised her that if she told, he would make her sorry. At the time he made his promise to her she'd been afraid and had not mentioned Lennie's cruel abuse to Christine or Mavis until later. However, once her aunt had learned that he had threatened her, she had promised her that she and few of the ladies from the church might have to straighten Lennie's problems out with their dead husbands' old forty-fives. That was all Christine Hart had to say about Lennie, but she had promised Carol that if he came near her or Mavis while they were visiting her again, she was going to see to it that he would have a talk with the sheriff. Carol glanced at Lennie and went back to assisting a customer who was looking at a wide-brim light blue hat. She hoped that he had not found out that she had told and that he planned to keep his promise after all these years.

"Now, this is pretty," the woman said, setting the hat on her head and twisting to the left and turning to the right in front of the mirror.

"Venus, I know you're not buying that hat," the woman that was shopping with her said.

"I might. It's nice and big," Venus said, twisting again and adjusting the brim on her head.

"As long as you don't sit in front of me in church,"

her girlfriend said. "Because I'm there to listen to the minister and I like to look at him when he preaches."

"You don't have to sit behind me," Venus said, still striking poses in front of the mirror.

"And stop twisting and turning. Prancing around does not make you look any better in that hat," her girlfriend said, and smiled.

"Oh, be quiet. You're just jealous because you didn't see this hat first."

"Huh!" The woman moved to the tray of multicolored gloves; she held up a pink pair. "I have a dress about the color of yours," the woman said to Carol. "Let me see." She held the dressy glove against Carol's dress. "I'm buying these," she said as Carol moved away. "These will go well with your dress, too," she said, and Carol glanced back and smiled. The gloves would have been perfect, except that she did not like dressy gloves. The accessories brought back to many hateful memories.

They had lived in a poor neighborhood when she was six years old. Like everyone in the community, they had no money but plenty of food, and lived in an old house that was clean, and warm in the winter and cool in the summer. During the summer her mother shopped for sales, buying her and Bretton winter clothes, boots, and thick mittens that matched her black coat and Bretton's gray coat. Their mother had attached a small clip to the mittens assuring herself that the children would not lose the mittens. One day while she walked the one block home from school, a boy who looked to be a few years older than herself, robbed her of her gloves, saying he was giving them to his little sister. Carol didn't need to be told what the fist shaking meant. However, in the short time she had walked home, Carol thought her hands would freeze. She pushed one hand inside her coat and carried her little book bag with the other, and had cried all the way home. When her mother asked her what had happened to her mittens, she was silent. "Tell me who took them and I will get them back for you." But she had refused to tell her mother for fear of what would have happened to her. "Okay, since you can't tell me, you'll have to wear these for the winter, because we don't have money to replace those mittens. At least not now, Carol," her mother had said. Carol knew her mother was a strong woman. But she feared that if her mother went out into the street and found the boy, there was no telling what would have happened to her because the boy's parents were as mean as he was.

For two weeks from that freezing day until the first day of spring, Carol wore the light blue gloves that her mother had brought her the last Easter. She had hated wearing them because her hands were still cold, and the children had laughed. Even the boy who took her mittens had laughed.

Tanika turned on the noonday music, and old soulful sounds floated out through the speakers, bringing Carol back to her present surroundings.

"Girl, that's my song." One woman stopped thumbing through a rack of blouses.

Mavis walked from the back of the store laughing. Her light brown smooth skin seemed to light up because the women were enjoying themselves shopping and loving the music that was playing. Mavis looked nice as usual dressed in fashionable clothes instead of the nursing uniform that Carol had often seen her wearing when she was returning home from work at the hospital. "I cannot believe that I am working in Mother's boutique," Mavis said, her long black hair bouncing over her shoulders as she walked to the front of the store.

After five years of marriage she was divorced, and had

explained to Carol. Her ex-husband had fought with
her, refusing at first to give Mavis the freedom she
needed. Then later, when he knew that she was not
backing down, he'd given in, and she was now a free
woman.

Carol noticed that Lennie was still staring into the
boutique. She understood from her aunt that most of
the people in town did not forget anything that had
happened, and she wondered again whether he was
thinking about that hot summer day. She pressed her
hand against her heart and prayed that Lennie would
get no ideas to carry out his threat. "Mavis, are we
going to lunch?" Carol asked, ignoring Lennie, who
was beginning to move away from the showcase window.

"I'll be ready in a few minutes," Mavis said. She was
showing the client a matching hat that went well with
a black-and-white dress.

"Okay," Carol said, going behind the counter and
taking her purse from the cabinet and making a hair
appointment for tomorrow afternoon. As she made the
call, she glanced out of the window and thought that
she had seen Terrence crossing the street. Her heart
fluttered and she composed herself. Saturday night she
and Terrence were going out. Maybe their meeting was
divine order, or maybe their meeting was a delightful
surprise to keep her from being lonely. She gave the
thought consideration and decided that her pondering
did not make sense, because she didn't date back home
and she was not lonesome for male companionship.

She finished making her hair appointment and
answered a call from a customer, and while explaining to
the woman that the sale would begin soon, she noticed
Lennie again, looking more dangerous than ever. She
said a silent prayer for the man, who was probably more
dangerous than Terrence's client.

* * *

Lennie had not known when Carol Grant had arrived in town. He had only known that she had because he had seen her driving downtown this morning. Had she moved to town to stay forever—or was she just visiting? He wondered whether she remembered when he had told her if she reported him to the police officer, she would be sorry that she opened her mouth. He had grown up and was trying to be a decent citizen in town. If she told now what he'd been attempting to do, he wondered what his son would think of him. *Maybe she won't say anything,* he mused, and hoped that she had forgotten that day.

Chapter Seven

In his downtown office, Terrence's meeting had lasted longer than he had intended. It was thirty minutes past noon and he felt as if he were starving. It didn't make sense to take another statement from the next young woman until after lunch. He thanked the gentleman for his time and walked over to the desk, seating himself on the edge, going over the notes he had taken, and began speaking into the handheld recorder.

So far, he was confident that the testimony from these witnesses would be the final evidence that would prove that the young man accused of the crime was innocent. Terrence rolled his neck to relieve the tension that had been building shortly after he had received his mother's telephone call, and had continued to build during the meeting. The pressure building inside him was also probably because he was anxiously anticipating his date with Carol tomorrow night, and he wondered whether she had liked the roses he had sent to her, roses that reminded him so much of her. He tossed the thought around—she was sweet and beautiful but had shielded her passion with a spiny cloak. However, he had never thought until now that being anxious over a date would have been a problem at his age. He was older, but maturity had only heightened his emotions for Carol.

Terrence turned off the recorder and his laptop and placed the equipment inside the filing cabinet as visions of Carol framed his thoughts, and he was not lucky enough to think of anything else as he slammed the filing cabinet drawer and checked the lock. He had been really busy when she'd first arrived this summer. Once he realized that she was in town, he began making plans to visit her. Now that his work was coming to an end, he hoped that at least they could spend plenty of time together. He took the cellular and his sunglasses from his tan suit jacket and left the room.

Taking long strides down the marble hallway, Terrence nodded to other court officials and office employees as he walked out of the building. He put on his sunglasses, shading out the brilliant sun. He moved onto the sidewalk, listening to the radio music drifting from the opened windows of an automobile. The lazy barking of a small dog floated out to him as he crossed the street. He gave a can a brisk kick as he moved toward the diner, inhaling the aroma of delicious home cooking.

If it had not been for the sign that read Ruby's in gigantic red letters, perched and rising from rich manicured grass, and sitting in the heart of town, one would have thought that the diner was someone's home. The porch was full of colorful flowers, a long white swing, and several white rocking chairs that beamed a familiar and friendly air of home.

Terrence took the steps to the porch and walked inside, removing his sunglasses and scanning the dining room. Several people sat at the counter, drinking ice tea or lemonade, while gossiping over the tones of soulful music.

For a moment he searched the dining room, hoping that Carol was seated at one of the round tables. "What can I get you today, Terrence? The special?" the waitress asked, holding a menu and drawing him out of his search for Carol.

"Yeah, give me the special, Miss Louise," he said.

"All right," she replied, laying the menu next to the cash register and pushing a gray strand underneath the white hair net. "I saved your table, and I'll be back as soon as I finish over here." She turned on the heels of her rubber soles to take care of another customer, while Terrence headed to his favorite table at the back of the room and waited for the Friday special. Fried chicken, mashed potatoes and gravy, a couple of homemade yeast rolls, and peach cobbler promised to hold him until dinner tonight. He pulled back a chair and sat, listening to bits and pieces of gossip after the music had stopped playing. Some of the discussions were about the trial, while others were about weekend plans.

Someone dropped more coins into the jukebox and once again music filled the room, relieving Terrence from listening to the conversations of others. He saw Carol and Mavis walk in and follow Louise to his table.

"I didn't think you'd mind if these two ladies sat with you." She winked at Terrence. "What're you having, honey—salad?" she asked Carol.

"I'll have the chef salad and a glass of lemonade," Carol said, and spoke to Terrence. "Hi." He tilted his head, held her gaze and smiled at her.

"What about you, Mavis? Are you having salad, too?" the waitress asked her as Carol and Terrence exchanged smiles.

"I need a menu," Mavis said, pushing herself closer

to the table and looking around the room, seeing one of her customers and waving.

"I'll be right back," Louise said, leaving them as she went to get the menu.

Terrence didn't mind having Carol sit at the table with him. Matter of fact, he was glad that all the tables and booths were occupied.

Several minutes later, Louise returned. "Here's your menu, Mavis." She gave her the blue book, then beckoned for the bus boy to hurry with the large trays that held Carol's chef salad and a tall glass of lemonade and several packs of crackers, and Terrence's lunch special. "I have no idea where you put all of this food," Louise said to Terrence, eyeing him carefully. "But I guess you need your strength if you're going to stay up half the night out on a date," she said with a teasing smile.

Carol felt her face warm, and Mavis chuckled.

Terrence felt heat rise to his face. Already his personal business was being strewn all over town, as well as back home. He looked at Carol as she unfolded the white napkin and covered her lap. Then her eyes met his again.

"Where're we going tomorrow night?" Carol asked him.

"Let me surprise you," he answered, unwrapping his silverware.

There was one thing Carol did not like and that was surprises. She'd had enough of those to last her a few years. "I don't like surprises," she stated calmly, spearing a small cube of turkey and eating the meat.

"Carol, you're taking the fun out of everything." He stuck his fork into the mashed potatoes and scooped a forkful, eating the buttery vegetable.

"I would like to know how to dress for the occasion," she said, closing her eyes as she ate a combination of lettuce, turkey, bits of cheese. "Mmm," she moaned as she crunched down on the fresh crispy lettuce.

"We're going to Atlanta," he said, knowing that it was only fair that he tell her.

"To what restaurant?" Carol asked between chews.

"I'm not telling you the name of the restaurant," Terrence said, narrowing his gaze. "But"—he held up one finger—"no jeans or shorts are allowed."

Carol decided then that Terrence reminded her of her ex-husband, At first she had thought Boris's surprises were fun, and romantic, especially when he gave her half of the information on what the surprise was about. Later she had thought his ways of surprising her were not romantic at all. Especially when he insisted that they go where he wanted, and she was not allowed to ask questions without starting an argument.

She raised an arched brow at Terrence. "What's the name of the restaurant?"

He chuckled. "Okay," he said, telling her the name of the fancy restaurant where he intended for them to dine. "Are you satisfied?" he asked her.

Carol lowered her gaze, almost ashamed that she was still carrying around with her the aftermath of her ruined marriage, like a bag of garbage. She looked over at Mavis, who still waiting for her lunch. "What did you order?"

"I'm having the seafood salad," she said, glancing at her watch. "But it seems like Louise has to go deep-sea fishing before I'll get my lunch today."

Carol grinned and looked over her shoulder. "She's coming now," she said, and lifted her glass, taking a sip of the lemonade.

Terrence turned his attention to Mavis, almost forgetting that he hadn't spoken to her since she and Carol had joined him. "How have you been Mavis?" he asked, as he speared the fork into the vegetables.

"I've been good," Mavis said as Louise set the salad in front of her.

"Would ya'll like something else?" Louise asked before she turned away to leave them to their lunches, but not before she gave Terrence and Carol a knowing look as if their friendship should have been a secret.

"No," Carol and Terrence said in unison.

"Mavis, can I get you anything?"

"No, Miss Louise. I'm fine," Mavis said, looking up and unwrapping the silverware.

Carol, Terrence, and Mavis made small talk while they ate their lunches.

Mavis was the first to finish, wiping her mouth and covering the half-empty salad plate with her napkin. "This is too much food for me," she said, pushing away from the table. "Beside, it doesn't taste good."

"Have Louise get you something else," Carol said, watching a frown that pleated Mavis's arched brows.

"I think that I have gorged myself out, since this is the second time this week that I've eaten this salad," Mavis said, getting up and going to the register to pay her bill. "Carol, I'll see you and Terrence later."

"I won't be long," Carol said to Mavis, before turning back to her salad, spearing a small chunk of turkey and preparing to eat, when she noticed Terrence looking toward the window. Lennie was standing on the diner's porch, peering through the window at them. Carol was beginning to think that her first trip to the small town might not have been a good idea. She couldn't stop him from ogling through windows, but his actions were making her uncomfortable. She dismissed the worrisome thought and the black fear she thought she had released many years ago, which was beginning to coil and snake its way through her. Peering into windows was probably a habit of his, she mused, as she ate the salad slowly, considering that the man probably did not mean her any harm.

"Are you all right?" Terrence asked as he looked away from the window.

"I'm okay," she replied, promising herself that she would not worry about the past any longer.

"I don't like the way he's looking at you," Terrence said, then added, "But I've noticed that he has a habit of staring at people."

Hearing his opinion was a relief to Carol, now knowing that Lennie just loved to stare. She took a sip of the lemonade, and from the corner of her eye, she noticed that Lennie had left the window. "Terrence, that was not a lunch," she said, noticing that he had packed away the heavy meal.

"What can I tell you? I like to eat." He lifted the glass and finished the ice tea.

Wiping her mouth, Carol pushed away from the table and lay the napkin over the salad plate. "I would love to stay and chat with you, darling, but I have a few personal tasks I need to take care of," she said, taking money from her purse to pay for her lunch.

"I'll take care of lunch." He touched her hand as she lay the money on the table.

"Thank you, but I can handle this," she replied, giving his hand a playful pat as they rose from the table.

"I hope the two of you enjoyed your lunch." The waitress smiled up at Carol and Terrence as they stopped at the register to pay.

"The food was good as usual," Terrence said, clasping Carol's hand and moving around the waitress. They headed outside, pushing their way through a small crowd that was coming in for a later lunch, when they bumped into one of his mother's old friends.

"Terrence." Mrs. Ernestine Gates switched her gaze

from him to Carol, a small frown pleating her thin salt-and-pepper brow as she looked at him.

"How are you, Mrs. Gates?" Terrence asked the elderly woman.

"I'm fine," she said, ignoring Carol. Her brown skin appeared fresh and free of wrinkles. "How are you?" She clutched her black purse underneath her arm against the sleeve of the light-colored summer dress she was wearing.

"I've been okay," Terrence answered and gave her a respectful smile.

"That's good," Mrs. Gates said. "I spoke to your mother yesterday, and she said that she was thinking about coming down. She probably wants to check on the window dressing that she wants my granddaughter to work on."

"Probably," Terrence said politely, remembering that it was Mrs. Gates who often kept his mother informed on his behavior when he was visiting with his grandfather.

"Well," she said, stroking the cluster of diamonds on her ring. "I don't think Samantha was pleased when she heard that you were seen with . . ." She glanced at Carol. "Oh, you know how people talk." She reached out and patted his hand.

"Mrs. Gates, this is Carol Grant. She's a very good friend of mine." He slipped his hand out of Carol's and circled his arm around her waist.

"So I heard." She gave Carol a blank look and walked away.

Terrence's arm was still circling Carol's waist as he walked her across the street to the boutique. "Are you sure you don't want to go out with me tonight?" he asked, slowing his step and looking down at her.

"If we hadn't planned a girls' night out, I would go out with you," Carol said, banishing her thoughts on why the women in town seemed to hate that she and Terrence were together. And while listening to Mrs. Gates, she was almost certain that his mother was still trying to choose the women in Terrence's life.

"If I don't see you tonight, we'll talk tomorrow?" he asked her as they walked into the boutique.

"Yes," Carol said, ignoring the eye contact that she and Terrence were receiving from the customers. "Thanks for the roses," she whispered.

"You're welcome," he whispered close to her lips, and leaned in farther, brushing his lips against her. "Don't stay out too late tonight," he said, sounding serious.

Carol stepped out of his embrace. "I'll talk to you later," she said, and ignored his warning. She and Mavis and Tanika always stayed out late when they were together.

Carol went to finish working on the books for Mavis, and placed a few orders to the jewelry company. And in between her work, she thought about Terrence, until Tanika joined her behind the counter. "You know, you're the first woman that I have seen Terrence talk to for a long period of time, and I have never heard of him or seen him having lunch with any woman in this town." She smiled and took her purse from the drawer.

"We're friends, Tanika," Carol said, and went back to her work.

"Yes, well, I guess having one dozen roses sent to me . . ." She paused, and cast Carol an amused glance. "Let me think," she continued. "You and Terrence had lunch today, which of course ended with a kiss." Tanika giggled.

"Is that a problem?" Carol could hardly refrain from smiling at Tanika's evaluation of her and Terrence's friendship. "We're just friends."

Tanika opened her purse and took out a pink compact. "In this town that kind of action is known as a couple, going together," she said, peering into the small mirror.

"Terrence and I are still getting to know one another," Carol said, and she was unable to conceal her smile from Tanika. But even though Terrence's kiss had been nothing more than a brush against her lips, she was still savoring the thrill that had slowly coiled its way to her heart. "Are you going to lunch, or what?" Carol asked through her smile at Tanika's sentiments concerning her and Terrence.

"Yes." Tanika gave Carol a playful pat on her back and laughed.

Chapter Eight

Terrence wished that he could have spent the rest of the day with Carol, but he knew that was impossible because he had to work.

As he walked the few blocks to his office for the meeting, passing the music shop and noticing a poster featuring a saxophone player, he allowed his thoughts to wander to the past. Once he left Georgia the last summer he had stayed with his grandfather, he wanted to take time out from his studies and take a job that would give him the ability to travel as well as earn money, and added to that he thought this was a perfect way to play his music. So one day he took the train to New York and signed up for the merchant marines. He could always return to college and earn the law degree that was the trophy his father, uncles, and two older brothers were so proud of. He wanted to play his saxophone while he was still young. And as the years progressed, he would be able to say that he had done what he wanted to do.

Two weeks before he was to take his physical for his new job, his father called him into the study. He needed to talk to him about a choice he had made. The only choice Terrence had made was to work instead of returning to school. No one in the family was supposed to have known about his decision, so he decided to keep quiet and play dumb.

"Son, I can't tell you how to live your life or who to work for, and I'm not going to make you feel guilty because you don't want to work in our profession." Terrence had opened his mouth to speak, but Cornell Johnson stopped him with a raised finger. "You need to figure out another way to play that saxophone, son, instead of working and hanging out with a gang of rough men." Terrence started to speak again and again his father stopped him. "But if this is what you want to do, go ahead. If you get into trouble, we'll defend you." With that said, Cornell walked out of the room, leaving Terrence to think.

His first thought was that Reese had probably eavesdropped on one of his telephone calls and had not stopped until he had tattled. Terrence's plan had been to travel, and when the ship would dock in different countries, he would play the nightclubs. Terrence knew that his parents would never support his idea to travel and play a saxophone, so he had figured out a way to earn a living while he enjoyed his music. However, his next sensible thought was that he would return to school, and during the summer, on the weekends, he would figure out a way to work for the law firm and at the same time play the local clubs.

A few hours later Terrence's meeting was over, and with nothing particular to do tonight, he had an idea.

He stopped by his house, picked up an important piece of equipment, and headed to the next town.

Carol, Mavis, and Tanika arrived at Adair's Place. The soft kaleidoscopic lights seemed to have pulled them farther inside of the packed club. It seemed that everyone in the surrounding area had the same idea on how they wanted to end their workweek. But still the club was more crowded than usual. Carol noticed the band was not the usual group that played the club. The music was awesome, and the dance floor was filled with friends and lovers, moving to the beat of hot soulful sounds.

With no one to dance with at the moment, Carol enjoyed the music, tapping her feet to the rhythm while Tanika and Mavis refused offers to dance.

"I don't know about you all, but I'm not coming here again without my boyfriend," Tanika complained, looking around at the couples who all appeared to be in love.

"Tanika, be quiet," Carol said. "You can be without that man at least one night out of the week." Carol chuckled.

"I know, but I don't like to dance with other guys," she complained.

Mavis shrugged. "Whose fault is that?"

"Mine," Tanika replied, and tossed her head. "If I dance with a guy, someone in this club will tell my boyfriend."

"He's jealous?" Carol asked, rocking her head to the music.

"He wouldn't be jealous if the people in our town would stay out of my business," Tanika said, and Carol had to agree with her. She had never seen so much worrying over other people's business. She never would have known this information about the town if she and Terrence weren't becoming very good friends.

Carol smiled as a thought crossed her mind. She suspected that before the sun had gone down today, the roses that Terrence had given would probably be the main topic at the dinner table. She chuckled at the thought that may or may not have been true, and settled back and looked out across the room at all the faces, realizing that she did not know one person in the room, other than the women she was out with. Anyway, she was glad that she had overheard one of the customers mention Adair's Place when she had first arrived in town.

Carol was snapping her fingers and rolling her neck to the music when the cocktail waiter stopped at their table and took their food and drink orders. Except for Tanika, everyone decided on old-fashioned barbecue chicken sandwiches, coleslaw, and a bottle of chilled Chablis. Tanika ordered the same food, but because she was the designated driver for the evening, she ordered a soft drink.

At any rate, Carol wasn't getting any invitations to dance, and this was all right with her. She wasn't particular about dancing anyway. "I'll be right back," she said, getting up and weaving between tables on her way to the ladies' room to wash her hands before her food arrived.

On her way back to the table, someone grasped her arm.

"Terrence!" Carol smiled, glad to see him.

Terrence was still dressed in the tan suit, just as she, Mavis, and Tanika had not bothered to change clothes after work, either. He smiled and gathered her to him, and without asking her, he began moving to the slow rhythm of blues as the contralto's voice lowered to a salacious mourn. As she moved to the beat, Carol had the strangest feeling that she and Terrence were supposed to be together. She did not believe in coincidences. *He is so nice,* she mused as she moved against the hard lines of his muscular body.

"Are you driving?" Terrence whispered in her ear.

"I'm riding with Tanika and Mavis." She rose on the tips of her toes, elevating herself close to his lips, and whispered back to him. At the same time, she felt a sense of excitement sweeping through her. Carol still could not believe that she was having more fun and enjoying herself more than she had in a long time. And she knew that she would never have had this much fun if she had gone for her vacation to another place. Maybe she was meant to be happy after all, she mused, feeling a warmth travel to her heart as Terrence hugged her to him even tighter.

"Can I give you a ride home?" he asked.

"Yes," Carol said as the cocoon that she had once wrapped her heart in, slipped completely away, and any distrusts she'd had seemed to have vanished. She knew then that it was time for her to live an eager and passionate life. She seriously considered her musing as she looked at him. His face seemed to have been holding a secret message for her. However, with all of her consideration to allow herself happiness, she still wanted to take her time. Usually, rushing into anything was the reason for her troubles.

The music was coming to an end when he touched his lips to her red mouth and brushed a feathery kiss against her. As he walked her back to the table, Carol felt as light as the kiss he had planted on her.

"Ladies," Terrence said to the women once he had pulled Carol's chair back and gave her one last kiss, before she sat down in front of the food that had been delivered while she was away.

"Hi, Terrence," Mavis and Tanika said to him.

"What brings you out tonight?" Tanika asked him.

"It didn't make sense to stay home," he answered.

"You got that right," Mavis said, bobbing her head to the music.

"I'm over there," he said to Carol, swinging his head to the section that was near the band. "Let me know when you're ready to go." Still looking at her, he moved away and Carol knew that she could not ignore her feelings any longer. The truth was simple: she wanted Terrence Johnson.

Carol nodded as she watched him leave her. At the same time she spoke to Mavis. "I'm riding back with him," she said when the music stopped. And then she saw Terrence join the band with a saxophone in hand.

"I'm not surprised," Tanika said, lifting the tall glass of cola. "Since both of you have gone completely nuts over one another." She giggled over the rim of her glass and sipped lightly.

Mavis laughed. "Tanika . . ." She stopped. "People are like that when they like one another." She pointed toward the bandstand, when the music started again. "I didn't know that Terrence could play."

"Me, neither," Tanika said, and returned to the subject. "I'm serious," Tanika said. "Miss Carol popped into town like this"—Tanika snapped her fingers—"and got Johnson's attention."

"That's because she wasn't trying," Mavis said, still smiling.

"And every single woman in town is upset at what you did." Tanika giggled.

"I didn't do anything," Carol said, taking a bite of her sandwich.

"Oh, yes, you did." Tanika giggled again and set the glass down.

Tanika was not that much younger than Carol and

Mavis and, although she wanted to marry, she was seriously thinking of breaking up with her live-in boyfriend.

For at least another two hours, Carol and the women enjoyed the evening. Then she decided to go find Terrence, since he was not on the bandstand any longer.

"I'm going home," Carol said, gathering her purse and getting up from the table. "I'll see you tomorrow, Tanika." Carol flung a glance at the young woman and said good night to Mavis as she moved away from the table.

She found Terrence at the table where he promised he would be, listening to several men talk and drinking a glass of fizzing water. Carol touched his broad shoulder and leaned close to his ear. "I'm ready to go."

She watched him push away from the table that he had been sharing with the men, whom he seemed to know well. While Terrence lifted the black case that held his saxophone, the men continued to talk to him, finishing their conversation and promising him that they would talk again soon. During that time, Carol tried to ignore Tanika's comments that she had made earlier in the day about her and Terrence's friendship.

Carol could not deny that Terrence had awakened and ignited a warmth in her that she had kept under guard. Nevertheless, she had to face the truth and facts that she could no longer dispute. She was wearing her heart on her sleeve.

One thought after another crossed her mind as Terrence reached back and covered her hand with his. "I'll see you guys later," he said, slipping his arm around her waist.

The weight of Terrence's hand resting on her waist pulled her out of sensual ambling thoughts, and she could no longer deny the warmth inside her.

Chapter Nine

Once Carol and Terrence reached his car, he handed her the keys. "I had about one drink," he said, "and I feel as if I've had at least three. I guess I'm tired." He circled his arm around her waist and put down his saxophone case. She went willingly into his arms, feeling the sexual magnetism between them that made her want him even more, and she grazed the side of his jaw with her fingers.

"I don't mind driving," she agreed, admiring his confidence in her to take them safely home, and glad that she had poured herself one glass of Chablis this evening and she only had taken one sip of her drink.

"Thanks, baby," Terrence said, drawing her tighter into his arms and claiming her with a sizzling kiss.

A tingling sensation rushed through her as their kiss deepened, and he demanded more from her. Finally he raised his head and moved out of her embrace to take back the keys and unlock the door.

She sank down on the soft leather seat and unlocked

the passenger door for Terrence, feeling different than she did when she drove her two-seater sports car or the Land Rover she'd rented and driven to Georgia. She turned the key, bringing the motor and music from the radio to life at the same time and stole a glimpse at Terrence. "Are you sure that you trust me to drive your car?" She smiled as she teased him. He was so unlike Boris who would not let her sit behind the wheel of his expensive car.

Terrence's husky laughter fused with the music. "I don't usually let anyone drive my car." He gave her a sideways glance as he slid down into the seat, after putting his saxophone case in the back seat, and leaned over close to her. "But I trust you." His warm breath stroked her neck, and she shivered.

"Behave yourself," Carol said, meaning every word, as she drove down the street. She would be unable to drive if Terrence continued to touch her with his breath, his hands, or his lips.

Driving at a moderate speed, and enjoying the slow sounds of rhythm and blues that filled the car, she stole another glance at him. He was quiet and seemed comfortable with his head resting against the headrest. His strong thighs and legs were parted, reminding her of the passion that she was no longer ignoring. But she would give herself time before she took their relationship to another level. She wanted to know more about him. "I didn't know that you played a saxophone." She spoke over the soft music, breaking the silence between them as she turned onto another street and headed south.

Terrence chuckled, thinking how he loved the instrument so much, he had once wanted to run away from home just to play his saxophone. "I enjoy playing in my spare time, and once I wanted to play professionally, but I love my work too much."

"Have you ever worked anyplace other than with your family?" Carol asked.

"No, and I wouldn't think about working with any other firm," he said.

"Not even for yourself?" Carol was curious. Although she had a feeling that the Johnsons might have been a tight-knit family.

"Maybe," he said as she stopped at the traffic light. His glance met and held hers, and even in the dim light of the car's interior, she could see the seriousness in his eyes. "But I'm in no rush to go out on my own," he said.

"Working with family can be nice," she said, thinking how well she and Mavis were getting along. But the boutique did not belong to them, and when their vacations were over, they would return to their careers.

"Sometimes my family get on my nerves, but I enjoy working with them most of the time," he remarked quietly as she turned off the main highway.

Just as I thought, she mused. *Terrence has strong family ties.*

"You and Mavis seems to make a great team," he said.

Carol smiled. She and Mavis *were* having fun working the boutique. "Yes, but our careers are so different," she said, speeding up. "I work for a loan-and-grant company," she answered softly, and smiled, proud of the career that she'd had for many years, while she noticed his quick glance.

"You enjoy your work, don't you?" he asked in a husky voice that was almost a whisper.

"Of course," she replied. She wasn't rich, but her career had afforded her a comfortable life. She worked long hours, but when she decided to take a break, she could travel wherever she wanted to go.

"Have you ever thought about opening your own business?" Terrence asked.

She smiled. "Matter of fact I have. I would love owning a business like that." She had begun saving to open her business in another year or two.

"I don't blame you," he said.

Carol turned into their street and slowed as she neared Mavis's mother's house. "Would you like to come to my place for a while?" Terrence shot her a warm glance. Carol didn't see any reason why she couldn't visit with him for a while. After all, the night was still young and if she did not get to the boutique on time the next morning, she did not have to worry.

"I—" she started, when he interrupted her.

"We could listen to music and finish this conversation." His voice tapered. He tilted his dark head close to hers, and the side of his soft mustache against her cheek.

"Sure," she said, not ready to end the night with him. She drove past her and Mavis's house, eased beside the row of rich green hedges near the curb of his grandfather's house, and cut the engine.

"I'm glad you're here," he said, his voice as warm as the summer night. And his eyes held the same gentleness. "I don't want to think what would've happened to me if you would've taken a flight to some faraway island or resort," he said.

Carol chuckled. "You would've been fine," she said. She was almost certain that if she had not spent her time in Georgia, he would've eventually asked at least one woman in the town to have dinner.

"I'm serious," he said, rising from his comfortable position, releasing the seat belt that strapped him in, and opening the door. He got out and took his instrument from the backseat, then waited for her to join him.

"I'm serious, too," she said, walking beside him, her heels striking lightly against the gray cemented walk as they passed bunches of polychromatic flowers assembled in orderly fashion on a bed of green manicured lawn. She felt the weight of his arm circling her waist, drawing her closer, as her hips brushed against the side of his hard thigh. "But I do admire you for helping Edmond."

He stopped them at the edge of the first wide step. "Is that why you're going out with me?"

"No!" Carol laughed, watching a smile curve his lips.

"Sometimes it's good to give back, Carol," he replied quietly, before he began to climb the six steps to the porch, which was radiating a warm, welcoming soft white light. He slipped his arm from around her waist and reached for his keys, unlocking and opening the door. "Come in," he said, reaching back and holding her hand while flipping the light switch in the foyer, radiating sunny beams.

Again Carol shivered from his touch, being mindful that spending an evening with him was the perfect ending to her day, while she admired the light-gray love seat, sitting against the foyer's wall, lined with three black throw pillows. She glanced around the foyer in admiration, noticing the two green silk plants perched inside silver buckets at opposite corners of the room.

The African-American painting hanging over the love seat held her attention. She had never seen this painting in any gallery or magazine and she wondered how she had missed this piece of art. Frowning, she turned around to Terrence who was standing behind her. "Where did you get this?" She would love to own the painting of the old house that was surrounded with tall oaks and Georgia pines. She wondered if the painting symbolized any particular success.

Terrence chuckled. "You love art, too."

"Yes," she said, waiting for him to answer her.

"This is a painting of this house when my grandfather first built it and before he renovated. We have lots of old photographs. I thought this would look good in oil, so I gave the photo to a guy I know. . . ." He smiled at her as they moved away from the painting, and she noticed a black baby grand in the living room.

"Can you play?" she asked, studying his face as he guided her into the living room.

"Yeah, I can play." He chuckled again, the velvety rumbling sound of his laughter floating out to her. "I once thought it was a disgrace for a guy to play the piano. . . . You know," he said between chuckles, "I kinda thought pianos were for girls."

"You're not serious." Carol smiled as she admired the rest of the room's décor.

"I was very serious, until my father took us to a live rock 'n' roll concert. After I saw those brothers playing, I thought the piano was kinda cool."

Carol was impressed with his talents and good taste and she was more certain than ever that she was not making a mistake with Terrence. "I can play," she said.

"Yeah?" he said, holding her at arm's length before leading her out of the room and down the hall to the den.

"Yes. Playing the piano soothes me," she confessed as they reached the large room that held everything from a wide-screen television, stereo, pool and card table, a huge box-shape sofa that sat behind a thick glass top resting on the back of a black jaguar serving as a cocktail table. Farther back at the end of the room was the largest bar she had ever seen in anyone's house.

"I enjoy the piano, baby, but my saxophone gives me the most peace," he said, standing the instrument in the corner where the stereo was stationed, and then he pulled off his jacket and laid it on a nearby chair before he unbuttoned his shirt halfway.

Carol looked at him, and held her gaze on his smooth muscular chest. "I understand," she said, and she walked to the sofa and sat, crossing her long legs, and watched him cross the floor to the bar.

"Would like a glass of Chablis?" He was behind the counter, standing in front of a rack of wines.

"Yes," she said, watching him take a chilled glass from the small refrigerator, popping the cork on a bottle of Chablis, and then filling her glass. When he was finished doing that, he made himself busy mixing himself a Scotch on the rocks.

Seconds later he was sitting beside her. "To us." He toasted their sizzling friendship, their glasses touching lightly, giving off a diminutive tingle, before she sipped the chilled wine.

Carol felt even more comfortable with him now. His quiet manner was natural and she knew it wouldn't take much for her to fall in love with him. She settled back on the thick blue sofa, taking another drink. "Terrence, I know that we talked about this before, but I'm serious now. . . . Are you dating anyone back home?" she asked, hoping that he was free for her to love him if things turned out the way that she hoped. She licked her lips, tasting the smooth drink. She did not want to hear from an old girlfriend of his, telling her that they had rekindled their relationship and did not want to receive a message from a woman telling her that she was dating Terrence.

"What did I say when we talked earlier this week?" he asked her in a smooth tone.

"I know what you said," she replied. "I don't want any surprises."

Terrence chuckled and set his glass on the cocktail table and turned to her. "I understand," he said, searching her face. "I don't compete with anyone for the love of my woman and I don't share." He moved closer to her then bending his head so close to her, she could hear his soft steady breathing. "And I'm glad you're not married anymore, but it's hard for me to believe that you're not in a serious relationship."

"I'm glad that I'm no longer married to Boris, and no, I'm not going out with anyone," Carol replied, freely admitting to him that she had made the mistake of her life by marrying Boris Myers. She felt the automatic frown pleat the center between her brows, a habit that she had acquired over the years when she had to talk about her ex-husband. On behalf of the misery he put her through, she usually kept the conversation short.

Terrence touched the place between her brows as if he could erase the wrinkles that had creased into a frown. "Just be thankful that you didn't have a child to experience that pain of being separated from one of their parents," he said as if he had read her thoughts.

"I agree." But she had wanted children. However, Boris was consumed with his control and she could not stay with him and raise a family in that environment.

Terrence kissed the place where he had touched her between her arched brows. "I'm not sure we'd be out tonight if you'd had a child," he said.

"Why?" Carol asked, not understanding. "Don't you like children?"

"Of course I love children and would love to be a father one day, but I had a bad experience once, and I promised myself that I would never make that mistake again."

"Okay, what happened?" Carol asked him.

"I was going out with this woman . . ." Terrence said, telling her how he had dated a divorced woman who had two children. The problem was when her ex-husband stopped by to pick the children up for the weekend.

The man had a habit of instigating an argument with him in front of his children. Later he had noticed that the children were actually blaming him for the disturbance. They were young and loved their parents, and of course, whatever their father said to them would hold more truth than any explanation he could offer. It was then that he made the tough decision to walk away from the relationship.

"I guess you have a point," Carol said, knowing that she probably would have made the same decision if she was dating a man whose ex-wife was showing up starting fights. "But I have my family," Carol said. "I love my nephews."

"Did you ever think of remarrying Boris?" Terrence lifted his glass and waited for her to answer him. He had to know if Carol was still pining over the man. He would not ensnare himself into a trap and learn later that he had made a mistake once again.

"No," she answered, watching him take a drink then setting the glass down.

"Where is he now?" he asked, searching her face and finally her eyes, a gaze that turned her heart over.

"I don't know," Carol said. "I haven't seen him in years."

"Was he unfaithful?" Terrence asked one question after another.

"Not as far as I know of," she said, willing to answer his questions since she was also interested in knowing about his life. In so many ways Terrence reminded her of Boris. He liked art and music, and did not mind asking direct questions. She was attracted to Terrence, but what if he was exactly like her ex-husband?

"So why did you divorce him?" He held her gaze as if daring her to tell him the truth, and she looked away.

"He was not exactly a nice man," Carol said. "I was

young, and too foolish to know what I was getting myself into.''

Terrence let out a groan. ''That's not the answer to my question,'' he said, looking as if he was ready to pump her for correct information.

''Boris was impossible to live with'' was all she said, because she was not ready to discuss her ex-husband's abusiveness. If she saw Boris years from tonight it would be too soon for her.

''I was wondering if you had hopes of the two of you getting back together, that's all,'' Terrence said.

Carol lay her head back against the sofa and laughed. ''I realize that you don't understand.''

''I don't know—I'm asking. It's not the strangest thing that ever happened between divorcees.''

''I understand,'' she said once she had control of herself. It was then that she noticed the concern. ''My ex-husband and I are through.'' She took another sip of the wine and savored the taste, wishing that she could change the subject. However, she had to be fair since she was the first to broach the subject of lovers. Nevertheless, discussing Boris Myers was not a subject she enjoyed, especially over a chilled glass of wine. ''Can we change the subject?''

''No, I think Boris needs discussing,'' he replied, stroking the glass with his thumb. ''Carol, I like you and I hope that we can continue to see each other once we're home. I don't want any problems.''

She studied the sensual look in his eyes. He was serious, worrying that she was still in love with a man who had mentally and physically abused her. ''You worry too much.''

''Not all the time.'' He lowered his gaze and continued to stroke the glass. ''Six months ago, I broke off a relationship.'' He looked at her and turned away.

''Do you still love her?'' Carol asked, glad for this

conversation now. She didn't want to get caught in the middle of Terrence's problems, either.

"No," he said. It had taken him a while to recuperate from the agony, since he'd wanted to marry the woman. But little did he know that she didn't love him, or at least not for the same reasons that he loved her. "She wasn't interested in me completely," he said, flicking a glance in Carol's direction.

Carol could not imagine why the woman was not interested in him. "What was the problem?" she asked.

"Like tonight when you went out with Mavis and—"

"Yes," Carol said, wanting him to get to the point.

"She used to go out with her girlfriends, and one evening I happened to stop at the club. I couldn't believe that she was bragging to her friends about how she was going to use me."

Carol wondered if Terrence's relationship were over. "Maybe you made a mistake, Terrence. After all, you were in a nightclub. Everyone talking at the same time and the music was probably loud . . ."

"I was standing behind her when she bragged to her friends. Matter of fact, she was talking so much, she didn't see her girlfriend's warning."

Carol raised an arched brow, not exactly knowing what to say. She was certain who this woman was, she probably was not going to give him up easily.

"Did you break up with her then?" Carol asked.

"Yeah," he said, and for a while they were quiet and Carol was beginning to wonder whether she was making a mistake with Terrence. Six months was not a long time for a couple to be apart, and they could rekindle their relationship. Carol pressed her lips together, not wanting to be too critical of his situation.

"Maybe there was a misunderstanding and you can work things out," she said, feeling as if all her hopes and dreams were dissolving.

"No." Terrence shook his head. "I want the woman that I plan to spend my life with to want me for myself and not anything else. I'm not interested in a one-sided love affair."

"No one likes a relationship like that," Carol said as he circled her wrist with his fingers and gave her a light squeeze. For too long she had fought a battle, restraining herself from becoming too serious with matters of the heart. "What?" she asked, noticing the faraway look in his eye. He lifted up off the sofa enough to remove his wallet. He slipped from the folds a white plastic card and handed it to her.

She read the medical information and was not amazed that he was health conscious. She gave the card back to him and removed a health card from her purse. "Thanks for sharing that information with me," Carol said, watching as he read her information.

"I believe that we are in the right place." He then lay the card on the table and cupped her face with both hands and caressed her lips with another kiss. "I like fairness." He kissed her and lifted his head. "I like honesty." He brushed his lips against hers again. "And I want you." He smothered the words with a soul-searching kiss.

Pleasure exploded inside Carol, and she struggled to harness her rising passion. She ran her fingers through his thick black waves, letting her hands slide down the back of his neck, and she felt him shiver from her touch. She turned her head, feeling the tense ache in her neck and shoulders and she pulled out of his embrace.

"What?" Terrence asked.

"I need a massage," she said. Not having gone to the spa in months was finally catching up with her. She had felt the tension in her shoulders today as she'd worked on the boutique's books.

"All right." Terrence slipped his fingers along her shoulder and massaged lightly.

"Mmm, it feels good." Carol spoke just above a whisper, enjoying Terrence's massage as he slipped his fingers from her shoulders to the bare space on her back. "Ahh!" Carol closed her eyes and allowed his touch to ease the stiffness.

"Are you feeling better?" he asked, touching his fingers to the center of her back.

Carol let out a satisfying lament. "Yes," she said. Then her cellular phone rang.

"Don't get that," Terrence said, stroking his fingers against her skin.

"I have to answer the phone," Carol replied quietly, taking her telephone from her purse and noticing the name of the town framing the cellular telephone window. She hoped there was not an emergency back home with her nephews, her brother, or her father. She settled back, only to be stopped by the gentle touch of Terrence's fingers. "Hello."

"Hi, Carol, are you busy?" Carol heard her girlfriend's voice. "Mmm-hmm," she said in a low moan from the touch of Terrence's strong and firm fingers that were lightly stroking her shoulders and back. She reached back, tapping his hand to stop him.

"Carol, are you all right?" Jay asked her.

"Yes, I'm fine," she said, watching Terrence cross the room to the stereo. "But, Jay, can I call you back tomorrow?"

"Sure, as long as you're feeling all right," Jay said.

"I'll call you around noon," Carol said, sounding more like herself.

"Okay," Jay replied, and the line went silent.

"Who's Jay?" Terrence asked Carol, shuffling through a stack of CDs.

"Jay is my girlfriend." Carol slipped the telephone back inside her purse and lifted the wine, taking a sip.

"Oh," he said, and went back to shuffling the stack of music. "How long have you been friends?"

"Since college. Why?" Carol asked, wondering why was he asking so many questions.

"Jay sounds like a guy's name to me," he said, pulling a CD from the stack.

"Yeah, but she's my best friend. You should understand. Don't you have a best guy friend?" Carol asked, studying his face.

"Yes, I have a buddy," he said, thinking how he and Conrad McCoy had been best friends since high school, when his telephone rang.

"Carol, will you answer that for me?" Terrence asked, and pulled out another CD. "If the call is not from Edmond, tell them that I'll call them back tomorrow." Terrence continued to shovel through the stack.

"Hello." Carol answered the call, and listened to the long silence on the other end. "Hello?" she said, wondering who had time to breathe on the telephone at eleven-thirty at night.

"Who is this?" The feminine voice floated out to Carol.

"This is Carol," she said.

"Carol, this is Wanda, and I would like to speak to Terrence. The man who I intend to marry."

"Hold please." Carol gathered her composure and held the receiver out to Terrence. "Wanda wants to speak to you."

"I'll talk to her tomorrow," Terrence said, pulling a CD from the stack and slipping the music inside the player.

"I think you need to take this call, Terrence," Carol said, and lay the receiver on the table and moved to the other side of the room. Her problem was with herself, easily seduced by a fine-looking man. Now she knew that his six-month breakup with his fiancée was not over. However, she had believed him, as she had allowed herself to fall into his trap. She was a monogamous lover, and wanted the same treatment in return because she took matters of the heart very seriously. However, being duped by a handsome face and by smooth, warm, heartfelt words and a few passionate kisses, and she could blame no one but herself for allowing herself to be pulled into a relationship with him.

"I don't know why she's calling me at eleven-thirty at night." Terrence went to the telephone grumbling and cutting into Carol's thoughts. He grabbed the receiver. "Yeah?" The sound of jazz filtered out of the speakers, filling the room and Carol's heart, since this was another one of her favorite artists.

Carol sank down on the sofa listening to bits and pieces of the call, while her thoughts rambled. Earlier, when Jay had called her, she could hardly wait to tell Jay about the man she had met. Now she didn't think that she would bother to mention Terrence to anyone that she knew back home.

"No, Wanda, you can't come here," Terrence said, and Carol's drifting reflections came to another abrupt halt. "Get a hotel," Terrence said, and hung up. He turned to Carol. "We were about to enjoy the music." He reached for her.

"No, Terrence, I think you need to tell me about Wanda." She settled back on the sofa.

"All right," he said, sitting down beside her. "My assistant has a sick child, and Wanda is down here to assist me."

"So why does she want to live with you?" Carol asked, withholding the information that Wanda had anxiously revealed. Carol had thought that he was an honest man.

And maybe Wanda was just talking, but she couldn't trust this information to be untrue.

He had hoped that he never had to explain this foolishness to Carol, but unless he wanted to lose her, he had no other choice but to tell her about his mother and her meddlesome friends. "Carol," he said. "Wanda and her family are friends of our family."

"Oh, really," Carol said, turning sideways to get a good look at him and not wanting to miss a word of this confession. "Tell me more."

"Wanda is a law student who should have been out of school years ago, but that's not the point. She's working as a paralegal in our office and has gotten herself transferred here to help me out."

Carol slowly waved her hand back and forth. "So, if you're not interested in her, what difference does it make if she works with you?"

Terrence held her gaze. "She—my mother—is trying to matchmake."

"Oh, I see," Carol stated firmly.

"I'm not interested in Wanda like that," Terrence said.

Carol did not think she was being jealous, she simply did not want to be caught up in a love triangle. What she feared most was loving and finding out that her partner's sincerity was not real. The only problem was she liked Terrence so much and wanted to believe him. But she had to wait and see things through before she found herself in an unpleasant situation. "Let me be honest with you," Carol said, standing. "I don't think it's a good idea that we continue our new friendship."

"Because of Wanda?" Terrence asked, standing and searching her face, as if he couldn't believe that she hadn't believed him.

"I understand that you need an assistant, but it seems that Wanda believes that she's going to marry you!" She calmed herself before she spoke again. "I wouldn't want you to disappoint her."

"Oh, come on, Carol. I'm not marrying Wanda." From Carol's expression and the tone of her voice Terrence knew that she was never going to speak to him again. He couldn't let that happen and he had to make her understand.

"What do you want from me?" Carol asked, mindful of how not knowing where she stood in their new relationship made her insecure and afraid. She felt the weight of Terrence's arm rest against her waist, and her heart fluttered with unwanted excitement.

"I would like for you to understand that I want us to become lovers," he said, drawing her closer. "And believe me when I tell you that I'm not engaged."

She felt his hot breath on her neck, and her good sense seemed to scream her a warning. But her heart, body, and soul did not listen or take instructions. Instead of tearing out of his embrace and running across the street, she stood before him, inhaling the heady scent of his cologne, which had faded but left just enough masculine scent to entice and force her into reconsidering being his lover regardless of the fact that she would have some reluctance to the woman that his family approved of and most likely wanted him to marry. Finally she was able to pull herself away from him.

"What are you thinking?" he whispered as she backed away from him.

"I'm going home," she said, taking her purse and heading toward the front of the house.

"Baby, you can't believe anything that Wanda said to you." Terrence followed her through the foyer and stopped her at the door.

She opened the door and stepped out onto the porch. "Good-bye, Terrence." Her stubborn streak had set in and she was finished with playing games.

"Are you still going out with me tomorrow night?" he wanted to know.

"Do you have other plans?" she asked, studying his face underneath the soft glow of the porch light. She had made a hair appointment and other plans, getting herself ready for their dinner date. Her time and money were valuable, and she was not wasting a good hairstyle, sitting in the house on a Saturday night.

"You know I don't have any other plans," he said.

"Then we have a dinner date," she said, and moved down the steps and started across the street with him beside her.

They reached the house and Carol turned to him. "Good night, Terrence." She turned to go inside, and when he wheeled her back to him, holding her gaze under the soft glow of the porch light, she noticed the tenderness in his eyes.

"I want to be with you, date you. I want to love you," he said.

Carol listened to the intensity in his husky voice. She wanted the same things for them, but her past experiences and her stubbornness stood strong like a mountain, blocking her from trusting him completely.

"After tomorrow night you're not going out with me again, are you?"

Carol looked away, not realizing that she was that transparent but realizing that she should not go out with Terrence at all. "I can't go out with you," she said, wishing she would never have involved herself with him.

"Carol, you have to trust me," he said.

"I trusted you," she said evenly. "I thought that we would continue to see one another once were home."

"I want the same for us," he said.

"Under the circumstances, I don't believe that is possible." She looked away, not wanting to look into his soft black eyes. She thought that she had finally found herself a man whom she could date and maybe love. But when it came to her heart, she was selfish.

"Carol, please!"

"I don't like placing myself in the middle of other people's affairs. And you knew that you were engaged to be married. You should have told me!" She snatched her hand out of his and walked inside.

"Carol." She heard him call her name, but she didn't answer. She double-locked the door and with measured steps walked to her room. Her heart was heavy, and tears were burning her eyes. She sat on the edge of her bed and stared ahead, and allowed the anger and hurt to rush through her. From the distance she heard the long whistle of a rusty freight train, a lonesome sound that seemed to enhance her sadness. Tears had settled in her eyes and were threatening to fall. Instead she squared her shoulders and calmed herself.

Many years ago, before she had met Boris Myers, she had not thought that loving would be a problem, but she had found complications too many times. Her hopes and dreams of meeting the right person were nothing more than a fantasy, or so it seemed. She had no time for sorting through lies and deceit. Terrence wanted her to believe and trust him, and yet Wanda had sounded sincere. Carol had found herself in the middle of a triangle that promised more agony than she was willing to accept. She blinked the tears away and was prepared to cleanse her spirit and her heart. After tomorrow night, she would become antisocial again, and by the end of the summer when she'd return home, she would bury herself in her work. The long hours would keep her so busy that she would never think about Terrence Johnson again.

However, keeping her plans to work long hours once she returned to New Jersey was already promising to cause a problem for her. It was going to take much more than the work that she loved to forget Terrence. She was certain that her memories of him would probably remain at the center of her thoughts for many months and maybe longer.

Even years from now she would probably think of him from time to time, recalling the memories like an old song that she once loved. And Terrence Johnson was like a love song. He was music to her soul. Her heart danced to the sound of his voice. He made her body move with an uncontrollable tempo from his sensual touch, and she could never forget how her lips burned from his kisses. As she let the thoughts reel through her mind, she wondered if she would savor the thoughts and hold dear to her heart her memories of Terrence until she was old and gray and was still regretting that special day that she allowed him to uncover the passionate wrappings from her heart.

Carol sighed at the thoughts that would not leave her. Why had she been so careless? But she was thankful that at least she'd safeguarded part of her heart. The only desiring passion that she had shared with him was the sweet drugging kisses. She had not allowed him to melt her body with hot, deep, soul-searching desires.

Chapter Ten

Two weeks had passed, and Wanda was beginning to think that Terrence was losing his mind. He had loaded her down with so much work, she'd hardly had time for a lunch break. Well, anyway, she had broken up his relationship with Carol Grant the night she had called him when she had first arrived in town.

Wanda sat at the dressing table, studying her reflection in the mirror. Her eyes that had been clear were now strained and red from the hot dry sun and all the work Terrence had piled on her. And just as she had crawled into bed for a good night's sleep, the harsh whistling sound of a freight train woke her. She ran one hand over the back of her neck-length hair and frowned.

She could not believe that she was sitting in a downtown hotel room, clenching her fists and hating the woman who had answered Terrence's telephone. Who did Terrence think he was? He should've known that his mother had chosen her for his wife.

She stood and paced the room. Because of Carol, she

had been forced to live in the tiny room instead of
sharing the house with the man she loved. She peered
out of the window at the street. Nothing was stirring
except her thoughts. She wheeled around on the heel
of her bedroom slippers. If Carol thought that she was
going to be her competition, she had better find other
things to think about, because Terrence Johnson was
her husband-to-be. She had known him since she was
a girl. It was no wonder that Samantha Johnson told her
to get to Georgia as soon as possible. She had planned to
fly down with the family while they were on their way
to Simone Island. However, Samantha told her that she
would be doing her a favor if she was with Terrence,
since he needed an assistant. Besides that, Mrs. Johnson
had heard some very disturbing news. Sure enough, the
news was true. Terrence had been seen all over town
hugging and kissing some woman from New Jersey.

Wanda flopped down on the bed, feeling like a
spoiled girl. She didn't care, because she could play
games of the heart like a professional sports team, and
that was to win. She was going to make Carol wish that
she had never seen Terrence. Carol Grant had no idea
whom she had chosen as her opponent. As for Terrence—she would deal with him later.

Wanda stood and pulled off the housecoat and lay it
at the edge of the bed. She was awake now and would
hardly get back to sleep for a long time, so she sat again
at the vanity table and peered at her light complexion,
while she allowed herself to revel in her successes. She
had broken up Terrence's last relationship, which was
not difficult because the woman did not like him anyway,
at least not well enough to marry him if he was a poor
man.

One Friday evening she had asked Terrence's woman
friend to join her and her girlfriends for happy hour
at the private club they often attended. Wanda had

made certain that she had chosen the perfect time, knowing that Terrence would be there. Wanda's scheme was to get Terrence's fiancée to brag about how she was marrying Terrence for his status, and how she believed that her true love for him would come later. When she saw Terrence walking from the back of the club to their table, Wanda began talking about men and marriage. By the time Terrence reached their table, his fiancée was blustering about her marriage to the man that she did not exactly love . . .

Wanda smiled at her wonderful deed. Dealing with Carol was going to be child's play. "Oh well . . ." Wanda said aloud, and smiled, and checked her purse, pulling out her credit card. As soon as she had some free time, she was going shopping. She was fed up with Terrence ignoring her.

Wanda went back to bed, pulled the covers over her head, and let out a sigh. Terrence was not getting any younger, and she had overheard him say lately that he was ready to settle down. She looked at her ring finger. *A diamond would look nice,* she decided, allowing that thought to slither across her mind.

Her days in Georgia were beginning to look promising. Soon she would have accomplished her task. She began to doze again and this time, visions of wedding gowns and chapel music promised her sweet dreams.

Chapter Eleven

Terrence looked at the telephone next to his bed, trying to remember Christine's telephone number. He doubted she had changed the number over the years. He finally remembered and ignored the late hour of the night. He had to call Carol and talk to her if she would listen to him. He had stopped by her house at night as soon as he'd finished working, and Mavis had told him that Carol was asleep. He had stopped by the boutique to talk to her and Carol acted as if he were not in the store. When he called her cellular number, she answered his first call and after that time, she never answered his calls again. This problem was causing him to lose sleep.

This was the last time that Wanda Mincy was going to tell a lie on him. He rolled over and grabbed the telephone and dialed Mavis's house, hoping that Carol would pick up instead of her cousin.

The telephone rang several times, and just when he was about to give up, Carol answered, sounding as if he had woken her from a deep sleep. "Baby," he said in a low voice. "Can we talk?"

She was quiet, but he knew that she was listening. "Can I come over?"

"It's late and we don't have anything to talk about, Terrence."

"Yes, we do," he said, hoping that she wouldn't hang up and at least let him come over. This was the first time that he had lived this close to a woman he wanted and had not been able to talk to her. "I can't sleep," he said.

"Take a sleeping pill," Carol said.

"I don't take that stuff."

"Then have a drink," Carol remarked. Her recollections of Wanda's message to her that she was going to marry Terrence buffed her like raging storm. And Terrence had been no better, leading her on, making her think that their friendship was heading to a serious relationship.

"I don't want a drink!" He set the receiver on the cradle and drew in a deep unsteady breath. Yes it was late, he thought, but he was not sleeping tonight until he and Carol talked.

While she was thinking what Terrence had done, she hadn't noticed the silence between them over the line until the dial tone buzzed, bringing her back to the present. It was just as well that he had hung up on her, because she was not talking to him anyway, she mused, getting out of bed and heading to the kitchen for a glass of water. She noticed one of Mavis's high heels scattered in the hallway, and her purse lying by her bedroom door. Carol decided that Mavis and Tanika must have partied this Friday night.

Carol had chosen to stay home the last two Friday nights. Going out only meant that she would run into Terrence, and she did not want to talk to him. She took

Mavis's belongings to the living room and lay her purse on the coffee table and set her shoe near the door. At that moment she also wished that she could talk to her girlfriend Jay, but it was too late, and she couldn't talk to Mavis, whom she knew was asleep by now, consumed by exhaustion and fun. Carol's vacation was turning out to be the worst. Her peace and serenity had left her and all she wanted to do now was go home.

Carol was on her way to the kitchen when she heard a light tap on the front door. The noise drew Carol out of her thoughts. "Yes?" she asked, wondering who could have been visiting at that time of the night.

"Carol." She heard Terrence outside. "I need to talk to you."

"I'm going back to bed," she said.

"Carol, I can't stand out here and talk to you without waking up the neighbors."

That thought had not occurred to her, although it should have. Carol opened the door. "I don't know what you want to talk to me about, but whatever it is that you need to say at this hour of the night, say it and go home." Her gaze swept over his handsome face, and the thick black waves tossed around on his head, before her gaze slid to his waist-length sleeveless polo shirt covering his wide chest, and baggy pants. He came in and she closed the door and stood before him. He reached out and touched her waist, and she wished that he would not touch her. "I'm listening," she said, waiting to hear what he had crossed the street to say to her.

"Can't we talk in a room instead of the foyer?" Terrence asked her. Carol started walking toward her room. "Go ahead and tell me what urgent message you have for me tonight," she said, waiting patiently for Terrence to say what was on his mind, once they were inside her bedroom and she was sitting on the edge of the bed, ignoring his warm sensual glances.

"All I want is for you to listen to me and believe me," Terrence said, sitting beside her.

"Okay," she said, understanding that she was not getting rid of Terrence tonight until he'd had his say.

"I'm not engaged to anyone. If I was, of course I would talk to you as I talk to Mavis or any other woman in this town. But I wouldn't ask you to have dinner with me, and I wouldn't touch you." He swallowed. "I wouldn't kiss you."

Carol looked at the painting of the mountain on the bedroom wall as she listened to him, and she could almost feel his gaze searching her face as if he were looking for signs that he had convinced her that he was being honest. "Can we start over?" he asked her.

She'd listened to him, and what he'd said made sense; now she was having second thoughts. Carol turned away from the picture and looked at him. "I was your friend because I thought that you were free to date, but now I don't know." She searched his face. "I at least thought that you were decent enough to tell me if you were . . ." She let the words trail.

"I try to be a decent man, but I'm not perfect. But I would never take advantage of you."

She understood Terrence. She tried to be a decent woman, and she never thought about perfection in herself.

"I don't know," she said, looking at him. Wanda had sounded upset to her and very convincing.

"Listen to me," Terrence said, covering her hand with his. "Wanda is not right. She had this image of us—" he started to say.

"Don't you bad-mouth her to me," Carol said. "If she has an image in her mind, you probably put it there!" Carol lowered her voice, not worried about waking Mavis, as much as she was concerned about her partially opened bedroom window that could give her neighbors even at this time of the night the pleasure of overhearing their conversation.

Terrence rested his hands on his thighs and stared at the floor. "You don't understand. There is something wrong with her. I have never asked her to go out with me. Our discussions are about work," he said. "Can we start over?"

He stood and pulled Carol up from the bed with him and gathered her against his muscular chest, and she did not resist him this time, but enjoyed the comfort of his arms.

"Trust me," he said.

Carol realized that if she was taking another chance, she had to trust him, and for reasons that she could not explain to herself, she believed him. "All right, Terrence." She moved to walk with him to the door. "I'm going to bed."

"Baby, are you agreeing with me just to get rid of me?" Terrence asked.

"No, but I'll let you know in the morning," she said with a teasing smile.

"Then we're going to bed," he said, kicking off his tennis shoes and discarding his pants and shirt. "I'm not leaving until I'm satisfied that you're all right."

From the look in Terrence's eyes, and the serious expression on his face, throwing him out tonight would probably cause one of the loudest arguments, which would have ended with her slamming the door. By morning the news would be scattered to the far ends of the town. "Get in the bed and go to sleep." She slipped out of her housecoat and slid beneath the covers, with the compulsive notion to stare at his strong muscled thighs and his beautiful physique.

Terrence slipped in beside her, his flat stomach

pressed against her hips and he felt her shiver against him. "Stay on your side of the bed," she said.

He pulled away from her. He did not want Carol to think that he wanted to use her for his physical needs. He wanted her to trust him, and tonight, if it drove him crazy, he would control himself. He had purposely come to her without one condom in his pocket.

And staying on his side of the bed was the best suggestion he had heard all night. So to remedy the situation that he had put himself in, he turned over on his back and stared at the ceiling.

"Baby," Terrence whispered to her.

"Go to sleep, Terrence," Carol said. She did not want to talk to him anymore tonight for fear that he might touch her. And there was nothing that she liked more than being caressed by the man she cared about. And even though he was in her bed, she was not that certain that having him beside her was the best idea.

Her memories of the past sailed across her mind like a bad dream, reminding her that moving too fast was not good for her body, but was even worse for her soul. What if she had rushed back to Terrence, rekindling what they had begun weeks ago, and realized that she had really made a mistake? She would be left to wait until the strands of her heart had woven back together and her body had stopped aching for the need she could no longer have for herself.

Memories of how she had once been injured began to flow back, flashing against her mind like still pictures in brightly painted colors. Memories that she knew she would never forget, but would use as her posting board, to keep her heart, body, and soul in check.

"Carol, you don't have to be afraid of me—of us— and what we can have together," Terrence said in a low husky voice, interrupting her drowsy pondering.

She couldn't compare him to any man in her life

whom she had kissed, held, or even talked to. "I'm being careful," she said.

"You don't think that I'm not being careful?" Terrence inquired, reaching over, touching her shoulder. His fingers lingered a while and she wanted him to stop.

"Are you?" she asked, wondering why on earth he would be afraid of her.

"Of course, I've had my problems, but I won't let the past or what anyone tells me about you ruin what we can have together." His fingers slipped along the small part of her back and he stroked lightly, then reminded himself that as much as he loved touching her, he had to keep his hands to himself. He locked his fingers behind his head and stared at the ceiling.

"I agree with you," she said. She had often allowed the past to dictate her future, ruining the chances that she might have had with a potential lover who might have brought joy into her life, and she in return could have returned the favor. Instead she had chosen her work and had allowed her hobbies to keep her happy.

"You need to believe me when I tell you that I'm serious about us being together," he said.

"Terrence." She rolled over and rose up on her elbow, studying him. His fingers were locked behind his head, his bare chest was rising with easy breathing, and he seemed to be studying with great detail the stucco designs in the white ceiling. "I believe you, and I think that we can have a wonderful love," she said, wondering what had happened to her patient nature. Having Terrence in her bed was so unlike her, even if they were just lying together and talking. At that moment, she was beginning to admire him even more. "But you know, I work a lot and I think you do, too," she said, realizing that she and Terrence weren't going to have much time for one another once they were back home.

"We'll make time to spend together, Carol. We can't allow our lives to be centered around our work all of the time."

This apparently was easy for him to say, she decided, feeling another sensual thrill circulating inside her. But she had to try. It would be a shame to walk away from a promising relationship and never know what the future might have held for her and Terrence Johnson. She would make time to know him now and then be with him once they were back in New Jersey.

"Yes," Carol whispered, "it would be a shame to allow our careers to take over our lives." She made a silent pact with herself then to let go of her past and allow herself to be loved and to give love in return. She had made the right choice, and if their relationship did not work out, she would not blame herself or hold him accountable. But still Wanda's words rang inside her head like a broken record, and she was so jealous, she did not know what she would do if she ever saw Terrence and Wanda together, even after knowing that they worked together.

He turned and looked at her. "I know our being together is right, and I wouldn't do anything to destroy what we're trying to achieve," he said, and while he spoke to her, his gaze traveled to her lips and lingered for a long time because he wanted to kiss her. Instead of following his sensual instinct, he controlled himself and turned his attention back to the ceiling.

As usual and without warning, Terrence always had the power to generate pure pleasure inside of her. "If you answered my telephone and a man told you that he and I were planning to get married, what would you think?" Carol asked him.

A disturbing shift of wind blew across his lips and he chuckled. "I would be angry, jealous, and probably ready to fight!"

"I'm not exactly ready to fight," Carol said, smiling, but I am a little—" She'd wanted to say "jealous," but thought it was in her best interest not to foster Terrence's ego. She leaned over and kissed the tip of his nose. "Go to sleep." Carol then turned over on her stomach and turned her face away from him. She was not sleepy but sleep would come.

Chapter Twelve

Terrence lay atop Carol's fresh sheets on the bed and stared at the ceiling. He was in no rush to sleep, preferring to savor the night he and Carol were spending together. Nevertheless, his lids grew heavy until he could no longer keep his eyes open. He was pleased that they were together. It was as if fate had given him another chance to meet her again. He dozed, slipping into a pleasant slumber at first, which was followed by a fitful repose.

Terrence squeezed Carol's hand, they climbed the grassy knoll. Holding on to one another's hand, they scrambled to keep from sliding backward. Her laughter rang out to him, splitting the summer day with merriment, and he stopped them, tilted her chin, and kissed her. When he looked into her eyes, he shivered from the chill that raced through him. Terrence kissed her again, hoping to recapture the warmth that he remembered when he looked at her. The eyes did not belong to her, and he shivered again from the fear that was racing through him. Quickly he released Carol from his embrace, backing away from this woman whom he did not know. She reached for him.

"Get away from me," he said, backing away from her long outstretched arm. In her other hand, she held bouquet of a white flowers and as she moved toward him, her bloodred lips moved, speaking words that he did not hear or want to listen to. "No!" he yelled, sliding down the grassy slope as visions of Carol faded and were replaced by Wanda. He struggled, but was unable to climb back up the hill to where he and Carol had been. He was tired and losing his strength. He couldn't allow Wanda to catch him; he wouldn't let her. "Oh, God— Carol!"

Terrence sat up in bed, his body wet with perspiration.

"Are you having a nightmare?" Carol stood beside the bed, dressed in a light blue tight summer dress and light blue heels. She sat on the side of the bed and gathered him to her. "Terrence?"

Terrence wrapped her in his arms. "I—ohh!"

"Are you all right?" she asked, running her fingers through his hair and straightening the waves that were damp with perspiration.

"I'm all right now," he said, releasing her. "What time is it?" He blinked against the golden bands of sun that slit through her partially opened bedroom blinds.

"It's nine o'clock, and I'll be leaving in a few minutes," Carol answered.

Terrence rolled out of bed and stretched. "I've got to get to the gym."

Carol studied his tall muscular frame and wondered what on earth he had dreamed that had put him in such a state. "I'll do just about anything to know what you were dreaming," she said.

Terrence pulled on his pants, shirt, and tennis shoes.

"I'd rather not talk about it. But please promise me that'll you'll trust me."

Carol frowned and watched him as he walked toward the front door. She was working on trust, and this work was not going to happen overnight. "I'm working on it," she said, and watched him leave her.

A few years ago, she had seen Terrence at a fund-raising party, and was about to go over and speak to him, but changed her mind when she had noticed all of the women chasing him and wanting his attention.

He had made himself clear to her last night that he believed that their being together was right. Still, she was not certain if she wanted the competition, as she realized the stress that came with dating a man like Terrence Johnson. He had everything that every woman in her right mind would want. He was handsome, well mannered, a nice dresser, had a successful career, and added to those wonderful qualities, he was rich.

Ten minutes later, her ringing telephone brought her out of her musing. "Hello," she answered, and heard Terrence.

"Baby, we can't go out tonight," Terrence said, explaining to her the problem that had surfaced in Edmond's case. Terrence had made the decision to ride with his investigators so that he, too, could have firsthand information and then there were a few people whom he needed to talk to in the town where they would be staying for a week.

"I'll see you next week." Carol sighed and hung up.

Chapter Thirteen

A week had passed and Terrence could hardly wait to see Carol. He had called her every night while he was away on business that concerned his client—and he had sent her roses and chocolates—except for last night when he arrived home. He'd been too exhausted and tense from the long ride to pick up the telephone.

Terrence tossed his duffel bag across his shoulder and took the steps two at time off the porch and out to his car. He cast a glance at the house across the street, figuring that Carol was probably at the boutique since her truck was not in the driveway. As soon as he returned from his workout, he was stopping by the store to see her. With that thought in mind, he slid behind the wheel of his car.

Just as he started the engine, his cell phone rang. Terrence pushed the earplug inside his ear and checked the name that flashed against the diminutive window. "Reese Johnson." He read the name aloud and pushed the talk button. "Yeah."

"I'm flying into Hartfield this evening, and I'll see you about seven tonight. Maybe we can get a bite to eat and hang out for a while," Reese said.

"Are you renting a car?" Terrence asked his brother.

"No. I was thinking that I could get a ride with you and I can rent a car when I get there."

"I'll be in Atlanta tonight. Why don't you stop by the club?" Terrence said, giving his brother the name of the club and restaurant where he and Carol had made plans to spend the evening last weekend before an emergency had come up.

"Will you be alone?" Reese asked.

"No," Terrence replied.

"I don't want to intrude," Reese said.

"I want you to meet Carol," Terrence said.

"Terrence, you know I don't like being a third wheel."

"Maybe we can work something out," Terrence offered as he pulled out into the street, driving slowly passed Mavis's house. He made a suggestion to his brother. "Are you sure?" Reese asked, and after more convincing from Terrence, was sold on his brother's idea.

"I don't see what could go wrong," Terrence said, easing up to the stop sign.

"You're right—yeah, do that. And if things don't go as planned, I'll find something to do and I'll meet Carol another time."

"All right. I'll see you later," Terrence said.

He cast another glimpse at Carol and Mavis's house while he waited for several cars to pass before he finally pulled out onto the highway, and allowed his thoughts to waver back to the last time he had seen his baby. He hadn't intended on sleeping in the same bed with Carol that night, but he had liked being close to her and talking to her before they slept. He settled back, driving along the almost traffic-free highway, passing tall thick groves of pines and oaks that seemed to stretch for at least two miles, before he drove past that next brick house sitting on acres of green freshly cut lawns and surrounded by thick jade bushes and crimson and canary flowers.

He took in the quiet landscape as he thought about the woman whom he knew he was in love with. Terrence counted his blessings as he remembered the late-night telephone calls he had made to her. She had sounded happy and alive when they talked, and the joy of hearing her voice had filled him with intense pleasure. He wished that he had been there with her. Thinking about her now only made him want to see her, so he quieted his thoughts. He would see her soon enough, he pondered as he turned on the radio to squelch the silence. But when a love song filled his car, his thoughts slipped to her again.

She was like a rock. Her mind was strong and hard, and like him she did not play games. Carol—the woman he needed and wanted—did not compare to any woman he had ever dated. She was honest and easy to talk to, and knowing that, he knew that he and Miss Grant could become partners for life.

Nonetheless, he had been as honest with her as she had been with him when she had questioned him for certainty on his love life. He was not in a relationship, yet he had not missed the uneasiness in her voice and the tension that had settled around her dark eyes. Her uncertainty seemed to have engulfed her and it was then that he realized that her marriage must have been tormenting. Or maybe her apprehensions had been spurred by another relationship. But there was one thing that he was sure of: he would never lie to Carol or intentionally cause her any emotional pain. Besides, he mused as the song came to an end, Carol was a determined and fiery woman and he would not want to do anything to her that would place him on her bad side. He allowed that thought to swing through his mind as other reminders from the past swept through him.

Years ago, when he was much too young to know what being in a serious relationship was about, he knew that he wanted Carol in his life.

Nevertheless, unlike himself, she had been so sure of herself that summer when he had first met her, and he had been disappointed, but he was impressed to say the least. Through the years he often thought about her and he had wondered if she was still happily married, if she had children, and if so, how many? He had suspected that she would have two or three children by now, all of which had been his reasons for not approaching her at the fund-raising party they had both attended years back.

Nevertheless, by the time he returned to college after the summer he had met her, all thoughts of the woman he cherished from a distance had not faded to the back of his mind. And when he returned the next summer for his grandfather's funeral, he had found himself staring at Christine's house, already knowing that Carol would not sit on the porch that summer.

Seeing her again was like a dream that had come true for him. Her integrity and openness were refreshing. It was as if fate had sent him to the small town to work pro bono for the young man. However, the underlying reason seemed to have been for him to meet Carol again and this time to love her as he always wanted to do.

Just as he turned into the street and was ready to cross the rusty railroad track, the red and white rails shut him out, refusing him access to cross. From the distance he saw the train's light and heard the sound of the long whistle. He settled back against the soft black leather seats and turned the volume up on the radio, listening to a song that he and Carol both loved, until the last box car whizzed by and the rails lifted, allowing him access. Terrence turned the volume down and eased across bumpy iron rails as his thoughts wavered back to her, but were interrupted by the ring on his telephone, drawing him back to the present. "Yeah," he answered impatiently, slowing to round a curve. His oldest brother, Devon, was on the line, wanting to know how his case was moving along.

"I intend to bring this case to a close very soon," Terrence said, telling his brother that he didn't need his help. He had things under control and should be home soon. They talked a few seconds more while he passed several stores and shops, until finally he pulled into the gym's parking lot. He found a parking space in the crowded lot and cut the engine.

He wove his way between the rows of automobiles to the building, then he paused in front of the glass door, thinking that he had just caught a glimpse of Carol walking away from the check-in counter. The woman turned slightly and he realized that his imagination was playing with him.

He went into the club. "Good morning," he said to the desk clerk, giving her his card. While he waited for her to check him in, he could not help but inhale her perfume, a fragrance that reminded him of Carol. "Thank you, Mr. Johnson," the clerk said, handing the card back to him. Terrence nodded and headed inside, steering clear of a group of women and men who were on their way to the lockers.

For a moment he stood at the edge of the rows of workout equipment, searching for a vacant treadmill. He spotted one on the far end of the room, and as he claimed it and jogged in place, his thoughts never left the lovely Miss Carol Grant.

Chapter Fourteen

"Mavis, I'm putting this dress aside for me," Carol said, lifting a short black dress off the rack and maneuvering her way around the three racks of expensive summer dresses standing in the center aisle.

"I was saving that dress for Mama," Mavis said, adjusting the music to a more soothing sound to relax the customers after the store was opened for the day.

"How can you save this dress for Aunt Christine, when it's on the first rack in the store?" Carol asked, looking at the size on the dress. "This dress is too small for her anyway." She held the low-cut dress out in front of her. "Besides, it's too sexy for Aunt Christine."

"Carol, you don't know Mama. She'll wear that dress." Mavis smiled as she rounded the corner behind the counter and inserted the key, unlocking the register. "But if you insist, take it and don't say anything when Mama calls you up and cusses you out."

Carol slipped the dress inside a gold shopping bag and unlocked the front door for several customers that were waiting. "Good morning, ladies," Carol said and walked behind the counter.

"Hey, how are you ladies this morning?" a stout light-brown-skinned woman said while checking the gold watch that hung loosely on her wrist. "I thought ya'll opened at nine o'clock instead of nine-thirty?"

"You know better than that," Mavis said, picking up a ticket from the tray on the counter. "Tanika, did you put a dress away for this woman yesterday?" Mavis asked, and Carol glanced over, noticing that the ticket was made out for Wanda Mincy.

"Yes, Miss Mincy will be in today for the dress." Tanika made a swift gesture toward the plastic bag that was hanging on the gold rack behind the counter. "She told me that she was down here to help Terrence and that she was going out tonight." Tanika swung her head from one side to the other. "All she talked about was Terrence Johnson. Carol, you'd better watch out." She giggled.

Carol pretended that she wasn't paying attention to Tanika. If she heard one more word about Wanda and Terrence, she did not know what she was going to do. It was taking her a lot of time to trust herself again, and she thought that she was progressing nicely, although she thought that she might have been moving too fast, especially when she was behaving like a wanton woman. She had allowed him to shower her with kisses, which she enjoyed. And last week he had sent her a dozen fresh roses every other day, except for yesterday, when he'd sent her a box of chocolates, too. Terrence's thoughtfulness finally revealed the shocking truth: she was in love with him. She had waited all week to see him, and late last night after she and Mavis and Tanika returned from their night out, she could think of no one but Terrence.

Carol began to make herself busy, ringing up the

customers' purchases, but as soon as she had taken care of them, her thoughts twisted and turned, forcing her to think of Terrence again. She banished the thoughts, only to be reminded of the telephone call, with Wanda reminding her that she and Terrence were planning to be married. An untrue image of Terrence and Wanda entwined in a loving embrace flashed across her mind, and Carol felt a twinge of jealousy coiling inside of her. She crammed her imagination to the far corners of her mind and prayed that the image stayed in place. She had reached a place and time in her life where and when she only wanted peace. But she had allowed Terrence to enter that special place inside her.

She shut out the thoughts that managed to surface again, and began arranging the jewelry on the rack that sat on the edge of the counter. When she was finished with the simple task, she kneeled down and began arranging the jewels in the glass case below the counter. She finished and rose from her position, and looked at the tall light-skinned woman standing on the other side.

"I'm Wanda Mincy. I'm here to pick up the dress." She gestured to the dress that was hanging on the rack behind the counter.

Carol had finally gotten to meet the woman she had spoken to on the telephone last week. Wanda was tall, with a light complexion and black neck-length hair. Her red lips curved into a smile that did not reach her cold narrow black eyes. "That will be sixty-five dollars," Carol said.

"I would also like that bracelet," Wanda said after glancing at Carol's gold nameplate, and leaned down and pressed the tip of a finger against the glass case.

Carol felt her heart flutter against her chest when she saw the man's gold bracelet that Wanda had chosen. The jewelry looked as if it was a perfect fit for Terrence's wrist. "Do you think Terrence would like this?" Wanda asked her.

Carol shrugged her shoulders and kept her cool. She would not allow herself to think any negative thoughts. She had to trust the conversation that she and Terrence had had with regard to Miss Mincy. "I don't know, but it's nice," Carol said more to herself than to Wanda as she closed the lid on the jewelry box.

"I have to buy something nice for my boyfriend," Wanda said, and smiled at Carol sweetly.

"Are you paying with cash or using a credit card?" Carol asked as she controlled the anger that threatened to rise and spill from her.

"Of course, I'm using the card," Wanda said, still smiling. "I don't have a cent on me. It's not that my job doesn't pay well." She stopped and looked at Carol while she gave her the credit card. "I'm Wanda and I'm down here to work with Terrence Johnson," she said. Her smile faded. "I could hardly wait until he's back from his trip." Wanda took her her card back from Carol.

"I'm sure you couldn't wait," Carol replied. If Wanda's intentions were to pluck her nerves, she had succeeded. Carol fiddled with that thought, recalling again how her heart had been broken twice and each time she had walked away as if nothing happened, and as if her spirit had been intact. Added to that, she had packed away the hurt and buried herself in her work to forget how she had allowed herself to walk into a trap. She would not keep quiet again, and Terrence would know her feelings tonight!

"Oh"—Wanda turned back to her—"do have gift wrap?"

"No, but we do have shopping bags," Carol said with a pleasant smile, as if anything that Wanda had said

about her and Terrence's love affair had not meant
anything to her.

"Anything in red?" Wanda asked.

Carol reached down and lifted one small red bag with
gold handles from the shelf. "I think your bracelet will
fit nicely in this bag," she said, and watched as Wanda
dropped the gift inside.

"I'm surprised that everything down here is so expensive," Wanda complained as she glanced around the
store and back to Carol.

"We sell quality," Carol said.

"But when you love someone, money doesn't matter," Wanda replied.

"I can imagine," Carol said.

Wanda smiled sweetly. "Have a nice day."

After Carol took care of several more customers, she
checked her watch. She had a hair appointment and
didn't want to be late. "Mavis, I'm going," she said
when Tanika came to take her place behind the counter.

"Okay, I'll see you later," Mavis said. "And you and
Terrence have fun tonight."

"I don't know about the fun," Carol remarked
sternly. She'd had about all she could take from hearing
Wanda bragging about her and Terrence's wonderful
love life.

Mavis laughed. "I had a good time last night."

"I suspected as much, since your shoes and purse
were all over the house again." Carol chuckled.

"You weren't doing too bad yourself. I heard you
pacing the floor while you were on the telephone. I
knew you couldn't have been talking to no one but
Terrence at that hour of the night." Mavis laughed.

"I was talking to Jay," she said quietly, taking her
purse from the drawer. She didn't want to discuss Terrence.

"I like this dohickey." Carol heard a woman admiring

a dress in the center row, as she was leaving. "Do you have this in a size twelve?"

"I hope she didn't forget that I ordered that black suit for her." Carol listened to the rambling conversation as she headed to the door, the soft jangling bells that hung over the entrance drowning the conversation among a group of women as the door slowly closed behind her. She stood outside the boutique for a moment and calmed herself. She had made many mistakes in love but nothing like this.

At that moment Carol experienced a disturbing quiver of uncertainty, and she tried to ignore the unsettling feeling coursing through her. She was here to relax and so far she had enjoyed herself more than she had planned to, which was an added spice to her visit. Nevertheless, all sorts of ugly thoughts about Terrence reeled their way through her mind as she walked to her truck. He was a disgrace, to say the least, and she had no one to blame but herself.

She unlocked the door and looked up, standing face-to-face with Lennie Cass, the man who made her recall memories from the past. Carol cringed at the sight of him as the fear that was supposed to have died sprang to life in her. She did not know what she was going to do or how she was going to stay in this town much longer, faced with the harsh memories that were wearing against her soul again, and wondering whether or not Lennie Cass had changed. Or was he still hanging around wooded areas and rising creeks?

Carol looked at him through a narrow gaze; she would not let her fear of him ruin her time in Georgia.

"What do you want Lennie?" she asked him.

"I just wanted to say hi," he said.

"Hi," she said to him and got inside her truck, started the engine, and drove away.

* * *

The parching Georgia heat intensified, covering Terrence like an electric blanket on a summer night, as he walked from his car to Christine's boutique. He was wearing the coolest clothes he had brought with him: wide-legged shorts, a sleeveless T-shirt, and a pair of African sandals. He swiped a thin trail of sweat from the side of his face and pulled his cap low over his sunglass-shaded eyes as he searched the parking lot for Carol's truck. When he did not see the Land Rover, he walked into the crowded store, and it seemed that every woman in town was shopping.

"Hi, Terrence." A young woman walked up to him and slipped her hand inside of his. "It's been a long time since I've seen you," she said, blocking his path to the jewelry counter.

Terrence smiled. "How are you?" he said, remembering that he used to play basketball in her brother's backyard when was visiting for the summer.

"I'm fine. You know, you should stop by Sunday for dinner. I can't wait to tell my brother that I saw you."

"Where is he now?" Terrence asked, just as another woman closed in on him.

"I haven't seen you in lately—working hard?"

"Pretty much," he said.

"Well, don't let work keep you from coming to church this Sunday," she said.

"I'll try to get there," Terrence replied. He had never gone to church regular. But it seemed that attending Sunday services in Georgia was mandatory, so he had tried to attend as many services as possible.

"I remember him when he was a teenager." Another woman spoke up while she rested her hand on Terrence's arm. "This was a skinny boy. But you're nice now since you got a little meat on your bones." She laughed loudly.

"It's nice seeing you ladies again," Terrence said, wanting to buy a gift then get himself some lunch before he went home and watched the Saturday-afternoon golf game.

"So, how is the case coming along?" another woman asked, and he raised his hands. Discussing the case was off-limits. "We're working on it," he said, moving to the jewelry case set below the counter and squatting to look at the jewelry.

"Are you buying that for Miss Christine's niece or is it for that woman who's working with you?" Terrence looked up from the jewelry that he liked and didn't answer her. He was not discussing his personal life. A few weeks ago, someone asked him why wasn't he married. He hadn't answered their question either.

"How can I help you, Terrence?" Tanika asked as he peered through the jewelry case at the gold and silver necklaces, with single diamonds. Terrence switched his gaze to the ruby and herring-bone necklaces and bracelets.

"I'll take that bracelet." He pointed to the herring-bone lying on the black velvet-covered shelf. "And the necklace." He hoped that Carol would like his taste in jewelry, he mused as he peered into the case.

The night she had come home with him, he had measured the width of Carol's wrist between his finger and thumb. If the bracelet did not fit her, he could always have links added. "I should've measured her wrist correctly," he said aloud to himself, and rose from his squat and glanced around the store again. This time he noticed that Mavis walking toward him. She was all smiles as usual and looking crisp and cool wearing a chic beige dress and gold accessories.

"Well, it's about time you stopped by," Mavis said.

"You're just the woman I want to talk to."

Terrence observed her, telling her his plan.

"I don't know, Terrence," Mavis said. She had a few issues with his suggestion.

"Please," Terrence pleaded with her while pulling out his credit card and giving it to Tanika.

"All right. Since you're begging so pitifully, I guess I'll do it." Mavis propped her hands on her hips. "Don't make this a habit."

Terrence chuckled and reached for his telephone.

"What's up?" he said, when Reese answered his call. While he spoke to Reese, he looked around the store, observing the women were mingling among dresses, hovering over shoes and purses that were in an array of summer colors. The shopping frenzy was enough to make him dizzy, so he cast a glance out the window and noticed Wanda standing outside the store, leaning against a white pole.

Terrence finished making his call and walked out, heading across the street to the diner, when Wanda fell in step beside him. "Terrence, I stopped by the house this morning to pick up the paperwork that you had on Edmond Sampson, but of course you weren't home as usual," Wanda said.

Terrence had a stack of work from his trip that he needed her to work on, but she could start Monday morning. "I'll take everything to the office Monday morning," Terrence said, taking long strides.

"Why can't I work at the house? That way you won't have to carry all those files to the office."

Terrence used the office for meetings, and he was glad he had acquired the space. The last thing he needed was Carol upset with him again because Wanda was making her believe that they were engaged. "You'll get more work done at the office and no one will disturb you," he said as politely as he could.

"It would be better if I started this evening," she said, reminding him that he would probably be in court all day Monday, and if she needed to ask questions she would have to wait until he was on lunch break.

If the regular paralegal that worked with him had come down instead of Wanda, he wouldn't have to discuss the work. He wanted to watch the game after lunch, tonight he was busy, and Sunday he was planning to go to church.

"I'll give you an idea what you need to expect."

"Thanks," she said. "Why didn't you answer my calls while you were away?" she asked.

"Wanda, after listening to your messages, I didn't think what you wanted to know was important. You had all the instructions that you needed."

"I think that you're as rude as all of the lawyers and paralegals in your office back home. You need to check your attitude," Wanda complained as they walked into the diner.

The cold air covered Terrence, cooling him from the dry scorching heat, as he walked to the back of the room toward his favorite table. He disagreed with her; he did not consider the lawyers and paralegals that worked on his team to be rude. They were all busy people. Wanda had gotten herself assigned to his case and did not have the slightest idea how to work on her own, or so she pretended, Terrence decided.

"Give me a few minutes," he said. He needed to bring her up to speed on what had happened while he was on his trip, but first he had another call to make.

Wanda pressed the back of her dress down and sat across from Terrence. She was glad that Mrs. Johnson liked her and had suggested that she go to Mr. Cornell Johnson instead of to Terrence's snooty secretary to ask if she could work with Terrence.

It had taken her a couple of days before she could

meet with Cornell Johnson, but the timing had been right. Mrs. Johnson had suggested that she talk to him just before he left work that particular day. Samantha and Cornell would be attending a social event that evening, and her husband never liked being late. All Wanda had to do was ask for permission and he would say yes. She had followed Samantha Johnson's instructions.

Wanda smothered a smile that she hoped that Terrence didn't see. Working with Terrence would give her the opportunity to convince him that they were as right for one another as Mrs. Johnson had thought they were. His mother wanted the best for her son, and as far as Wanda was concerned, she was the best woman for Terrence Johnson. Her family had money, businesses, and clout and knew all of the right people that the Johnson family knew and associated with, so of course she would make Terrence the perfect wife.

Her plan was moving along smoothly, Wanda mused. Carol would soon be out of Terrence's life. She did not understand why Terrence wanted to date a Miss Nobody like Carol, a woman who had been married and divorced and had no substantial background. She glanced over at him while he held the small telephone to his ear, and wondered who was he calling. She hoped he was not calling Carol. Carol had seemed sure of herself, and was not disturbed in the least when Wanda had purchased the bracelet and mentioned that she was buying the gift for Terrence. She had purchased the bracelet just to see the reaction on her face, but Carol had acted as if she was not bothered, not even at the sound of Terrence's name. However, she was not going to relax in her fight until she won Terrence over—and she would get him one way or another. She had worked too hard all of these years not to have gotten the man she wanted. And Carol Grant would not stand in her way.

She glanced at Terrence. He was still making calls and Wanda wondered if he loved Carol. She wouldn't be able to tell unless she saw them together. Wanda's brow pleated and she began figuring out a way to learn if Terrence and Carol were friends or lovers. She watched him punch the close button on the cellular then punch in another number.

Chapter Fifteen

Terrence did not like to give Carol short notice, but he'd thought that she would be at the store when he'd stopped by for her gift.

"Carol," he said when she had finally answered his call. He wondered why she had taken her so long to answer the phone.

"Hi, Terrence," she said.

"Where are you?" he asked her.

"I'm at Jack's beauty salon," she answered.

"Oh." Terrence groaned, understanding what she was going through. Jack's Beauty and Barber Salon was a place he'd always dreaded going to when he'd spent summers with his grandfather. The husband-and-wife team was the slowest. He understood that the couple was still working, but had added a few of their children to the team and they were even slower. He allowed his memories from the past to fade.

"What's going on?" Carol's voice reached out to him

and he took a deep breath. The sound of her voice made him wish that he was with her.

"I need to toss an idea your way," he said, wishing that they could be alone, not because she made him realize his needs, but because he loved being with her.

Carol said, "Go ahead."

He stood and moved around, turning his back to Wanda as he talked to Carol. It appeared to him that Wanda was listening to every word he was saying. He lowered his voice, telling Carol that Reese would be joining them for dinner tonight, and telling her of the other plans that he had made. "I hope you don't mind," he said.

"No," Carol replied. At least he was keeping his promise to take her to Atlanta. But he didn't have to involve his brother and Mavis, just to keep from spending all of his time with her. "I wished that you would have told me before you made plans," she said. "Because we didn't have to go out tonight," she added.

"Terrence, what're you eating today?" The waitress stopped beside him.

"Give me a minute," he said to the waitress.

"What did you say?" Carol asked.

"I was talking to the waitress," he said, realizing that Carol was not sounding as if she was upset. "Are you feeling all right?"

"I'm fine," she said.

"Good," he said, realizing that she did not sound as if she was delighted to hear from him.

"Terrence, I have to go. I'll see you tonight."

"All right," he said, not pleased with the cheerless discord in her voice. But everything will be fine, he mused. It had to be . . . he loved her.

Carol closed the call and settled back in the chair, ready for her hair to be blown dry and curled. At least someone would have fun tonight, she mused. Tonight would give Mavis a chance to have fun with someone other than Carol and Tanika. As far as she knew, Mavis had not gone on a date since they had been in town. Carol suspected that if nothing else, Reese was probably as much fun as his brother. He was probably equally as handsome, and Carol hoped that Mavis didn't make the same mistake she had made, and leaped before she looked. However, tonight she would deal with the problem she was having with Terrence.

Silence from the wireless telephone greeted Terrence and he joined Wanda, who seemed to have been waiting patiently for him to fill her in on her next list of duties.

"Are you ready to order now?" The waitress stopped at their table before he could get started with Wanda. He ordered a steak sandwich, a large glass of cola with extra ice, and a large order of homemade potato wedges.

"I'll have a salad," Wanda said, and named the dressing while taking a small recorder from her purse.

"All right," Terrence said once the woman had left them. I need . . ." He began giving her the task list of information. He hadn't quite finished when the waitress set their lunches before them.

"Wow, Terrence, I'm not going to have time to do anything but eat, sleep, and work," Wanda complained to him.

"That's what you came down here for. Right?" He bit into his sandwich, and in between bites and chews, he filled Wanda in on what was happening with case and their client and why he'd taken an emergency trip.

"I thought I would have time to go out. But with this and all the other things you want, I'll have to get started tonight," she said.

"That takes care of everything," Terrence said. "You can get started anytime, just as long as you have the work done by Tuesday." He lifted the soft drink and drank half before he set the tall glass down. He then bit into the sandwich again, chewing slowly, taking his time enjoying his lunch. Between giving Wanda more instructions, his thoughts slipped to Carol. He hoped that tonight they would enjoy their time together. A strange sensation settled inside him and he prayed that nothing would go wrong that would keep them from enjoying their evening.

Carol's hair was finally dried, and curled, and the beautician was combing her hair into a loose flowing style. As soon as she was out of the chair, she paid for her services and stopped at the soft drink machine hoping that she could buy a bottle of juice. The only refreshments left in Jack's machine were mineral water and lemon tea. She headed toward the diner, preparing to quench her thirst with a nice cold glass of juice.

Carol composed herself when she noticed Terrence and Wanda involved in what appeared to be a serious conversation. Right after Carol paid for the juice, she cast another glance at them. Wanda looked past Terrence's shoulder and smiled at Carol as she reached out and stroked the side of Terrence's face.

Carol walked out of the diner and across the street to her truck. At least she knew she had been right all along; if Mavis weren't going with them tonight, Carol would be staying home.

Terrence arrived home just in time for the beginning of the golf game. He stretched out on the wide blue sofa and pushed the button on the remote control. A few hours later, he woke up to the sound of the cheers; Tiger Woods had won the game.

Working long hours, and staying up half the night

since he had been in town, and then meeting and spending time with Carol—a treat that he didn't mind—was finally catching up with him. In a short time the trial would be over, and he would be able to go away and relax.

Terrence checked the time on his wrist. If he didn't hustle, he was going to be late. With that thought crossing his mind, he hurried to get ready.

Carol was beside herself. She was absolutely sure that the only label she could give to the feeling circulating inside her and stopping to hover at the edge of her heart was unadulterated jealousy. An emotion she had no right to claim when she thought about Terrence and Wanda. But seeing Wanda smiling sweetly at her twice in one day was not only nerve-racking but an indication that she was not in a competitive mood for Terrence's love or friendship. Nevertheless, she was not going to refuse his invitation to have dinner tonight, and maybe she would have a little fun. Afterward, she intended to tell Terrence what she thought of him. She was looking for total commitment and not some fly-by-night love affair.

Nonetheless, nothing seemed to stop the green-eyed monster from spiraling to the core of her soul. Carol squared her shoulders and took the black slender bareback dress that she had bought from the boutique to wear for the evening.

She had allowed herself to enter into a web of one-sided passion, and she was determined to untangle herself from it. However, if she was to straighten out the emotional chaos within her, she was going to have be strong. She fought to control the ugly jealousy that threatened to send her into a rage and destroy her spirit. She sighed, stilling the anger.

Today when she had spoken to Terrence, she had kept any feelings that she may have had earlier for him out of her voice. Admittedly, she had allowed herself to be distracted by too much sensuality that he showered on her. Carol loved him for his tenderness, but she had no time for imitated lovely acts when her emotions were involved. If Terrence wanted another lover besides Wanda, she was certain that he would have no problem finding someone to stroke his overblown ego. But the busier Carol kept herself, the quicker she would get over this disaster. Carol pressed her lips together. She planned to keep things simple when she told Terrence that they could not remain friends. A tear rolled lazily down her cheek and she brushed it away.

Chapter Sixteen

Huge chandeliers hung from the ceiling, filling the room with a dim glow. Waiters dressed in black tuxes moved gracefully as they carried large trays filled with delicious food and colorful drinks. And while quiet conversations mingling with soft music filtered through the large dining room, Carol sat quietly, listening to the conversation and forcing herself to be polite to Terrence.

Once during dinner, Carol glanced at Terrence's wrist, checking for the bracelet that Wanda had bought for him today. However, she only saw the gold links that held the cuffs of his cream-color shirtsleeves together. Terrence, Reese, and Mavis were discussing everything from last night's eleven o'clock news to the days they had all been in Georgia many summers ago.

Nevertheless, Carol thought it was better if she listened while she finished the pinwheel-stuffed steak, the tiny carrots, and the sugar peas.

"So, tell me, Carol, how are you enjoying your summer in Georgia?" Reese asked her, drawing her into the conversation against her will.

"It's nice and quiet," she said, studying the man who resembled his brother. Carol glanced at Terrence, and lifted the wineglass. "It's a change of pace," she added.

"I have to agree," Reese replied, and turned his attention to Mavis. They began talking about her work as a registered nurse, and in the meantime, Carol almost squirmed beneath Terrence's smoldering gaze.

They finished their dinner and talked more, when the band began to play. Reese and Mavis moved to the floor, joining several other couples, and Terrence pushed his chair closer to her. "What's wrong with you?"

His warm, low baritone voice floated out to her and she was determined not to fall into his magic web or be pressured into discussing her feelings and her beliefs fearing that she might start a scene in the restaurant.

"Can we talk later?" she asked in an even tone. It wasn't the place to end the relationship that she thought had meant as much to him as being his friend had meant to her.

Terrence reached for her hand and began lifting her from the chair. She wanted to refuse his offer to dance with him, but if for no other reason than for herself she needed to be as graceful as possible to get through this evening. She would soon have plenty of time to keep her distance from him.

In spite of her reasons for breaking up with him tonight, she felt good being in his arms, moving to the rhythm of the music and feeling his masculine body against her. The heady scent of his masculine fragrance and the soft kiss he planted on the side of her neck were enough for her to change her mind. "Can we wait until the band plays something faster?" she asked, pulling out of Terrence's embrace.

"Are you ready to go home?" he questioned her. Terrence walked beside her as they went back to their table.

"I'm ready whenever you are," she said.

Without speaking, he sat and waited for Reese and Mavis to join them. When they returned and were seated at the table again, Terrence and Reese began talking among themselves in low voices. Carol turned to Mavis. "Are you enjoying yourself?"

"Yes," Mavis said. "But you don't seem to be having much fun."

"Let's go to the ladies' room," Carol said, excusing herself. She was unable to hold in her feelings much longer. Telling Mavis what was on her mind probably would not help, but hopefully she would feel better. She let the thought wheel its way through her mind as she and Mavis moved down the wide aisles and into the plush black-carpeted corridor to the powder room.

Carol pushed open the door, entering the powder room with its two cream sofas and matching chairs on opposite walls. She caught a glimpse of herself in the wide mirrors, noticing the long mass of thick black hair that fell over her slender shoulders. She sat on the sofa and crossed her legs.

"What happened?" Mavis stood in front of Carol with her hands on her hips.

"Mavis, I like Terrence a lot." She paused. "But I'm not going to put up with him and his lies."

"What lies?" Mavis asked, pressing her hands across her soft peach dress as she joined Carol on the sofa.

"Terrence and I had a long conversation before he left for his trip. I thought we had gotten to know one another better. And he swore that he was not in a relationship. He even told me that Wanda Mincy, the woman that's a friend of their family, is not his lover." Carol cast her gaze toward the ceiling, and explained to Mavis the problem she was encountering with the man—that she thought she could not trust him enough to continue their romantic friendship.

"He's probably being honest," Mavis said, eyeing her cousin carefully.

"I don't think so, since he seems interested in Wanda."

Mavis touched the tip of her short red nail to her bottom lip. "Terrence doesn't seem like the type of man who would lie and cheat, Carol."

"Then will you please tell me why on earth Wanda was in the boutique this morning buying him a gold bracelet?" Carol's voice rose.

"And you know all of this and you're out with him anyway?" Mavis asked, lacing her fingers together.

"For two reasons," Carol said. "First, he pulled one of Boris's old stunts, making plans and then telling me what he'd done. My second reason . . ." Her voice ebbed.

"Don't you think you're overreacting?" Mavis asked, arching her brows. "Maybe he and Wanda are friends," she added.

"I have had platonic friends, but I've never told his girlfriend that we were planning to marry," Carol remarked hotly. "I don't need Terrence and his drama in my life." She waved her hand close to her crossed legs, striking the clusters of jade stones against her silk. "Gosh, I ruined my pantyhose." Carol got up and went to a stall, pulled off the stockings then dropping them into a wastebasket on her way out of the ladies' room.

"Carol, why don't you just ask Terrence if he's dating Wanda?" Mavis asked her with a very concerned expression on her face.

"For what—so he can lie to me again?" Carol asked, annoyed at herself for feeling her jealousy rising.

"I mean, Wanda is working for him, Carol." Mavis stopped walking and forced Carol to look at her.

"And what a lovely arrangement," Carol replied. "You know, I have seen Wanda before, but I can't remember where."

"You know, ever you since you divorced Boris, you have been unreasonable, and it seems to me that your last relationship has left you unreasonable when it comes to men," Mavis said as they walked back to their table.

"I suppose you left your ruined marriage in high spirits?" Carol spoke quietly as they neared Terrence and Reese, who were rising and pushing their chairs close to the table. "And of course Reese is the first man that I've seen you with since your divorce."

Mavis and Carol stopped several feet away from the men. "I know that. But what I'm saying is that I think that you're being too hard on yourself and Terrence," Mavis whispered.

"Hard on him?" Carol replied in a hushed voice before they joined the men. She was not being hard enough on Terrence. He wanted a relationship with her, and she wanted the same, but she needed stability— and the truth. "If he does not want a romantic friendship with me, then he needs to be man enough to tell me."

"Is everything all right?" Reese directed his question to Mavis.

"We're fine," Mavis said, and stood beside him.

"Good, because we're not riding with Terrence. I've rented a car." Reese reached out and covered Mavis's hand. "You guys have a good night." Reese glanced at Carol as he and Mavis walked away from her and Terrence.

Carol's plan to talk to him tonight began to taper off. She should probably wait until tomorrow or some other time because tonight she feared that she would be a bundle of emotions. And when she was upset, it was hard for her to make her point. "I'm ready to go whenever you are," she said to Terrence, her thoughts fading into the soft din of a love song that filtered out to them from the band that sat at the back of the room.

Once inside the car, Terrence pushed the overhead button, switching on the light, and pulled out a CD from a leather case. "Are you ready to talk to me now?" He slipped the music inside the player, filling the cab of the Mercedes with a warm and passionate melody.

"We'll talk tomorrow," she said, hoping that the music had camouflaged the anger swelling in her voice. She cast a side glance at him and noticed the shadow of faint light against the side of his face. It was no wonder that she'd had problems with male romantic companionship. She realized that she had placed too much hope in all of her relationships. However, the more she considered the discussion, she thought it would be better if she said nothing at all, or at least wait until she not angry.

"I think we should talk now." Terrence gripped the steering wheel while resting his arm against the window.

"I think that we should wait," Carol said, unable to control the anger that bristled inside of her.

"I thought we had settled everything and had come to a decision that we wanted to continue our friendship," Terrence said, his voice as warm as ever and filled with sensuality, as if they did not have one problem.

"But apparently it seems that we have a misunderstanding," Carol said, breaking the promise that she had made to herself to keep quiet while she was still angry. Nonetheless, having said that, she relaxed against the soft black leather satisfied that he had quietly accepted her decision. "I think it would be better if we talked when both of us are calm."

"I don't think so," he snapped, as he drove the car out into the street. From the corner of his eye, he noticed that Carol was stealing glances at him.

She stole another glance, noticing that he was unblinking and still looking at what was in front of him, as the tension between them filled the interior along with the love song that was playing, reminding her of the love that she could not risk herself to enjoy. She was more than ready to settle into her own peaceful world, to bury herself in her work, and to free herself of the passion that Terrence had ignited inside of her.

The music changed to an even more sensual sound, and Carol turned her attention to the street as the lights from lanky street lamps cast shadows on them as they rode out of the city. She wondered whether Terrence had chosen the music because he also loved it, or whether he thought that the particular tracks of music would enhance the spell that he wanted to cast upon her soul, making her forget how angry she was.

An hour later Terrence pulled into their street. "Are you coming home with me?" he asked without looking at her as he slowed the speed of the car to a crawl.

"No, I'm going home," Carol said.

Terrence turned into Mavis and Carol's driveway and cut the lights and the engine, got out, and pulled off and tossed his black suit jacket onto the back seat. He closed the door with a firm snap and took long strides around to the passenger side and opened the door.

She was going to talk to him if it took him the rest of the night to take care of the problem that was standing between them. He had given her no reason to think that he was disloyal, and thought he had proven himself to her the last time that they were together, showing her that he did not want her just to satisfy his physical needs. He rolled that thought around while waiting for her to get out.

"Good night," Carol said as she was inching her way around him when he closed the door.

He pulled her back to him, blocking her path and pinning her against the side of the car while he removed his tie and unbuttoned his shirt halfway. "We're talking now," he said, following the motto that he had learned from his grandfather—*strike while the iron is hot*—as he unlocked the back door of the Mercedes and waited for her to get in. When she didn't, Terrence got in sank down, planting one foot on the floor and one leg on the seat. He pulled her between the vee of his thighs, pushing himself back and resting against the door. When Carol was safely inside, he reached around her and closed the door. "We're not leaving this car until you make sense out of why you're mad at me," he said, circling a tight grip over her flat stomach and slender waist, drawing her closer to him until her hips were pressed against the crotch of his trousers.

Carol kicked out of heels and turned around to face him. Folding her legs underneath her hips, she sat on her heels and clenched the sobs that were rising inside of her. "You are a liar," she said, hating to be controlled by anyone except herself. "You know I'm right," she added, noticing that he was too quiet.

"How did you come to that conclusion?" His voice was like the first chill of a winter's night, forcing her to look away.

"Terrence, I saw you in the diner with that— woman!" Carol felt the jealous rage swelling in her, and she turned to get out of the car, when she felt his strong hand grip her waist again, pulling her closer to him. "Take your hands off me."

"Not until you listen," Terrence said.

"What's to listen to?" she asked, turning back to him. There was nothing he could say to convince her that she was wrong. "She couldn't keep her hands off you."

Terrence had had no control over Wanda brushing the side of his face and he had wondered why Wanda had suddenly found it necessary to touch him. It was clear now about her reason for the sudden performance, a gesture that she had never done to him before. He had asked Wanda why was she touching him, and she could not give him an answer that made sense.

"I thought that you believed me when we talked?"

"I had no reason to disbelieve you until later," Carol said, fighting the overwhelming battle not to lose control of herself.

"How can we have a relationship when you don't trust me?" He covered both her hands with his, and pressed them against his chest.

"We can't," she said, managing to stay calm and sounding more like herself.

"Carol, you're upsetting yourself for nothing," he said. His deep tone floated out and challenged her.

"I am?" she asked, staring at his watch before switching her gaze to his bare wrist. "It must be nice to have Wanda buying you an expensive gold bracelet because she's a friend of the women in your family!" Carol snapped, holding to the scanty control that she had managed to maintain during the evening. She swallowed the hot salty tears that threatened to spill from her, and she tried to pull her hands off his chest, feeling the beat of his heart as if nothing she said had upset him. This made her more angry.

"What?" he asked, tightening his hold on her hands as he switched his gaze from her face to the skirt of her tight dress that had inched up around her thighs as she struggled to free herself.

"Where's the bracelet that she brought for you today?" Carol's voice was intense, rising and echoing against the fine interior of the Mercedes.

"What bracelet?" Terrence questioned her, studying

her as though he wished that he could ease her pain and the suspicion that Wanda had so skillfully managed to insinuate, tearing away the fibers of the relationship that he and Carol were trying to build. And he hated Wanda. Realizing that he could not convince Carol, Terrence closed his eyes and rolled his neck, tossing his head from one side to the other.

It was too late to get another assistant. However, he expected within the next few weeks the trial would be over, and he would be rid of Wanda and her lies. But if he had to put her on the next flight out of Georgia before the trial ended, he would do that, too, because he would not have her ruin what he was trying to build with Carol. "Wanda may have brought a bracelet but it wasn't for me," he said, remembering the jewelry that he had wanted to give Carol tonight. "Baby, I love you," he said, drawing her closer to him, making her dress ease up farther over the top of her thigh.

"Save it," Carol said. She would not let herself believe that he loved her.

"You can't break up with me now, baby." He tried to draw her even closer to him, but she was stubborn, so he let go of her hand and circled her in his arms.

"Yes, Terrence." Tear tears began to blind her vision, and she looked around for tissues. He rose up and opened the console between the parted seats, then lifted out a small box of tissues that set next to a red bag with gold engraving that read *Christine's Boutique.* "After tonight there is no we—no us—no anything!" She rose from his embrace and snatched a soft powder-blue tissue from the box and wiped her eyes. It seemed as if her good sound senses were warning her not to make another mistake. But she had made mistakes time and again, and now she was repeating the process, or was she? Terrence did not seem the least bit disturbed now.

"You just can't walk away without giving us and yourself a chance," he said, trying to make her understand that Wanda was lying in her roundabout way and Carol had believed her.

"I have given myself a chance to trust you—and where has trust gotten me?" she asked him, swallowing back the fresh tears that swelled up inside of her, remembering the gift that she had sold Wanda. Through her blurry vision the bag appeared to be much larger. She spoke to Terrence, holding his gaze, but not seeing him. "I will not be lied to. I will not be controlled and I will not be abused!" Her tears spilled then, leaving a wet trail down her cheeks. She didn't resist when he gathered her to him. Slowly, he rocked her back and forth.

"What did he do to you, to make you like this, Carol?" Terrence was beginning to understand that her marriage must have been horrible.

She looked at him then, studying his tender gaze, and lifting another tissue from the box, not realizing that he understood that she was talking about Boris. Nonetheless, she was quiet and unwilling to discuss her awful marriage and the husband who had been controlling and overbearing. But the one thing she had given Boris credit for was that if he had ever been unfaithful, she'd never known. Unlike Terrence, who was in her face being unfaithful and wanting her to believe otherwise.

"Did he hit you?" Terrence slipped his thumb and finger underneath Carol's chin, tilting her head back, intensely watching the tears that were brimming in her eyes. "Huh?"

That horrible night of her and Boris's ugly encounter swung back to Carol and she couldn't control her tears. She had buried the pain deep inside her with intentions to forget. That particular evening her hate for Boris had grown stronger, and after she had freed herself of him and moved on with her life, she'd had a problem with the first signs of a normal social life. If there were ever any signs of her date having a controlling nature, or if she thought he was lying to her, she had retreated into her safe cocoon, and any friendship that she was building with her potential lover had ended and she had moved on with her life. But for reasons she could not explain, Terrence was relentless and unwilling to give up. "Yes," she whispered in a strained voice.

"You aren't ready to love me. Are you?" he asked, forcing her to look again at him.

"Yes, I'm ready to love you" she said, her voice much clearer now.

"Then why should Wanda's silly games and your ex-husband's cruelty have an effect on how we feel about one another?" Terrence took another tissue from the box and began wiping her eyes, but she took the tissue from him.

Carol knew that her problem was more with herself than with the blame she was laying at the feet of Boris and Wanda. She cupped the tissue in her hand and buried her eyes against the cottony soft paper. "I'm trying to change," she said, and wiped her eyes and face.

He gathered her back to him then. "You need to relax and let yourself go instead of worrying about something that's not happening," he said, speaking close to her lips. His quiet voice was calming. Terrence seemed sincere enough, pointed out details of her life that she had never told him about.

"I don't play games and I'm not out here to stroke your ego," Carol said. She was determined to rid herself of the triangle she had permitted herself to enter, knowing that getting out was much harder than she'd realized. That thought crossed her mind when Terrence's mouth covered hers and caressed her lips. Carol knew that she shouldn't, but she couldn't help slipping her arms around his strong neck and returning the drugging kiss that short-circuited her.

Terrence's hands swept over the top of her thighs. "Come home with me tonight."

Carol pushed away from him, realizing that resisting Terrence was even more difficult than the past that had followed her through the years. "I think we should give ourselves more time," she said. She hadn't intended to go this far with him tonight since her plans were to break off their friendship. Now she needed time to put her past behind her and allow herself to think about what trusting Terrence meant to her. The fear and pain and distrust that she'd thought were dead were still alive and tearing away at her soul. Beginning tonight, she would work on pulling her life back together, but not in Terrence's bed. "We'll talk," she said, reaching behind her for her purse.

"When?" Terrence quizzed her. He was willing to wait however long it would take for her to get in touch with herself.

"I can't give you a date and time," Carol replied, pushing herself forward and opening the door.

"All right." Terrence said, and straightened. He unlocked the door that he had rested against and got out and walked around the car to her. He was willing to give her time to sort through the hellish memories of her past, and he hoped that when she was finished she would come back to him. In the meantime, he would wait, hope, and pray. If for any reason he and Carol did not come to an understanding, he would thank God for the time they had spent together. He gathered her to him and brushed his lips against hers. "You know I don't want to do this," he said, while he searched her eyes with his.

"I need time to think," she said, untangling herself from his embrace and slipping her feet into her heels before she began walking to the front door. "Good night, Terrence."

He pushed his hands in his pockets and looked out into the night, which was lit with soft and dim porch and streetlights, and the million stars that decorated the dark royal blue sky. "Good night." Terrence walked past his car, not bothering to drive across the street. He didn't want to inhale the lingering aroma of Carol's perfume, and the damp tissues that she had left behind would only remind him of how hurt she was and how much he loved her. He stopped and almost went back to the car for the gift he had brought for Carol today. His second thought was to leave the jewelry until tomorrow.

Wanda stepped out from behind the thick tall pine that set at the edge of Christine's property. She brushed her hand against the black long-sleeve top she was wearing and hoped that there had not been any bugs awake who had transported themselves to her clothing. She brushed at her sleeve, thinking she had felt an insect crawling on her. But it didn't matter; she knew what she had to do and she was prepared to take the next step. Carol Grant was a real problem. Wanda had never seen Terrence that involved with anyone, she pondered as she slipped up the street and around the corner to the black sports car she had rented today. Earlier, she'd eased around the corner, hiding between the trees that stood at the edge of the neighbor's property, when she caught the first sign of headlights beaming from an automobile. She hated Carol for interfering with her life. She was now being forced to take actions that could possibly ruin her own life, which meant that she could forget about Terrence and her career. But her plan was airtight. She slid behind the wheel of the car, and brought the engine to a soft roar. She had come to terms long ago that Terrence didn't want her for his lover. *But,* she mused, *by the time I finish consoling him because Carol will no longer be available, he'll be my husband.*

That thought weighed on her as she pulled away from the curb. And the thought of her sharing Terrence's bed made her vibrate with uncontrollable flames. She had set everything in motion today when she and Terrence had left the diner. Terrence thought that keeping her busy was a way to keep her away from him. Wanda smiled, thinking how after she had set her plan in motion to destroy Carol forever, she had called her girlfriend, who had thought she was fatally attracted to Terrence Johnson. She was not fatally attracted to him, Wanda decided, she knew what she wanted.

Chapter Seventeen

All week Carol had battled with herself, keeping herself busy at the boutique to refrain from thinking about Terrence. Since the last time she had been with him, everything seemed to have gone awry. Even her meals had been distasteful. She sat over her lunches and dinners, spending more time picking at her food than eating. At night, she did not sit on the porch, looking at Terrence's black Mercedes and the house that reminded her of him. Instead, she quietly sat at the piano in the living room and stroked the keys, playing old spirituals, until she could barely keep her eyes open. At times she had caught Mavis looking at her strangely, but her cousin had respected her privacy and did not ask any questions.

The next Saturday evening when Mavis and Reese went out for dinner, Carol, too tired to read or watch television, found herself thinking about Terrence again. Her thoughts of him played in her mind like an old movie, moving in slow motion.

Later at night, she lay awake listening to sounds of small critters and the low lonely whistle of the train, and she fought to stop the tears that lay inside her. By Sunday morning before she joined Mavis in the kitchen for coffee, she knew what she had to do. If she was wrong, then she would be strong enough to walk away forever from the happiness that she thought she had found.

"Carol, are you listening to me?" Mavis cut into her thoughts.

"What were you saying?" Carol asked, taking her favorite mug from the tree, while the last thoughts of Terrence faded.

Mavis looked up from filling her coffee cup. "I was saying that I liked Reese, but I'm not interested in being his lover."

"Are you saying that you're still pining over Andrew?" Carol asked lightheartedly.

"No, I'm enjoying the peace and quiet of having no one to think about but myself," Mavis replied, crossing the room, and taking a cheese Danish off the platter. "I hope you weren't serious about that Andrew remark."

"I wasn't serious," Carol said with a chuckle, tightening the sash around the red silk robe before she joined Mavis at the table. She understood Mavis's point. It was taking her a long time to get her life back on the social track. Her past relationships had been like a phantom, haunting her and making it almost impossible for her to love again.

Mavis took a sip of coffee and held the cup midair. "I think Reese is the nicest man I've met in a long time, but still I have my reservations," Mavis said.

"Are you going out with him again tonight?" Carol was curious.

"Yes, we're going out again tonight," she said as she

broke the sweet in half, then licked the cheese off the tips of her fingers.

"He might make you a nice friend," Carol said.

"I wouldn't want to get too close to him," Mavis replied. "I'm sure Reese is not totally free to date without complications."

"Why? He doesn't seem bad," Carol said, after she had sipped coffee.

"We talked a long time last night. Reese has been divorced for several years and he has recently ended a relationship."

"Oh," Carol said, thinking that Mavis might have been interested in being Reese Johnson's lover.

"I'm not ready to get tangled up with his problems." A serious expression shadowed on Mavis's face. "Reese may need time to cool from that relationship."

"I understand," Carol said. Last weekend Carol had been a disaster because of the suspicions she had of Terrence. Imagining him and Wanda sharing the same bed had almost driven her to the brink of madness.

"I had my share of problems with Andrew, and I don't ever intend to find myself in a situation where I must distract a man I care for, to get his attention," Mavis said, before she bit into the cheese Danish. "Why don't you eat, Carol, before you make yourself sick?" Mavis was changing the subject as swiftly as she had begun explaining her reasons for not getting herself seriously involved with Terrence's brother.

Carol lifted the pastry, breaking the sweet in half and pinching off the edges, putting the food inside her mouth. Lately her food had tasted like sawdust, but the Danish was delicious.

"Carol, what's wrong—did you and Terrence have a fight?" Mavis lifted her cup and took a sip while she looked at her over the rim. She had been wanting to ask all week, but when Tanika began suspecting that maybe this was Carol's problem, she had kept quiet. In the evenings she had noticed that Carol ate as little as possible, and sometimes at night after she had returned from spending the evening with Reese, she often found Carol sitting at the piano playing spirituals that brought tears to her own eyes. Still Mavis had decided that it was better if she did not question her, thinking that eventually she would talk to her. But this was Sunday and Carol had not mentioned the problem that seemed to have been bothering her, and Mavis was worried.

"Let's just say that I needed to put space between myself and Terrence," Carol said, hoping that Mavis wouldn't pry further.

"Are you talking about a permanent space?" Mavis asked her and set the cup down.

"Not really," Carol said, knowing what she had to do. But if her plan did not work, she would not have to explain to Mavis why she had failed.

"Well," Mavis said, changing the subject again. "Mrs. Gates called me last night and asked if you could play for the choir at today's services. I told her that maybe you wouldn't mind donating a favor for a good cause."

"I wish she would've asked me," Carol said, being mindful of how Mrs. Gates had scoffed at her when she and Terrence were leaving the diner. Carol closed her eyes. Everything she did and thought about lately had Terrence connected to it. "Okay. Did she give you a list of the songs?"

"No, because I wasn't certain if you were going to play today." Mavis eyed Carol closely. "After all, you were asleep last night when she called, and I didn't want to wake you since you hadn't been sleeping lately."

Carol thought about the request for several minutes. Her music always calmed her and kept her grounded. "I'll do her the favor," Carol said, since she was attending church services anyway.

Mavis arched her brows. "I'm glad that you're going to do this, because if you don't, Mrs. Gates is going to tell Mama and everyone else who'll stand still long enough to listen. And when I tell you that we'll become the worst two women who ever stepped into this town, I'm not kidding."

"I can imagine." Carol smiled and her lips felt as if they would crack, since she hadn't smiled all week. "I'll see you at church," she said, getting up to get dressed, when the telephone rang. She crossed to the wall and lifted the receiver. "Hello?" Carol said, then held the telephone away from her ear.

"Who is that?" Mavis mouthed.

"Aunt Christine," Carol whispered loud enough for Mavis to hear her.

"Yes, Aunt Christine," Carol said. "Would you like to speak to Mavis?"

"After I talk to you." Her aunt spoke in a firm voice as if she was ready to chastise a small child. "What is this foolishness I'm hearing from my neighbors about Wallace Johnson's grandsons traipsing in and out of my house all hours of the night? And I don't want to even think about the one that spent the night with you!"

"Aunt Christine." Carol started to explain that her and Terrence's night had been innocent, when her aunt stopped her. "Behave yourself and let me speak to that daughter of mine!"

Carol held the receiver out to Mavis. "She wants to yell at you, I think."

Carol watched as Mavis took the phone, listened, frowned, and opened her mouth to speak, but as Carol suspected, her aunt was not giving Mavis time to speak and defend herself. "Mother, we're going to church," Carol heard Mavis say. She changed her mind about getting dressed right away and sat down to finish her coffee.

Carol had intended to go to church last Sunday, but she couldn't find the strength, and when Tanika announced to her Monday morning that Terrence had been sitting in the front pew, Carol was glad she hadn't attended services.

"Carol, I'm tired of these neighbors taking care of my business," Mavis said when she hung up.

"That one next door needs to be put on punishment for meddling." Carol agreed with Mavis. It did not seemed that much passed their next-door neighbor, and Carol knew she should have closed the window the night Terrence had slept in her bed. She thought of that night as she excused herself and went to her room.

Twenty minutes later, Carol had twisted her hair into a loose knot and dressed in a powder-blue collarless suit, and rolled the long sleeves on the jacket up over her wrists, displaying a clustered pearl bracelet that matched the pearls that hung from her ears. She slipped her feet into a pair of white heels and covered her head with a wide-brim hat matching the color of her suit. "Don't be late," she said to Mavis as she left.

"I'll be on time." Mavis smiled.

Carol smiled, remembering that her aunt Christine had been the one to encourage her parents to have her take the free music lessons that the community center offered after school three times a week and during the summer. During those years, Mavis and her aunt had been their neighbors. After school, she'd run across the backyard to play with Mavis and while there, she had found her way to her aunt's brown piano. She would touch the white ivory and stroke her tiny fingers against the black keys, until one day, Mavis sat beside her and taught her to play "Do-ra-me." Carol's memories of the first real sounds she had played were still with her. She had been amazed at the timbre she'd had the ability to create and by the time she was in the second grade, she was playing a few of the songs that she and her classmates sang at school. Carol dismissed that thought as she parked in the church's parking lot and went to meet with Mrs. Gates to see what music she had for her to play.

Ten minutes later she took her seat at the piano, and while the church got crowded, she played the music to "Our Father's Prayer." Once the minister began the service she continued to keep her eyes on the piano keys or on the music sheet before her. When she could stand it no longer, she glanced out into the congregation and locked gazes with Terrence. She inclined her head again before lifting it to see Mavis, Reese, Wanda, and Lennie who were also seated in the second pew.

From the corners of her eye she cast Terrence another sensual glance and noticed quickly the dark-blue suit that he was wearing. He wore suits most of the time, Carol considered, but today his suit seemed to be the top of the line. She cast her eyes back on the piano keys and listened to the sermon. When the minister was finished, she struck a note and the choirmaster led the choir into song with "Touch the Hem of His Garment." Carol played the music, and the choir serenaded the congregation with their beautiful voices. It wasn't long before she played the final song, "Save My Soul," for the services. It seemed that Mrs. Gates had chosen a few of the songs especially for her. Although she hadn't exactly gotten through the storm and rain, she was releasing the pain. When the song was over, she stole another glance to the pews and studied Terrence. He looked good, but he appeared tired, as if he had worked too hard and not slept much.

Finally the minister spoke the words closing out the services, the choir rose, and she played the last chords to "Amen."

Carol waited until the church was empty before she

walked outside to the truck. As she went to the Land Rover, she noticed Terrence, Reese, Mavis, and Wanda standing on the church grounds talking to several people. For a moment she cast a glance at Terrence and he met her gaze, pushed his hands in his pockets, and looked away from her as he dug the heel of his shoe into the grass.

Carol headed home, coming to terms with her reality. All men were not Boris; no one shared the same mentality and beliefs. But when Terrence took charge, making decisions for her, she resented his actions. She fiddled with the thoughts as she drove home. Once at home, she changed out of her suit and into a comfortable flare-tailed spaghetti-strapped red dress and a pair of two-inch-heeled red sandals.

She stood at the kitchen counter, not thinking of anyone or anything except the quick meal she was preparing. She cut the lettuce for the salad, took the frozen spicy wings from the freezer, placing the meat inside the oven. Mavis had wanted to make their lunch, but Carol had needed to keep busy. But the more she thought about Terrence, the more she was losing her nerve to carry out her plan.

"You played your heart out, girl," Mavis said after she had changed into an oversize, long, sleeveless black housedress and joined Carol in the kitchen.

"Thanks," Carol said, feeling much better than she had all week. She felt as if she could take on the world again.

Mavis took out the cranberry salad dressing from the refrigerator and set the bottle on the counter. "Everyone seemed to have enjoyed themselves," Mavis said. "Lennie Cass was clapping his hands to the music."

"I guess he has changed," Carol said.

"Maybe, but I don't trust him, so be careful," Mavis warned as she began making homemade ice tea.

"I will," Carol said, checking the wings. "I'm not working tomorrow," she said, telling Mavis about the errands she had to take care of.

"No problem. Tanika can handle things. Because I'm going on that buyers' trip tomorrow," Mavis reminded her.

"In that case, I can help Tanika," Carol offered.

"Don't worry, Carol, this is the most help Tanika has had since Mama left town." Mavis smiled. "Even when Mama is in town, she practically runs the place alone. But I'll let her know that you won't be in when I stop by in the morning to pick up one of the orders that I forgot."

It wasn't long before Carol and Mavis were sitting around the kitchen table enjoying spicy wings, a garden salad, and tall glasses of Mavis's ice tea. They talked about mostly everything, including what their friends and coworkers were probably doing back in New Jersey. But neither breathed Terrence and Reese's names, except when Mavis mentioned that she and Reese were going out for the evening. An hour later, after enjoying their lunch, they tidied up the kitchen before Mavis went to get dressed for her date.

Soon the doorbell rang and Mavis, who was now ready, checked her watch. "That's Reese," she said, heading toward the door. "I'll see you later."

"Have fun," Carol said. And to keep from thinking about Terrence and the decision she had made, Carol began re-wiping the kitchen counter and the table, and when she had finished with those chores, she went to the living room and dusted the furniture that appeared to have been dusted earlier that day.

Carol opened the drapes and looked across the street, noticing Terrence's car, which reminded her of her decision. Every fiber inside of her insinuated that she was right. She carried the duster to the broom closet, picked up the telephone, and dialed Terrence's number. "Are you busy?"

"No" was all that he said. He wanted her to come to him, but he would not ask. She needed to believe that he would not do anything to ruin their relationship.

Carol held the receiver to her ear, taking in the sound of his husky voice and considering how foolish she would be to let her distrust stand in the way of feelings for him. If she lost Terrence because of hearsay, she might deprive herself of a love that she may never know again, and she would have no one to blame but herself. "I'll be over in a minute."

"I'll be waiting for you," he said. "Baby, will you pack an overnight bag?"

"Yes," Carol said, holding the receiver, waiting for him to say more. She wondered what he had in mind for the evening. "What type of clothes?" she asked.

"A change of clothes for tomorrow," he said. They talked for a few seconds longer before hanging up.

Minutes later, Carol Grant rang Terrence's doorbell.

"Hi," she said when he opened the door, feasting her eyes upon his bare muscular chest, flat stomach, and the loosely tied black string that held the black baggy pajamalike pants on his narrow waist, before she settled her gaze on his firm hips.

"Come in," he said, and she didn't miss his dark sweeping gaze.

Carol walked into the foyer and he gathered her to him. She rose a few inches and covered his mouth with a hot burning kiss. She was not depriving herself or Terrence of their happiness. "I love you," she whispered when she had pulled away, ending the kiss.

Terrence smothered her lips again, clutching her against his bare chest. He lifted his head a half an inch from her lips, "I love you, too." He squeezed her to him. "I'm glad you're here." With that said, he smothered her lips with another kiss.

They freed themselves from their embrace and Terrence circled one arm around her waist as they began to walk slowly through the foyer to the den.

"Can I get you a glass of wine?" he asked, and locked the door once she was seated on the comfortable sofa and waiting for him to join her.

"Yes," she said, realizing that she had made the right decision to visit him. She looked around the room, taking in the many family photographs framed in gold, and the bowling trophies lining the shelves.

"One glass of wine for you." He grinned and set the tray with the bottle of Chablis on the cocktail table, and crossed to the stereo, turning on the music to a low volume before he sat beside her and lifted his Scotch on the rocks from the tray.

Soft romantic music filled the dimly lit room, casting a warm amorous atmosphere, and again Carol never thought that she would have found herself miles away from home living one of her dreams. "I've had time to think." She expressed herself quietly as she shifted her gaze back to him and his muscular chest. "I want to continue our friendship," she maintained evenly, and lowered her gaze.

"Do you think that you made the right decision?" Terrence asked, scooting back on the sofa closer to her and crossing one leg over his thigh.

"Yes," she said as he stretched his arm along the back of the sofa, and she felt his fingers stroking the top of her shoulder, sending a trail of thrills through her.

"I love you. You know that." He stroked the side of her neck with the side of his thumb, sending another spiral of warm waves through her, and she moved closer to him.

"I had a lot of time to think," she said, tracing one

finger against the tip of his moustache. "I have chosen to let go of the past. That part of my life is over." He touched his lips to hers then and she parted them, allowing him entry to a long tender kiss.

They slipped into an embrace, drinking the sweetness from their kisses and cherishing every minute, as if they were making up for the time they had lost. He slowly pulled away and out of their embrace, and reached for his drink as if he were having serious thoughts about a particular matter.

"Carol, are you sure about what you're doing?" Terrence sounded doubtful. He had suffered during the time that they had broken up over Wanda's lies. Who was to say that Wanda would not play another trick?

He lifted his glass to his lips. Not taking his eyes off her, he set the glass down.

"Of course, I'm sure," she said. "I would not be here if I was not serious." She had not struggled with the decision to rekindle their friendship. "I know that I've had problems listening to and believing—" She stopped, not wanting to say Wanda's name. "But, Terrence, I don't want to hear any more about you being engaged. If I do, I can't promise you that I'm going to continue being your friend or your lover." However, she would not deny herself or Terrence the pleasure that they both enjoyed. She loved being with him and he seemed to enjoy her.

"Promise me that you won't listen to Wanda."

"I promise," she said.

"Now that we have settled things . . ." He chuckled and gathered her to him. "Baby, this is not a summer fling."

"I understand," she said, realizing that she once thought that he had wanted an intimate fling to carry him through the summer. She slipped her hands behind his neck and drew him down to her. "I want us to be together for a long time," she whispered, and he leaned in farther to meet her parted lips.

"What about forever?" He cupped her face in his hands and raised his head.

"Forever sounds good," she said, and smiled, and kissed the tip of his nose.

"I want us to be more than lovers, sweetheart." His soft voice floated out to her, mingling with the music. She wanted more than to be his lover, too. But it was too soon to think about marriage, she pondered as she stroked her fingers against his wide chest, tracing a trail over the mounds and peaks, feeling the dark nubs harden like pebbles beneath her fingertips. Her breath caught in her throat as his strong fingers curved beneath her flare red dress, stroking and caressing her hips. She heard his breath become unsteady again, and she joined him with similar actions as soft lamenting sounds slipped across her parted lips as his broad hand eased between the silk and her round hips, caressing sweet ambrosia. A thrilled charged her, jumbling her thoughts when Terrence stopped.

"Are you sure you want to do this?" Terrence asked, and hoped that she could hear him, because in his excitement he was unable to speak above a hoarse whisper.

Carol rolled her head in a feverish nod, and she shivered under his touch, when he raised her in his arms again and slid the zipper down on her red dress, then peeled away the thin straps.

Chapter Eighteen

Through a slanted gaze she watched as he studied the black lace bra, and without hesitating further, Terrence unsnapped the bra with one thrust of his fingers, peeling away the black lace, exposing firm beige breasts. She shivered even more as a soft moan slipped from her as he kissed between the crevice of her firm round mounds, leaving a fiery trail showering her with slow, hot kisses, igniting a sizzle through her. When she could find her voice, she whispered his name. "Terrence."

"Hmm?" he murmured, kissing her again.

The flame flickering through her smoldered and sizzled, heating her body until she could barely stand his fiery touch as he explored her with kindling kisses and stopping momentarily to move the flare skirt of her dress up around her thighs. Without warning, he eased away from her and took a protective packet from his pants pocket, unloosened the knot, and stripped. For a moment he looked at her before he gathered her to him. His breathing was labored, as he calmed himself. "Oh, Carol."

"Hmm?" Carol stroked his wide shoulders as he slipped his fingers underneath the band that held the twist in her hair. Waging war not to lose control Terrence slipped the straps of her dress off her shoulders. No words were spoken as they explored every inch of each others body. They stopped only to skim each other's lips with a kiss, then slowly as if their lovemaking was a dance, move their hands magically against each other's body. Their sensual touches ignited soft murmurs, slipping across their lips and mingling with the love song that floated out from the speakers. Their bodies were moist and damp from prolonging their destiny to enter and lay claim to that world belonging to them.

Without rushing, they entered into their own magical world, slowly exploring crevices and secret places that made their blood sizzle through their bodies as they slowed and tasted the sweetness of each other's lips. As they moved along a rocky path, Carol and Terrence felt the pleasure of sweet harmony.

Their world began to spin and reel, swirling and swaying and they held on to one another as if doing so would refrain the explosive moment that would return them to the real world. They were successful and their passion continued to spiral through their bodies.

The prickly heat that Carol had felt earlier seemed to have grown hotter and intoxicating and without warning she felt herself skidding off their passionate path, and Terrence's response joined hers. They slipped from the peak of uncontrolled rapture and embracing and basked in the golden-glow of pure satisfaction.

Minutes later, Carol and Terrence rolled in the waves of flames and hot passion. They climbed rocky mountains, and slipped along paths laced with pleasure, dipping and reeling as they climbed to higher peaks.

Carol skidded and short-circuited as the flames burned deep in her body, her heart, and to the core of her soul. As they inched their way through crests of confectionary bliss, weaving their way farther up a spiral path to another place that only later they both would remember, she thought she heard a door slam. She wanted to speak, to tell him that someone was inside of the house, but again her speech was a tousle of delirium. And still they inched together as one to a sizzling peak, filled with gratification and unabashed passion, lost and lingering in their own private world. Without warning they exploded, spiraling and clinging, and finally they basked in a warm glow of wanton pleasure.

Carol tightened her arms around him and they savored the moment. "Terrence, did you hear a door close?" Carol asked drowsily. "I thought that you locked the den door."

"I did," he answered. His voice tapered, and he kissed the tip of her nose. "It was probably the wind blowing the back screen door," he said, remembering that he had not locked the screen door. He also had opened the windows in the living room and study earlier, he remembered as he gathered her closer to him. They lay together quietly, listening to the sound of crickets singing from the creek and the lazy croak of frogs, before they climbed the stairs to his bedroom and slept.

Around midnight, Carol and Terrence slipped again into their private world of passion, savoring each shivering kiss, every tender caress, until they could no longer stand the smoldering heat. With nothing or no one to stop them, they entered their passionate world, filling one another's desires and quenching the reckless cravings that they had waited so long to share. When they had reached the peak of sensation and tumbled back to the real world, Carol lay beneath the covers, still glowing in the lovemaking that she and Terrence had enjoyed.

"Baby," Terrence cradled her in his arms.

"Hmm," she said, dozing in and out of sleep, because she was a happy woman. She had no worries or problems. Her life was finally falling into order; nothing or no one could stop her or take the joy that she had found.

"I love you," he said, squeezing her against his hard body.

"I love you, too, sweetheart," she murmured. Freely, she had given love and affection to him and they had shared a passion that she had never known. She was beginning to feel the stability that she needed; her emotions seemed to have healed and her worries had ceased. Her dreamlike reflections brought her to a fully awake state and she lay comfortably in his arms, her curves resting against the straight hard lines of his muscular body as she listened to his quiet breathing. She watched through the partly opened drapes the many stars set against the dark blue sky. It was as if a miracle had been bestowed on her and she knew that she would never be the same again.

Had it been plain old-fashioned luck that she had found Terrence in the deep red clay hills of Georgia? Carol couldn't believe her luck had changed for the better. It was almost too good to be true. She had begun to think that she was undeserving of a very good man. Just when she had finally given up, she had found him. Carol closed her eyes, thanking the stars above that she had found him. She felt his arm tighten around her waist and she let out a breath of contentment. Feeling his smooth skin against her was like a balm. In a short time he had filled the empty space that hollowed that part of her heart and soul. He had the ability to change her mind, and to her this was not an easy task. But Terrence's sexy magnetic air had the ability to entice her into his orb of passion. Finally, she had conquered the loneliness that had held her prisoner in her own private world of distrust. Because of her choice, she believed, she had brought happiness not only to her life, but to Terrence's life, as well.

Monday morning, Carol woke to a half-empty bed. Feeling the space where Terrence had slept beside her last night, she sat up and pulled the black satin sheet around her shoulders. The bands of faint sunlight lit the bedroom as golden beams streamed through the partially opened gray draperies.

She observed her surroundings. The black sofa was scattered with two black-and-white pillows, while the third pillow lay atop the cocktail table, nestled against the gold potted green plant and a fat white candle. Her red dress and underwear were draped neatly on the gray recliner farther across the room. The sound of footsteps stopping outside of the bedroom drew her out of her observation and she slid out of bed. Her bare feet sank into the thick gray carpet as she went to the bathroom for a shower. Again she wondered who was inside the house. It was almost past 10:00 A.M. and Terrence and Reese were working by now, she considered as she entered the huge bathroom with its Jacuzzi tub and vanity that stretched along one wall. She stood between two black cushioned vanity stools and opened the top cabinet, finding a thick white washcloth and towel, before she stepped inside the shower, filling the room with thick foggy steam.

Enjoying the hot shower, Carol closed her eyes, allowing memories of her and Terrence's night together to return. As she sorted through the private recollections, she made it clear to herself that regardless of her career, she would make time for him. She was thankful that she had reached a point in her life where she would not wait any longer to give herself the gift of love. She would not allow herself another minute of loneliness. Because of her decision, she had finally opened her heart to him, allowed him to enter places that no man had gone for years. She felt no remorse and she was content. She had Terrence to thank for showing her again how to unleash the savoring affection that hovered inside her. She felt good, knowing what it felt like again to love a man. To truly believe and know that he loved her, too, was enough to make her want to spend the rest of her life with Terrence.

As she allowed her thoughts to unravel, she heard the bathroom door close. Carol turned off the water and wrapped herself in the towel before she looked out to see if there was anyone around or whether her imagination was playing a trick on her. Or maybe Terrence was back, she decided, then glanced into the bedroom. Terrence had told her last night that the wind had probably blown the door downstairs. There were no open windows in the bathroom. Not liking the feeling that she was being spied on, Carol took the shorts set from her overnight bag and she packed the clothes she had worn last night. Carol slipped into the white shorts and a coral top and put on sandals, anxious to go downstairs and leave the house, since there seemed to have been people walking in and out, peeking in the bathroom and slamming doors.

"Good morning." Samantha Johnson spoke to Carol.

Carol had reached the last step when she heard the feminine eastern accent, and noticed a fair-skinned woman wearing blue jeans, black shirt, and a pair of black toeless heels.

"Good morning," Carol said, and continued to walk toward the door.

"My name is Samantha Johnson, I'm Terrence's

mother," she introduced herself. "I was waiting for you to come down." Her full dark red berry-colored lips tipped into a wide smile.

Carol let out a breath of relief, thankful that she was not losing her mind. "It's nice to meet you. I'm Carol," she introduced herself, watching as Samantha's sweet smile faded, and with the toss of her head, a more serious expression crossed her face. She ran four dark berry-red fingernails over the center of her shoulder-length hair, sweeping back several black-tinted strands that had swung loosely over her high cheekbone.

"Well, I'm glad that I met you. It's too bad I didn't get here in time to stop you from making that mistake you made last night."

"Excuse me?" Carol turned, fixing her eyes on Mrs. Samantha Johnson and waiting for an explanation, when she remembered the doors slamming. Had the woman been in the house and the den? She was sure that Samantha had opened the bathroom door now. "What mistake?"

"You see, I arrived in town early last evening, and thought I'd stop by and let my sons know that I had a safe trip." She let out a short chuckle. "It was a good thing that I stopped by and picked up Wanda from the hotel." She chuckled again. "I hated that Wanda had to witness the scandalous sight . . . you and Terrence entertaining one another."

Carol focused on the tall corn plant standing in the corner of the foyer instead of looking at the woman who seemed to hold a dislike for her that she didn't understand. "I spent the night with Terrence. Do you have a problem with that?" she asked. After all, Terrence was a big boy and hardly needed his mother holding his hand.

Chapter Nineteen

"Matter of fact, I do," Samantha said, eyeing her carefully. "You see, my son is already spoken for. Wanda is the woman he loves and eventually will marry. I'm sure he plans to marry her soon," she said. "So, why don't you stop wasting your time, and find yourself a man who's interested in you and not just to entertain himself?" Samantha's arched brows rose in a manner that seemed to make Carol certain that she was making a mistake.

Carol swallowed the aching, rising sensation inside of her. "Terrence never told me that he was engaged," she remarked hotly.

Samantha Johnson slapped her hands together and let out a soft laughter that reached out to Carol, touching the uneasy feeling coiling up from the pit of her stomach. "Most of them don't tell you if they're engaged, honey."

"Thanks for enlightening me." Carol felt the anger rising even more as she pulled the door open and walked down the front steps. How had she been so stupid? She felt as if she had been wearing a sign on her forehead for the world to see, only, Terrence had seen the sign first. Hadn't she heard that he was involved with Wanda? She asked herself the question while she hurried across the street, feeling as if she needed to hide herself from the world.

Hot tears swelled and burned in Carol's eyes as she walked inside the house. She brushed the tears away, refusing to cry as she lifted off the foyer table the note that Mavis had left for her. Carol read it, recalling that Mavis would be out of town this week on a buying trip. She stuck the note inside her shorts pocket and went to her room. How had she misunderstood her own feelings and the small voice that counseled her to enjoy herself to trust again and to love and be loved?

She sat on the edge of the bed as one question after another winged its way across her mind. She'd had problems trusting Terrence; now she had problems trusting herself. Had she allowed the peaceful nights and hot summer days to coax her into being unreasonable with herself—make wrong decisions? She weighed the questions and finally determined that she was too old to make this mistake. She tried to swallow her tears; instead, the hot salty water spilled from her eyes, and she had no control over her heart-wrenching sobs or the ceaseless questions that continue to riddle her. Why hadn't he been honest with her? The next round of questions began to flow, reminding her that it was men like Terrence who gave her reasons to lose trust and to make the decision to never love again.

Carol felt as if she had lost her soul for the love of passion. This love business was not for her, she considered through her tears. And she wouldn't allow herself to fall prey again to a vindictive man like Terrence Johnson. She would move on with her life and would not have anything more to do with the rapture that she hungered for, she mused, realizing that finding Terrence was the biggest mistake she had ever made in her life. She had given her love to him and he had taken it without bothering to mention that he was engaged.

Carol snatched a tissue out of the box and wiped her face, determined not to shed another tear. And Terrence would be the last man that she would allow to hurt her. She stopped herself from thinking and pushed every bitter thought from her mind, promising herself that she would stay calm and be still.

But she could hardly stop thinking how smooth Terrence had been, playing the innocent man who needed a friend. She had never thought in a million years that she would have been hoodwinked into thinking that she had found a gentleman. She had to stop thinking about what she had done. Worrying and scolding herself would do nothing to cure the pain that she was feeling now. She needed something to do; she needed to get away. She couldn't stay across the street from Terrence for the rest of the summer.

It was as if her prayers had been answered when the telephone rang—but not in a way that was a blessing. Her aunt's nervous voice reached out to her. "Carol, your father is ill. He's in the hospital and I need you to come home." Carol didn't miss the fear in her aunt's voice.

"How bad is he?" Carol asked, already calculating the time that it would take her to drive home.

"I don't know. The doctors are running tests and we won't know how bad he is until we get the results. But he was really sick this morning," her aunt Betty said.

"I'm on my way," Carol replied after giving her aunt more comforting words and hanging up. Right before she reached the closet for her suitcase and clothes, the doorbell rang. She hurried out, wishing her visitor would go away. "Who is it?" she asked, not needing any interruptions.

"Mailman!" His cheerful dry voice sounded almost rehearsed.

Carol opened the door and reached for the letter while the mailman reached inside his shirt pocket for his ballpoint pen. "I need your signature," he said. Who was sending her a registered letter was beyond her, Carol thought, as she took the ballpoint pen and signed the green card. "Thanks," she said, taking the letter and closing the door.

On her way to begin packing, she noticed that the letter was from her job. Her first thought was to open the letter, then she decided that her boss was probably calling her to work sooner than she was scheduled to return. She slipped the envelope inside her purse and stopped in front of the telephone, then decided that since she was going home anyway it didn't make sense to waste a telephone call.

However, she called Mavis and left a message in her hotel room, informing her that she was leaving because of her father's illness. She then decided that she needed to get her clothes from the cleaners before she packed. With that decision settled, she drove to the cleaners in the next town for her clothes, calculating her time, realizing that by the time she arrived in the next town and returned home, packed and filled her gas tank, by early afternoon she would be on her way home.

Driving down the street, Carol passed several older women standing outside, dressed in housedresses. Black, yellow, and crimson turbans covered their heads, as they rested against their brooms at the edge of the yard, laughing and talking with their neighbors. Carol raised her hand and waved, making sure to not to forget the customary manner, as sadness swept her, knowing that it would probably be a long time before she saw these women again. However, her thoughts quickly drifted from the women resting on their brooms to the elderly men whom she passed, taking their morning stroll downtown to stand in front of the convenient store or the supermarket and catch up on the latest gossip or to discuss the trial that Wallace Johnson's grandson was working on. That thought of Terrence seemed to have enhanced her sadness, because she also knew that she would never see Terrence again.

Thoughts of Terrence and his dishonesty stood front and center in her mind, and she realized that when it came to the affairs of the heart, her instincts had become impaired over the years.

Carol stood at the dry cleaners counter, paying for and picking up her clothes. Then she drove to the fast-food restaurant, realizing that she had managed not to think about Terrence for the last twenty minutes. She sat eating alone, a habit she had become accustomed to over the years. But today she needed to be in the company of others, which usually kept her from thinking about her problems.

She watched a small boy having a tantrum, three tables across from her. It seemed that he wanted another orange juice. She imagined Terrence looking and acting the same when he was a child. She looked away from the boy and his flustered mother, who was now pulling the boy to the counter with her and ordering him another juice. She wondered whether Terrence had used a sophisticated tantrum on her and had gotten what he wanted. A tear stung her and she blinked, wiped her mouth, and carried her tray to the waste container before she made a public spectacle of herself.

Twenty minutes later, she was back at home, sorting and packing her clothes and forcing herself not to think about Terrence. The telephone rang and she reached for the receiver, then thought it was better if she checked to see who the caller was before she answered. It was noon, a time when Terrence was probably on his lunch break. Sure enough, his cellular number framed the caller ID window. She let the telephone ring. With each ring her heart fluttered because she wanted to talk to him, but instead she kept her promise to herself.

Carol was almost finished with her packing when she overheard her neighbor outside her bedroom window discussing the trial. From the bits and pieces of information she heard her say, the jury had plans to decide the verdict after the closing remarks this afternoon. She dismissed idle talk, and locked her luggage, rolling the suitcases out through the back of the house where she had parked the Land Rover. When she had stored everything inside the vehicle, she returned and made sure all of the windows and doors were locked.

With that done, Carol headed downtown, with thoughts of Terrence at the center of her mind as she pulled up behind a truck at the gas station. She pulled up behind a truck at the self-service gas tank and dismissed her rambling thoughts and read the red and white sign next to the gas tank: PAY INSIDE BEFORE PUMPING GAS.

Just as she was about to head inside to pay, a car's horn honked, followed by, "Hey Carol." She turned and waved to Tamika. She dismissed her rambled musings and headed inside to pay for the gas, turning around to wave to Tanika who was the one who'd blown her horn and yelled, "Hey, Carol!"

It was then that she noticed Terrence, Reese, and Wanda crossing the street, heading in the direction of the courthouse. A sinking feeling curled in the pit of Carol's stomach and she stilled herself, recognizing that this was the price she was paying for not listening to her good sense and moving too fast. She had been a fool, having wasted her time with Terrence, but the mistake she had made was over and she promised herself that she wouldn't make the same mistake again.

She filled the gas tank, remembering the advice that Christine had given to her and Mavis long ago: *Look before you leap.* She had looked, but still she had been wrong in her judgment. The bell tingled, an indication that her gas tank was full, while drawing her out of disturbing deliberations.

She was hanging the gas nozzle into its slot when Lennie Cass approached her. "How are you doing, Carol?" he said, and she jumped at the sound of his voice.

Lennie stood there, looking as evil as usual, his face beaded with perspiration from the noonday humid heat. His eyes were like black marbles sitting deep inside yellow skin.

"Hi," she said, wondering what on earth he wanted. It seemed that he had finally gotten the nerve to speak to her after she had been in town for almost an entire summer. She felt her heart quicken with a hint of fear because he was standing close to her, but she soon banished her fears. She was surrounded by several people who were meandering in and out of the station.

"Going somewhere?" He peered through her slightly tinted windows and she suspected that he had noticed her luggage.

"How have you been, Lennie?" she asked, getting into the Land Rover and not answering his question.

"I guess I've been doing okay," he said in a quiet voice that held her captive along with his dark wide-eyed gaze. "You know, I'm glad you stopped me from hurting that girl," he said.

A quiver of fear struck her then, and she forced herself to calm down as she closed the door and inserted the key in the ignition. "That was a long time ago," she said, starting the engine. But knowing that he held on to a memory for that long was even more disturbing.

"I was just kidding when I told you that I was going to hurt you if you told," he said, grinning at her and reaching inside his trouser pocket, his hand resting on a short square bundle.

"I have to get going, Lennie." She put the truck in gear and began easing away from the tank.

"Wait. I have something to give you," he said, walking beside the truck, pulling the brown leather pack from his pocket and removing a business card. "I'm a changed man. I'm a member of the church and I got married and . . ." He stopped and looked as if he were in deep thought. "Well, we're divorced now, but I do have a son," he added with a proud smile.

"That's nice," Carol replied, glancing at the card that advertised his hand-made office furniture. She tried giving the card back to him. She wanted nothing from Lennie.

"No, keep it," he said, pushing his hands in the back pockets of his brown pants. "My prices are good, so if you need anything just let me know. I take orders from people living up north."

"That's nice," she said, driving slowly to the edge of the street and waiting for traffic, noticing that he was walking beside her moving truck. Once she might have believed him when he said he was a changed man, but recently her judgment of character had been poor and Lennie could never have changed as far as she was concerned.

"I noticed that you were over to the Johnsons' house, and I know that you couldn't miss the desk in the study," Lennie said.

"The desk is nice," Carol said, wishing he hadn't mentioned the Johnsons.

"Yeah." He grinned at her as she was about to pull

out into the street and banish the recollections of Terrence that waited at the crevices of her mind, ready to spring forward at any given moment.

"Take care, Lennie," she said as he walked away from her. The thoughts that were centering her mind captured her again and she shook her head slowly. It never occurred to her that Terrence could have been so trifling, knowing full well that he was seriously involved in a relationship and had used her for his own advantage. She allowed that thought to slip away from her as an even more disturbing thought replaced it. He was disgusting to say the least, she mused, wishing that she could forget the lovemaking they had shared. But images of that early evening and that night reeled across her mind like a motion picture and she could not force the images away. Finally she turned on the radio, hoping the music would drown her thoughts. But it was her luck that a song both she and Terrence loved filtered out from the speakers. The lyrics and music filled the cab, reminding her of her mistake.

A flare of mixed emotions engulfed her, anger mingled with the pain that hovered close to her heart. Even before she'd met Terrence, she knew that she had no time for a romantic relationship, but she had realized her starving need for affection. He had made her realize that essential part of her that swirled up inside her and took a front seat at the center of her heart. He had quenched her hungering desire with a passion that she had never known. Hadn't she learned anything? she questioned herself as she drove along the turnpike, scolding herself for allowing Terrence to ignite the passion inside her that she was aware she had no time for.

Carol eased up off the accelerator when the headlights of an automobile flashed, signaling that a state trooper or an accident was below the hill. She heeded to the warning signal, and while doing that, she promised herself that she would keep herself so busy, she would not waste another minute of her time thinking about love and primrose paths. She only had time for herself, her family, and her career, and one day she would put that time into the business she intended to open. In her rearview mirror she noticed a vehicle following her. As the van drew closer, she recognized Lennie Cass.

Tears rose and swelled in her, and not because of her fear of Lennie, but because of the love that she thought she had found. She snatched a tissue from the box and wiped the tear that slid over her cheek, and she prayed that when the pain had finally gone away, her soul would still be whole.

Chapter Twenty

Wanda Mincy felt as if she were walking on air. She knew that she could depend on Samantha to straighten out the havoc in her life, whether the trouble was with her part-time summer career or her personal and social life. But this was her first time asking the woman to take charge of her love life, Wanda mused as she stopped working on the assignments that Terrence had left for her.

She'd been devastated when she'd walked into the house with Samantha and headed to the den to get a bottle of wine for them. Wanda turned the knob to the den's door. Locked, she thought, wondering why would anyone lock the door to the den as she went to Samantha, asking for the key. After fingering through a row of keys hanging on a rack near the pantry, Wanda hurried back to unlock the room. She had almost fainted when she noticed Terrence and Carol were wrapped in a passionate embrace. He kissed her, then stopped to whisper sweet messages against her lips. For a moment

Wanda had felt as if her feet were stuck to the floor, while she fought the hateful sensation that had raced through her. She'd wanted to destroy them both. But she could not destroy Terrence. She had loved him from a distance for too many years. He couldn't have wanted Carol; she was from the wrong side of the tracks, and had probably been taught to throw herself at men from the time she was old enough to pay attention to boys!

Wanda fussed while she tried to figure out why didn't Terrence love her. She could not figure out what his problem was. If he gave her a chance, he would know that she was a passionate woman. Maybe he did not like her because she was outspoken and sometimes a little ill-tempered. But she was loyal to the people whom she loved. Wanda considered Terrence's reasons for not wanting her. Maybe he did not like her because of all the lovers she'd had over the years. But Terrence did not know that she had not liked them. Most of the time she had wanted to make him jealous, but Terrence had not seemed the least bit concerned when she flaunted her newest boyfriend at the Johnsons' family New Year's Eve party.

Her patience had worn thin and she was becoming more temperamental as the days passed. Wanda stared in front of her and then down at the papers. This was the last year that she was going to work as a paralegal. She would get her law degree. Maybe then Terrence would respect her. However, she didn't know what difference her being a lawyer would make to him. Besides, she had only wanted to become a lawyer because he was in the profession. It seemed that she had wasted her money and time, since Terrence was in love with Carol and she was not a lawyer.

Wanda turned back to her computer and glared at the screen. She was sick and tired of being ignored by Terrence. And for that reason, Miss Carol Grant was going to suffer. A smile curved her red lips and she returned to her work.

Chapter Twenty-one

Terrence called Carol for the third time and this time he was calling her from the steps of the courthouse. When he didn't get an answer, he called the boutique and Tanika told him that Carol hadn't come in to work.

Court had lasted longer than usual today, and between recesses, he had slipped away and called her. Even shortly after he had called his last witness to the stand, he had tried to contact Carol. Right after he and the prosecutors had met with the judge, and the jury had gone out to decide if his client was guilty or not, he had called her, and still she had not answered her telephone.

Terrence decided that he should not worry, he had enough to think about tonight, praying that the jury's verdict would set his client free. He considered that maybe Carol and Mavis had gone to dinner. He lifted his attaché case and caught up with Reese. "Did you talk to Mavis today?" he asked his brother.

"Mavis is not speaking to me," Reese said, and headed toward his car.

Terrence did not have the energy to make sense of his brother and Mavis's problems. Most likely Reese had done or said something that had upset her to the point of her never speaking to him again in her life. At any rate, he intended to catch up with Carol as soon as she was home for the evening, and he didn't care how late that was. He was hoping that maybe they could go away together before they returned to New Jersey. He needed a vacation, and spending time with her was at the top of his list.

Terrence turned the key in the ignition and eased backward out of the parking space, recalling his memories of last night with Carol. She was a sweet woman and there was no doubt in his mind that he wanted her. If it was at all possible, tonight he would ask her to marry him. He considered this possibility, realizing that it was probably too soon to ask her to marry him. But the thought was worth the warm, satisfying coiling power that was beginning to circulate to his heart. With that concept wheeling its way across his mind, he drove to the supermarket instead of going home. He didn't feel like eating at the diner tonight, and he was too tired to drive to the neighboring town for dinner. He didn't dare ask Reese to drive, halfway wondering what had happened between Reese and Mavis.

He reached the supermarket just before the store closed, and he picked up two steaks, a lettuce, and a pack of precooked dinner rolls, and headed home. He turned into his street and slowed to a crawl, noticing the warm light illuminating Mavis's front porch, casting a soft glow over the crimson roses and the many shades of carnations and tulips that added a rainbow effect to the edges of the porch and driveway.

Terrence was noticing that neither of the women's

cars was in the driveway, when he recognized their neighbor rolling her fist in a winding motion, signaling him to slid his window down.

He stopped the car and opened the window. "Good evening," Terrence said, waiting to hear what Mrs. Benson had to say to him.

"Hi, Terrence," she said, taking her time walking to his car while pressing her hand against the hem of her flowered housedress to keep the early-evening breeze from blowing it up.

"How are you, Mrs. Benson?" Terrence leaned back against the seat and rubbed his eyes. He was tired, aggravated, and fed up with the prosecutor's closing remarks, and all he wanted was to have dinner and to talk to Carol, and afterward he wanted a hot shower and his bed—with Carol beside him if at all possible.

"How's the case going?" she asked, resting her one hand on her broad hips.

"I hope we'll know by tomorrow if we won, or sometime before the week is over," Terrence said, uncovering his eyes and looking at Mavis's house.

"Oh, neither one of them has been home all day. I know that Mavis is out of town. But Carol—I don't know."

If something had happened, why hadn't Carol called him? He kept his cellular on vibrator mode when he was in court and he would have returned her call as soon as he'd had a break.

"Did something happen?" Terrence asked, feeling a bit nervous as he began to interrogate the woman who seemed all too pleased to give him information on the disappearance of the women who lived next door to her.

"Well, Christine told me before she went on her vacation that Mavis was going on a buying trip for the boutique. I can't say what happened to Carol or why she left, but I do know that Minnie King said the last time she saw Carol, she was getting gas and Lennie Cass was talking to her."

"How early was this?" Terrence asked, with worry lines forming between the bridge of his nose. He did not like the sound of this information. He had heard rumors when he had visited his grandfather that Lennie was often suspected to have attacked a couple women in the town, and once Carol had mentioned to him that she had stopped him from committing an attack on a young girl.

"It had to be after twelve, because Minnie is always downtown at that time, taking lunch from the diner to her grandson," she said, and paused, looking into the distance as if she wasn't certain if she should continue. "You know, Terrence, I believe that Lennie has changed, but I don't allow my granddaughters to speak to him or his son."

"Thanks for the information," Terrence said, praying *God, please don't let anything bad happen to Carol* as he drove away from the woman and pulled up to the curb in front of his house. He noticed that his mother's car was parked beside Reese's in the driveway.

As he got out of his car, a vision of Carol being hurt flashed in his mind and he discarded the horrible image. This was not the time for negative thoughts, he told himself. Carol was fine and he would see her tomorrow. He pushed open the door, entering the house and inhaling the delicious aroma of home cooking.

"Terrence," Samantha called out to him just as he was taking the groceries to the kitchen. "You don't have to worry about cooking, because I've already made dinner," she said, taking the bag out of his arm.

He looked at her, wondering what had gotten into his mother. The last meal he remembered her cooking was in his senior year in high school. And when she did prepare food after that, it was for very rare occasions, and she supervised those meals. "I'll eat later," he said, and climbed the stairs to his room to change into comfortable clothes.

The doorbell rang and Samantha hurried to the door. "I thought you had forgotten," she said to Wanda.

"I got here as fast as I could," Wanda said, casting a gaze up the stairs to where Terrence was. "I didn't finish my work until late," she said, laying her purse on the foyer table and following Samantha to the kitchen.

"Did you take care of that problem?" Samantha asked.

"Everything is all done." Wanda giggled, slipping off her gray suit jacket, dropping it on the chair. "I'll be right back," she said to Samantha. "As soon as I go upstairs and pry Terrence and Reese out of their rooms."

Samantha gave her a sugary smile. "Put these away first," she said, handing Wanda the grocery bag. She loved Wanda and her family. The young woman was going to make her son a wonderful wife.

In his bedroom, Terrence set his attaché case on the love seat and kicked out of his shoes, and dialed Carol's cellular number again, and still he did not get an answer after the telephone rang at least ten times. However, he got her pager and left his number. Then he walked down the hall to Reese's room.

"Reese." He slapped the door with the back of his hand. A second later his brother opened the door, wearing nothing but his underwear. "Did Mavis give you the phone number to her hotel?" he asked.

"No," Reese said. "What hotel?"

"I can't find Carol, and I was thinking that she might have gone with Mavis on that buying trip."

"I told you that Mavis is not speaking to me," Reese said.

"Do you have her cellular?" Terrence asked, getting more nervous by the minute.

Reese went to his trousers, pulled out his wallet, and copied Mavis's cell phone number. "Thanks, man," Terrence said, and went back to his room.

He took off his suit, stripping down his underwear, and sat on the edge of the love seat while he dialed Mavis's number.

Two rings later she answered his call, sounding as if she was rushing. "Hello?"

"Hi, Mavis. I'm sorry if I disturbed you. . . ."

"Terrence?"

"Yeah," he said. "Reese gave me your—"

"I don't want to hear messages from your brother, and don't call me on behalf of that man anymore!"

"Wait. Mavis?" The line was dead. Terrence hung up, and while he crossed to the closet for his pants, he grumbled to himself. "The stuff that Reese gets himself into with women!" He put on a pair of comfortable pants and headed back to the telephone and opened the telephone book, when he heard Wanda outside his door.

"Don't keep us waiting, Terrence," Wanda said.

"I'll eat later," he said. Terrence didn't mind having dinner with his mother, but why did she have to invite Wanda? He picked up the pillow that was lying on the cocktail table and tossed it on the love seat. As he leafed through the telephone book looking for the number that he wanted to call, he was thinking that Carol could not have disappeared into thin air. He decided to call Information for her home telephone number. If she had left town today, Terrence knew she would not be home by now, but when she did arrive tonight and listen to her messages, maybe she would give him a call. He considered that if she was with Mavis, he would have thought that Mavis would have told Carol that he had called her, instead of hanging up on him because she thought he was carrying messages for Reese. However, the neighbors had seen her talking to Lennie and his fears swelled up inside of him once more.

Stay calm, don't get upset! Just because Carol was seen with that man does not mean that he has captured and is torturing her. He let the awful thought return to nothingness, back to the place from where it came.

Terrence's only thought now was to find Carol. With that in mind, he dialed Information, only to learn that Carol's New Jersey number was unlisted. "Damn!" He cursed the dead end that he had reached as he dropped the receiver on the cradle.

Suddenly, it occurred to him that Carol's family also lived in New Jersey. However, that idea led to a dead end, because he didn't know her aunt's name and he had forgotten what Carol said her father's name was.

Feeling trapped in his own worries and intensifying fears, he knew he had to make the call that he'd intended to make when he'd opened the telephone book. He found Lennie's number and gave the man a call.

"Hello," a woman answered.

"Hi, this is Terrence Johnson and I'm calling for Lennie," he said.

"Lennie is not here and he won't be back until early in the morning."

"Where did he go?" Terrence asked.

"He went to New Jersey. He's visiting his son," the woman said.

"What time did he leave?" Terrence asked, and held his breath. According to the neighbors, he was aware of the time Carol had been seen talking to Lennie.

"I think he left around noon today," the woman said.

Terrence's breath caught in his throat. But he controlled himself. "Who am I speaking to?" He wanted to know for later references if needed, especially since she hadn't identified herself.

"This is his mother, Elaine Cass," she said, dragging the last name out in a Southern drawl. "Lennie is not in any trouble . . . is he?"

"No," Terrence replied. *Not that I know of,* he mused.

Elaine Cass let out a sigh as if she was relieved that her son was not in trouble. "Well, I'll tell him that you called."

"Listen," Terrence said quickly. "Is there a number where I can reach him?"

"Yes, I have his ex-wife's number here somewhere," Elaine said. "Give me a second. She changes telephone numbers so often."

Terrence waited, anticipating the best, because he did not want to believe that Lennie had any crazy ideas about Carol. *God, please let Lennie be at his ex-wife's home,* Terrence prayed.

Elaine Cass was back in a few seconds giving him the number. Terrence thanked her and placed a call to New Jersey, hoping that Lennie's wife was expecting Lennie. He hadn't yet arrived. Unfortunately, Lennie's ex-wife was not expecting him until next week.

Fear reared it ugly head again and Terrence began to panic. Without saying good-bye, he set the receiver back in its cradle and buried his face in his hands. If God would bless him to stay sane until the next morning, he would call Lennie's ex-wife again and pray that Lennie was with her and his son.

Terrence's appetite had escaped him completely, because his one need was to know that Carol was safe. He dialed Carol's cellular again. The phone rang until the voice mail answered his call. "Baby, give me call," he said, hoping that she would call him tonight. He rose from the sofa and paced the length of the floor for a few minutes.

"Terrence, dinner is getting cold because we were waiting for you and Reese." Wanda was back at his bedroom door again.

"Don't wait for me," he replied, and went to open the door. "I'm not hungry."

"If you're worried about the verdict, I think we won," Wanda stated, and smiled at him.

"Where's Reese?" he asked, dismissing Wanda's statement.

"He's in his room, acting like you. Grouchy and rude." Wanda turned and walked away, then stopped and looked over her shoulder at him. "Terrence, if you want to talk, I'll listen," Wanda said.

The only woman he wanted to talk to was Carol Grant. And if didn't find something to do, he was going to lose his mind from worrying. He headed downstairs and sat at the baby grand piano in the living room, stroking his fingers lightly over the keys. One of his grandfather's favorites came to mind and fit his spirits. "Sad Mood" was an old song that his grandfather often had asked him to play. As he stroked the keys, his mind wandered to the woman whom he had met and fallen in love with.

Terrence stopped playing, went to the study, and grabbed the telephone book. "Tanika," he said, flipping the pages and trying to remember if her last name was Williams. He thought he'd seen Williams on her name tag. He reached the last names that began with *W* and scanned the page until he came across her name and number. Terrence dialed and waited for someone to answer his call.

"What's up?" A male voice answered.

"I would like to speak to Tanika," Terrence said.

"Anything you got to say to Nika, you can say to me," the man said. "Who's this, anyway?"

"This is Terrence Johnson, I need to speak to her about—"

"Who's that?" Terrence heard her in the background.

"That lawyer, Terrence Johnson. What's he calling you for?"

"Boy, give me that phone," Tanika said. "Hi, Terrence."

"Hi," he said, too tired and worried to think about her jealous boyfriend. "Did Carol go with Mavis?" Terrence asked her.

"I don't think that she went with Mavis," Tanika answered. "But I did see her around noon at the gas station while I on my lunch break." She paused for a second. "Lennie Cass was talking to her," Tanika said, and this reminded Terrence that this was the second time he had heard that Carol had been seen with Lennie.

"Thank you, Tanika," Terrence said, and hung up, not feeling any signs of relief.

"You can't find your girlfriend?" Wanda stood in the study's doorway, wearing a sheer black silk lounger that stopped at the top of a pair of black furry-top heels.

Terrence turned around slowly, noticing Wanda's seductive attire clinging to every curve. "Why are you wearing those clothes?"

"Mrs. Johnson said that I was welcome to stay here, so I changed into something comfortable."

Terrence walked out, knowing that his mother was probably up to her matchmaking tricks again. He headed toward the kitchen and found her seated at the island counter flipping through a magazine. "What time did you get here today?" he asked, and stood on the other side of the counter, remembering that he had left Carol in his bed that morning.

Samantha raised her elegant head and searched her youngest son's face. He was too young to know what he wanted, she mused. He had everything in life that he needed and would ever want except for the right woman. "I arrived late afternoon," she answered him quietly. "And of course I stayed the night," she said. "Why?"

"Did you see Carol this morning?" Terrence studied her while he waited for her to answer his question.

"I saw her," she said, and flipped another page.

"And what did you say to her?" Terrence asked.

"Oh, Terrence, you wouldn't be interested in women's conversations." She smiled up at him, then cast her eyes on the page.

Terrence thought about that statement for a second and hurled a swift glance to the wall clock and headed back to the study to call Carol's cellular again.

Her telephone rang several times before he was asked to leave a message. "Baby, I'm worried about you—please give me a call."

Chapter Twenty-two

Carol Grant glanced at the number against the window of her cellular telephone and ignored Terrence's call as she had ignored his earlier message, while she continued to put away her last piece of clothing. She was feeling much better now, after she left the hospital and had found out from the doctor that her father was going to be all right. After listening to her aunt, she'd thought that her father was taking his last breath. She stored the suitcases at the back of the closet, and headed back to her bedroom, recalling her aunt Betty's telephone call. She took the cellular from the dresser along with a pen and pad and went downstairs to check her messages.

Carol sat on the sofa, curling her long legs underneath her and listening to a message from Jay Lee Prescott. She smiled and made a note to call her girlfriend soon. Her next message was from Mavis in New York. Carol jotted the telephone number to the hotel and went to her next message. "Baby, give me a call." The

sound of his voice was upsetting, and she was determined to control the anger that rose without warning.
Carol exhaled and managed to stay calm in the presence
of her adversity. Forgetting Terrence was her first prior-
ity, but how was she to forget him when he was calling
and leaving messages? She erased his message and finished listening to her other calls.

With that task settled, Carol returned upstairs to
her bedroom and took the registered letter from her
purse and read the contents. Terror flickered inside
her and she could hardly believe what she was reading.
As the horror of losing all that she had worked for
over the years tore at her, she clutched the letter and
read the information again.

How had this happened? She wasn't a thief, and had
never stolen anything in her life. It seemed to her that
as soon as she had accomplished one problem, she was
riddled with another. This was worse than having
learned of Terrence's trifling ways and attitude.

Nevertheless, Carol held on to her control, forcing
the rising tears to sink inside her again. She had managed to control herself on the long drive home, and
she had not thought about him much, even after she'd
listened to his messages and heard his warm voice. She
was a strong woman, and although she was hurt, she
would contain her composure.

When she had steadied herself, she paged her lawyer,
Gregory Stetson. He had been her lawyer for years; his
first time working for her was when she'd divorced Boris.
Since that time, she had gone to Gregory to handle
other minor services, but nothing as harsh as the problem she was facing. She knew that he wasn't the best
lawyer for this kind of work, but he was all she could
afford.

Carol was not certain if Gregory would return her
call tonight. Most times, he would answer her message

the next day. But just in case, she took the portable telephone to the bathroom with her, along with her nightgown.

She'd had a long day, arriving in town late and spending as much time as possible with her father before he slept. What she needed now was a well-deserved bath and a good night's sleep.

She filled the tub with hot water and coconut-fragrant bubbles. As she stepped inside the scented water, her thoughts returned to her newest problem, and merging with that, came the reflections of Terrence. She was determined to get over the humiliation that she had suffered and allowed to happen. If Samantha Johnson had not set the record straight, she would have still been allowing herself to be made a fool of.

Carol breathed, sinking deeper into the bubbles, letting the heated water ease the tension in her body. Unfortunately, the effect did not reach her heart or shut out the pain that threatened to return, reminding her that she would be all right in all of her misery.

Right then, she wished that she could afford Terrence's family's firm, but even if she could, she wasn't certain if she would retain the famous lawyer. She knew that just seeing him would be too unsettling. He had all the morals of a perfect lawyer in business, however, the morals of an ally cat hadn't escaped his personal life.

Carol sank back, closing her eyes, shutting out all thoughts. She pressed her lips together, stalling the sob that reached her throat, and she swallowed the salty tears as she remembered the passion of her and Terrence's lovemaking. The memories clung to her, making it impossible for her to forget, when her telephone rang.

She finally lifted herself from the tepid water and the bubbles that were now dissolving and wrapped herself in a thick white towel, before answering the phone. It was Gregory, and she spoke to him for a few minutes, explaining her problem. Of course, he agreed to help and she was satisfied. Her next task was to meet with her boss, since he had requested in the letter that he wanted to speak to her.

Carol said good-bye to Gregory, and she headed to her room, thinking of her so-called vacation. She may not have gotten much rest and relaxation if she had gone any other place than Georgia, but at least she probably would not have taken anyone she had met as seriously as she had taken Terrence. Nevertheless, she had chosen to participate, and for this disaster she had only herself to blame.

Tense from holding back her tears, she slid beneath the bedcovers. Her throat ached and her eyes burned from fatigue, and she felt mentally and physically drained from traveling and the added troubles that had found her. She sat up and rotated her shoulders and stretched her tired, aching arms and hands. After several minutes, she lay back and closed her eyes. For the first time in many years, Carol wished that her mother were alive and she could go to her. She drifted in and out of sleep, remembering her first prayer.

"Now I lay me down to sleep . . ." Her lids were heavy as she recalled the childhood prayer that her mother had taught her. "I pray the Lord my soul to keep . . ." She could barely keep herself from drifting. "If I shall die before I wake, I pray the Lord my soul to take." She drifted in and out of sleep, awaking abruptly each time her dreams slipped to Terrence. She prayed that any memories of him that were stored in her subconscious would fade. When she was awake and thinking of him, she controlled her thoughts and she would think of other pleasant or mundane things. But when she slept, she had no control over Terrence Johnson entering her dreams. Finally, she drifted, allowing herself to sleep, dreaming of Terrence and the love that they had shared . . .

He gathered her to him, his mouth covered hers, and she drank the sweetness of his tender kiss. His fingers slipped beneath the straps of her bra, slowly peeling away the silk, and he covered the firm round mounds, building a fiery flame inside her. He raised his dark head, regarding her with satisfaction. His gaze felt as if he had touched her soul, and she shivered with pleasure from the effects. She had no worries now, no hurts or pain. She had rid herself of those emotions and watched them scatter into the wind. She was with the man whom she loved, and he loved her. . . .

Carol rolled over, frowning in her sleep. Terrence didn't love her; he had made a fool of her and she had been responsible!

She sprang up in bed, covering her face with her hands, not wanting to free the pent-up tears that she had buried and forced to stay in the rightful place inside her. Anger kindled her but she could not hate Terrence, because she still loved him too much. Her eyes filled and finally she freed the painful overflow of tears, crying until she slept.

At the crack of dawn, Carol's telephone rang and, still half-asleep, she answered the call. She got out of bed, dressed, and left her home.

Chapter Twenty-three

"Terrence." The soft voice floated out to him, at the same time that he felt soft fingers stroking his naked back, a sensual touch that drew him out of his sleep. God, he was glad that Carol was safe and had returned from wherever she had gone. And he was thankful that she was in his room. First, he was going to kiss her, and when he was finished doing that, he was going to give her one more good lecture on disappearing and having him worry himself almost sick. He stretched as he allowed those thoughts to swirl drowsily across his mind.

"Terrence!" Wanda called his name.

"Huh!" He sat up startled, realizing that the voice he was dreaming was Carol's belonged to Wanda. "What—what do you want?" he asked, covering his face with both hands, shading the brilliant sunlight that illuminated his room.

"You need to wake up," Wanda said. Her voice mingled with the low resounding voices coming from the television that he had left on last night, after the eleven o'clock news. "You're going to be late for work. Mrs. Johnson suggested that I make breakfast for you this morning, so here it is," she said, gesturing to the silver tray on the nightstand.

"I'm not hungry." He swung his long legs to the side of the bed and sat on the edge, wishing that his dream had been reality.

"Why are you being difficult?" Wanda asked, walking around to the side of the bed, searching his face, as if being in his bedroom and making him breakfast was what she did for him every morning. "And you slept in your pants."

"Why are you in here?" Terrence said, not caring whether or not he had slept in the baggy drawstring pants that he wore around the house.

She pointed at the breakfast tray, then reached for the ringing telephone. "Yes?" she said, and held the receiver out to Terrence.

He listened for a moment. "Thank you, Tanika," Terrence said. He was relieved to know that Tanika had called Mavis last night and found out that Carol had gone home because her father was in the hospital.

"Get that tray out of here." Terrence stood, yawned, and stretched as he half listened to the television, catching the tale end of a story on the world news show. ". . . A woman has been found battered and robbed near the turnpike in New Jersey early this morning. She was found unconscious and with no identification."

Terrence felt as if his heart promised to stand still, and he gasped as he listened to the announcer read the woman's estimated age, complexion, and height, all which fit Carol's description. He began moving backward to the bathroom.

This woman could not be Carol. The jumbled thoughts raced inside his head while he pulled off his pants and stepped into the shower, washing up as quickly as he could while Wanda banged on the door. "Terrence!" He heard her over his rambling thoughts and spray of hot water. "Oh, God, I'm sorry for that woman—but please don't let this be Carol," he prayed aloud.

"Terrence, what's going on? Why are you talking to yourself?" He ignored Wanda and soaped himself for the second time, and rinsed, being careful to get out of the shower without falling and breaking his neck.

A few seconds later, he began shaving. "Ouch!" he whispered, watching the thin trail of blood ooze from the small nick and roll down the side of his jaw.

"Terrence!" Wanda called out to him again. She didn't know what was going on, but she suspected it had something to do with the woman who was found. She set both hands on her hips. She had been paying attention to him and not much attention to the news, except for the descriptions of the woman. She wished she had gotten all the details, because she had an inkling that Terrence thought the woman might have been Carol. Wanda stopped her musing and rolled her eyes toward the bedroom ceiling. *What a shame!* "Terrence." Wanda moved to the bathroom door. When he did not answer her, she left his room.

Terrence made a call to his office in New Jersey and spoke to one of the members on his investigative team. Hopefully, by the end of the day or at least tomorrow he would have found Carol.

However, there was good news for Terrence Johnson. Late that afternoon, the jury made a decision, and he would be going home soon.

Chapter Twenty-four

"Terrence." Wanda walked into his bedroom the next morning, noticing that his bed was empty, but from the partly opened bathroom door, she knew he was taking a shower. She moved closer to the door and called out his name again. "Terrence."

"Wanda, tell Reese not to leave. I need to talk to him," Terrence yelled through the door.

"Why?" she asked, still not sure what was happening. Ever since yesterday he and Reese had their heads together discussing one issue or another, and as soon as she entered the room they were quiet.

"Just tell him," he yelled at her. Terrence then took a tube of first-aid cream, and a small round Band-Aid, covering the healing cut that he'd given himself yesterday morning. Before he left the bathroom, he looked out to see if Wanda was still in the room. When he didn't see her, he secured the towel around his waist and locked his bedroom door. He then went to the closet, and chose a dark suit.

A few minutes later, Terrence was dressed and downstairs in the study, checking his briefcase, assuring himself that he had packed all the important papers for the final day of work. When he finished doing that, he picked up the receiver, preparing to call his investigator, when he saw Lennie Cass from the window walking past the house. Terrence dropped the receiver in the cradle and ran from the house, not stopping until he reached the sidewalk. With one hand clutching Lennie's collar, Terrence held him tightly around the neck. "Where is Carol?" Terrence's jaw clenched as he spoke through the small space he left between his teeth.

"I don't know." Lennie struggled to speak. "I've haven't seen since the day she was at the gas station."

"You went to New Jersey—didn't you?" Terrence pulled his collar tighter, slamming him against his car.

"Yeah, man. But I didn't do anything to her," Lennie said, struggling to pull out of the tight grip.

"If you're lying to me, you're going to be sorry!" Terrence said, releasing his hold on Lennie and ducking to miss the blow Lennie swung at him.

Terrence rushed into him, wheeling him around. The men had tumbled into the stack of green hedges when Reese ran down the steps. "Hey, Terrence, man, what's wrong with you?" Reese grabbed his younger brother, pulling him off of Lennie.

"I didn't do nothing, man!" Lennie struggled to stand up, and straightened his clothes.

While glaring at Lennie, Terrence brushed a few leaves off his blue suit jacket. "If I find out that you have hurt my woman, I am going to—"

"Lennie, are you all right?" Reese asked him, hoping that the man would not call the police and have Terrence convicted for assault and battery.

"I'm fine. It's your crazy brother who you need to talk to." Lennie gave Terrence a mean stare. "If I would've known she was your girlfriend, I wouldn't have said anything to her," Lennie said, brushing at the grass stains on his light-colored pants.

"You remember what I told you," Terrence said.

"We're not going to have any problems . . . you know, no cops involved?" Reese asked Lennie.

"No. I can understand a man being jealous of his woman." Lennie looked at Terrence, who had his back to them, resting his hands against his car. "But I would like to know what he's talking about and what's wrong with him," Lennie said, walking away from Reese.

"I understand," Reese replied. "Take it easy, man," he said as Lennie headed down the street, looking over his shoulder every once in a while.

"What is wrong with you?" Reese turned on Terrence.

"I'm upset because I didn't know what happened to Carol, and Lennie was the last person seen with her." Terrence explained to Reese how Lennie had threatened Carol years ago. "I thought he might have known something, since he was out of town the same day that Carol was for a few days." Terrence was breathing hard because he was afraid of what might have happened to Carol, and angry because no one from his office had found out who the murdered woman was. And added to that, he did not trust Lennie Cass.

"You need to behave yourself. All we need is everyone in this town to get the news about this fight."

"I know, but if Lennie Cass has harmed Carol, I will not stop until he's in prison," Terrence stated flatly while he headed inside to receive the call he had been waiting for. He listened and nodded, then hung up. He had the information that he needed, and he could work in peace today. Edmond Sampson needed him strong, not angry and upset because of his personal problems.

"What's going on?" Reese asked him.

"I have found Carol or at least I know where I can

find her," Terrence said, grabbing his briefcase. "Let's go to work."

"I'm glad you've found a way to get in touch with her, because I was beginning to worry about you," Reese said, and chuckled. "I wish I knew where Mavis was, but I guess I'll run into her when I get home."

"Yeah, but yours and Mavis's friendship is different from mine and Carol's," Terrence said.

"What do you mean—different?" Reese stopped on the bottom step and eyed Terrence closely.

"Carol and I are in love," Terrence said, heading toward his car.

"Mavis and I are working on it," Reese said. "Or at least we were."

"Terrence, why were you and Reese talking to Lennie?" Wanda stood on the porch. The question slipped from Wanda as if she needed to know all the details.

"Nothing that concerns you," Terrence answered her with a grunt, which sounded more like a low growl, as he unlocked his car door.

"You guys are so grouchy!" he heard Wanda say as he slid behind the wheel.

For a moment Terrence sat behind the wheel, calmer than he had been in twenty-four hours. As he pulled away from the curb, Terrence dialed Carol's cellular and still the only answer he received was her voicemail, asking anyone who called her to leave a message. His fear of never seeing her again had subsided, but still he worried because he only knew where he could reach her, which did not mean that she was all right. But the team was working on that for him, too. He pushed the thought to the back of his mind and prayed that she was safe, regardless of what he had heard and thought had happened to her. He hoped he was wrong, because if anything had happened to her, he did not know what he was going to do with himself. He could hardly wait

until this day was over so that he could be free to find
Carol Grant.

The courtroom was crowded and buzzing with curiosity and excitement. This had been the day the entire
town had waited for. Terrence leaned over and looked
at Edmond, recognizing his fear in his tense facial
expression. He leaned back and patted Edmond's back,
reassuring him that he should not worry. "Calm down
and relax," Terrence said.

"What if the jury finds me guilty when I'm innocent?"
Edmond asked Terrence.

"Edmond, I defended you to the best of my ability,
I gave everything that I had to offer and more. All you
have to do is stop worrying, and do not have a nervous
breakdown on me now!" Terrence said, and looked
over his shoulder around the courtroom. It seemed that
every mahogany seat was filled with the familiar faces
he had become accustomed to seeing over the many
months he had lived in the town.

Bailiffs dressed in black pants, white shirts, and black
ties, armed and ready to escort from the courtroom
anyone who became overexcited or made any angry
outbursts, were posted near the door and in certain
locations around the courtroom.

"I didn't do anything wrong Mr. Johnson." Edmond's
voice trembled with fear.

"Sampson, don't fall apart on me now!" Terrence
whispered. He understood the young man's fear, and
the thought of spending years in prison for a crime that
he did not commit was enough to drive anyone crazy.
But he needed Edmond to compose himself. Terrence
knew that his client's life was hanging in the hands of
twelve jurors, even though he had read their faces well
and believed that he had proven to them in every way

possible, especially in his closing. He had stated that his client was innocent.

Terrence noticed that the teenager had crouched over, burying his face in his hands. "Sit up straight."

"All rise!" The bailiff's voice boomed inside the crowded courtroom and Terrence and Edmond rose from their seats with the others. "The Honorable Willis ..." Terrence had stopped listening, and was becoming more concerned about Edmond, feeling the need to comfort him. He tugged at the sleeve of Edmond's black suit jacket.

It was not long before the judge gave instructions to onlookers, stating that he would not tolerate any outburst when the verdict was read.

Finally, the time had come, and the jury captain read the verdict. "We find the defendant, Edmond Sampson, not guilty." A scream of relief escaped from Edmond, and outbursts from his parents were quickly silenced with the strike of the judge's gavel.

Court was adjourned and Terrence reached out to shake his client's hand. The boy wrapped his arms around him. "Thanks, Mr. Johnson," he said, and released him and turned to Reese, giving him a firm handshake.

Terrence stepped out into the aisles and he extended his hand to Edmond's parents, but instead of a handshake, Edmond's mother hugged Terrence while her husband waited patiently to thank Terrence for a job well done.

Terrence said good-bye to his brother and left the courtroom. While he still had a few loose ends to pull together, he had business of his own to take care of. If he had stayed calm, he may have thought of the idea himself, instead of pulling on the investigators from the team to find what he needed. Terrence stopped the smile that tipped his mouth and hurried to his car. His fears were disappearing and at last he had hope.

Devon Johnson ducked through the door of his St. Simons Island villa. His fair complexion was flushed from the sun, but he had walked inside just in time to catch the tail end of the midday news segment on Terrence's victory. He had no doubts that his younger brother could prove the Sampson boy's case and have the jury find him not guilty. He watched the news, noticing that Terrence was leaving the courthouse, and in the background he spotted Wanda.

Devon tilted his wavy-haired head to one side, the skin between his brows pleated into a disturbing frown. He hoped Terrence was not being duped by their mother's matchmaking. She was the best mother anyone could want but her overprotective nature was more than he could bear. She did not think that her sons could choose their wives, and because of her, he had once blindly fallen into a trap. He never regretted his divorce, but he hated the fact that the time he spent with his six-year-old sons was limited. So far, Terrence had escaped their mother's desire to set him up with the perfect woman. But Wanda Mincy seemed determined, having gotten herself in the same town with him, and ultimately, according to Reese's telephone call last evening, she had managed to get into the house. Terrence was a strong man, Devon figured, and wheeled around, heading outside. "Are you ready, sports?" he asked his twin sons.

"Yeah!" they said in unison. Devon patted each boy on a shoulder and headed for the park.

Chapter Twenty-five

Carol moved two or three steps to the wide window in Paul's office and stopped, observing the buildings stretching toward puffs of white clouds, which reminded her of soft cotton on a hot summer's day. A bird flew from the limb of a black oak, spreading its wings and soaring with not a care in the world, or so it seemed to her. She remembered just months ago her life had been simple and easy to manage. Now she was being bombarded with one fiasco after another, finally with this recent disaster that would probably land her into poverty forever—or worse. She dismissed the fearful deliberation.

Carol pressed her hands over her dark blue suit and turned to stare blindly at the plaques covering one side of the wall that she had seen so many times. She turned away, noticing the photographs of Paul's wife and children on his desk, thinking how once her visits to his office had been pleasant. But today she was visiting him because someone thought that she needed sabotaging, and if Gregory could not prove that there was not a drop of truth to the lie and to this evil deed, she could spend years in jail.

Carol was rubbing the back of her neck and clutching her purse with her free hand, a nervous habit she had acquired through the years, when the door opened and Paul walked in. "I'm sorry I'm late," he apologized, moving swiftly around the desk and rolling his chair back. "Have a seat." He spread one hand to the chair in front of his desk.

"I'm fine," Carol said, preferring to stand. She was too angry and nervous to sit. "What is it that you want to talk to me about?" she asked, looking into his eyes and watching him shift uncomfortably before he sat on the thick black leather chair. The letter she received had stated everything she needed to know as far as she was concerned. What more did Paul want to tell her?

"I wanted to say that I'm sorry that you are caught up in this dilemma."

"You're sorry that I'm in trouble?" Carol set her purse on the desk and folded her arms across her chest. She was furious at having been accused of stealing and writing grants for her friends. She could hardly speak fast enough. "How dare you bring me up on this trumped-up charge?"

"Carol, when the problem was brought to my attention, I didn't have a choice but to report this to the authorities," Paul assured her with much sincerity.

She continued to stare at him. "Paul, I have worked for this company for years. Do you actually think that I would ruin my career?" She unfolded her arms and planted both hands on her hips.

"Carol, you don't understand," he said, swinging one arm outward to her.

"Oh, yes, I understand. You have been trying to take my job for the last year, especially when that little niece of yours trotted into town." She lifted her arm and waved a long, pointed flesh-color nail in Paul's face.

"That's not true." He rose from his chair.

"Oh, no, but you would rather that I spend sixteen to twenty or more years in prison, and that's true, Paul." She tossed her head from one side to the other as she spoke to him.

"Carol, what can I do?" He pulled open the desk drawer.

"Apparently nothing, because none of this is true. It's all lies," Carol said, wishing that this was one of her nightmares instead of reality.

"You're right, and I wish there was something that I could do to help," he replied calmly and adjusted the lapels on his dark suit. "But giving money to people just because you know them is not exactly a lie."

At this point, she was quiet. There was nothing she could do to free herself from this evil trap of lies and deceit that had been brought against her. She watched as Paul removed the white envelope from the drawer. It was clear to her that he meant her no good, and he would do anything to save his own neck. Carol was beginning to think that he was the one who had stolen from the company, and since she was on vacation he had probably signed her name to the documents.

"Here's your check." He handed her the envelope that held her severance pay and the last check owed to her for the last week she'd worked for the company.

Carol's face turned hot as anger welled inside her. She would have loved to slap the phony serious expression off his face. "Paul, I hope you're enjoying yourself with this vicious lie, because you have not seen or heard the last of me." She stuck the check in her purse and snapped it shut.

"We'll definitely see one another in court," he said. "I'm sorry, Carol."

Without replying to his shameful remark, she turned on her three-inch heels and walked toward the corridor.

"Carol," he called after her.

"What is it, Paul?" she asked, keeping the anger out of her voice as she swirled around to hear what other lie she thought he might have to tell her.

"You can't deny that this is not your signature," he said, holding the copy of an application, while he slowly spaced his words with a force that only an evil person could do with pleasure.

Carol looked at the signature on the copies of the forms that claimed she had made it possible for several people to own businesses. "This is not my signature. Paul, you are a liar."

"The only reason that this application didn't get to your brother is because there was a bit of vague information that needed checking." He pointed a pencil to the yellow circle on the application.

"Bretton has never had a grant written from this company, and the only loans that he has ever received were from his bank."

"Maybe." Paul gave her a bland smile. "But the record shows—"

"The record should show that you're full of anything but the truth." Carol spoke slowly, being careful to keep the fear and anger out of voice. Her brother was raising three boys alone, he was the owner of one of the finest marketing companies in the state, and Paul was ready to drag his name along with hers through the mud.

"I'm sure that you were only trying to help him." Paul slid the paper inside the beige folder.

"You are disgusting," Carol said, understanding that he was ready for whatever reason to destroy her and her family's life. Her brother worked hard, acquiring the finest clients, doctors, lawyers, and major companies that needed his services. His sons depended on him for their welfare, and Paul had nothing better to do than smear both their names with his lies. "Paul, trying to ruin me is one thing, but leave Bretton out of this," Carol said.

Paul shrugged his narrow shoulders. "I'm not doing anything—you did it all," he said.

Carol turned to walk out of his office. She knew he was vicious, and she had watched helplessly as he ruined other people with his lies. But never had she had a problem with him. As far as she was concerned, she and Paul had had a wonderful working relationship until now.

"I suggest that you get yourself a lawyer," he said as she stepped out into the hallway.

Carol hurried to her old office for the Bantu mask that Jay had given her when she returned from Africa, along with other knickknacks. But in the meantime, she pulled the door behind her and buried her face in her hands and said a silent prayer. She had often promised herself that when she retired or left her job for whatever reason she chose, she would open her own company. The competition, and all the responsibilities that came with her work, were exciting to say the least. Now she wasn't certain if she would have enough money to open a Popsicle stand after she finished paying her lawyer. She swallowed back a tear and reached for the mask, laying it on the desk beside the telephone, when she lifted the receiver and dialed Terrence's home number. He would be in court by now, she mused, but God, it would be nice to hear his voice.

Then she realized that she had not been thinking straight. Terrence wasn't interested in her. He had toyed with her heart and her affections and he, too, was a liar. She set the receiver in place and blinked back another blinding tear, promising herself that whoever was trying to ruin her would be sorry.

Taking the mask and a shopping bag full of other odds and ends, she hurried to the elevator, quieting her thoughts. She did not want to think about the dirty game that someone, who had chosen to play with her life, had thought would be fun. The elevator door slid open and Carol walked inside, taking her last ride on the elevator to the lobby.

The elevator door opened and Carol stepped off, ready to get away from all the disgusting deception that was threatening her life. *What if I'm convicted?* The question slid lazily across her mind and she quickly shut out the negativity. She couldn't afford to think such thoughts, especially since she was all she had to depend on.

She could hardly go to her father at this time and ask for money if she needed more to pay her lawyer. What if she needed his services longer than she expected and her money ran out? And going to Bretton was out of the question. His three boys needed all that he could give and more. Besides that, he was saving for their college funds and they grew like weeds and ate like horses. Then there were the extras that he provided for them: summer vacations and winter camps, and the list went on. She knew for a fact that the new home he had recently purchased was expensive. Carol considered that maybe if she needed him, he would give her a loan, when another thought hit her. What if she was convicted and she could not repay him?

She had no one to turn to for help. *Terrence will help you,* a small quiet voice whispered, and she ignored the suggestion. All she had was her savings and the money that she had sued Boris for during their divorce. But she would survive this disaster without the help of anyone.

"Carol, you have a phone call," the receptionist said as Carol walked through the lobby.

"Who is it?"

"He said his name is Terrence," Violet said. Her bright eyes held a seriousness that caught Carol's attention. Violet tossed her head and went back to her typing.

Slowing her steps at the sound of his name, Carol wanted to answer his call. But she had made one mistake: getting involved with him in the first place. Why didn't he leave her alone? Couldn't Terrence call Wanda, the woman he was planning to marry? Thoughts swirled in her mind, one after the other. Just when she thought she had emptied all the tears inside her, her eyes filled and she blinked back the tears.

"What line is he on?" she asked the receptionist. The least she could do was to tell him to never call her and give him her reasons for her not ever wanting to speak to him again, since he didn't seem to know the reason.

"Line two," the receptionist said, looking up from her work.

Carol crossed to the office where clients were allowed to use the telephone and pushed the door closed with the heel of her shoe. For a moment she stared at the telephone and flashing clear light before she punched the button.

"Yes, Terrence." She glanced around the room, noticing the green plants and the two racks of magazines sitting beside the black leather sofa.

"Don't you speak to me in that calm voice. You left town and didn't tell me where you were going!" he yelled, and she held the receiver away from her ear.

"I didn't think my leaving town was any of your business," she said in the same calm voice.

"I was worried sick about you and I hardly slept." Terrence's voice was even louder now.

"Terrence, I can't talk to you now because I have pressing business to take care of, and stop yelling."

"Don't you tell me to stop yelling. I deserve the right to yell! Do you know how upset I am?" Terrence asked Carol in a lower voice.

"No, I don't, but I'm certain you were not half as upset as I was when learned about your little secret," Carol remarked hotly.

"What secret?" he asked.

"Terrence, I understand convenient amnesia—I've had a few of those spells myself. So, why don't you wrack your brains?"

"What are you talking about?" he asked, his breathing floating out to her, cutting through the silence that stood between them.

Carol sighed. She had no use for him in her life. Their feelings for one another were as different as night and day. She wanted him and he did not want her. "Terrence, our summer fling is over."

"Stop playing games, Carol. That's not what I asked you," he said.

"No, you're the person who's playing games, Terrence!"

"Answer the question," he snapped.

"I don't believe that you're interested in having a serious relationship with me." She paused. "Since you left out a few major details, such as the fact that you are planning to marry Wanda Mincy."

"Baby, I'm not marrying Wanda," Terrence said, and Carol thought that she heard signs of anger in his voice.

"And, oh, I almost forgot," Carol continued, "the night that I thought we were making love—I was not aware that I was your entertainment for the night."

"Carol . . . baby, listen to me—"

"Terrence, have a wonderful life." She set the receiver down softly, because if she would have listened to the rage inside her, she would have slammed the receiver down in his ear. She stood quietly over the desk, forcing her pain to settle down before she left the office. She knew that she would never have another relationship, but she also knew even after learning about Terrence, that all men were not like him. She was as responsible as he had been. Wanda had shown her all the signs, and she had chosen to ignore her.

Carol considered her choice. She'd had her share of disappointments, and she had no room or time in her life to play games. Her choice was to move on gracefully with her life. She and Terrence were good together, but all good things eventually came to an end, at least for her. Her plan was to stay away from matters of the heart, because the agony of going through the same torture again would be too much for her to bear.

"Carol," Terrence called out to her until he heard the dial tone in his ear.

Terrence sat in his bedroom. He had just won another case, saving a young man from the hells of prison. He should have been rejoicing over his victory, but instead, he was angry because Wanda had lied, and he was hurting because Carol had believed her and now she did not want him. He covered his face to hide the angry and painful tears that brimmed his eyes. He'd had many relationships and love affairs over the years until recently, and he understood that he would never find another woman like Carol. From the sound of her voice he knew that she never wanted to see him again, and he suspected that she wouldn't believe any explanation he would give her.

Entertainment? Terrence let the word totter at the edge of his thoughts. That sounded like a word any one of the Johnson women would use, but since his mother was the only Johnson woman in town, he hoped that she had not been the woman to ruin his relationship with Carol.

Terrence got up, crossed to the closet, and began packing. He had intended to take a nap before he headed back to New Jersey. But he couldn't sleep and he would not waste another minute worrying. He intended to visit Carol at her home, thanks to his prompt investigative team.

Ten minutes later, he was packed, and calling Hartfield for reservations. When he finished that call, he called an auto shipping company and made reservations for his car to be shipped home. He intended to show Carol how much he loved her, whether or not she wanted him to love her.

Reese had not considered that he was moving too fast with Mavis. However, she seemed to have thought just the opposite. She had thought that their dates were all fun, when he'd wanted to get serious. He understood that she had recently divorced and probably did not want a serious relationship, but when he kissed her and told her that he was interested in more than a friendship, Mavis seemed to have drawn herself into a cocoon after she told that she was not interested in having a love affair with him. He tried to reason with her, or at least suggest that they could be friends. Mavis was not interested and he had taken her rejection seriously. He'd told her that he was not her ex-husband. That statement had started an argument between them and she'd gotten out of the car without mentioning that she was going on a buyers' trip. And that was the last he had seen of her. He was not a man who gave up easily, and if he wanted something badly enough, he did not stop until he had what he wanted.

It was not often that he knew what he wanted, but

when he made up his mind, he was right about the choice. Now all he had to do was to convince Mavis that they were right together. Reese considered that convincing Mavis was not going to be an easy task.

Chapter Twenty-six

Carol sat on the tan leather sofa in Gregory Stetson's office, nervously sipping the spring water that his secretary had set on the table for her after she had ushered her into her lawyer's office and explained that his meeting would be over shortly.

Carol did not want to wait, because the extra time would give her the opportunity to sort through and worry too much about the disaster that her life was falling victim to. Falling in love with Terrence was the first disaster. She didn't think that she had to have special standards to love him. However, it would be impossible for her to even fantasize about a harmonious relationship with him or his family at this point, since his mother was determined to point out that Carol was not good enough for her son.

If she and Terrence had an honest relationship and remained lovers, she was certain that there would not be one peaceful moment between them. She understood the importance of family, and she did not expect him to defy his mother because of Carol's love for him. She lifted the clear crystal glass and took another sip, cooling the nervous heat that was moving through her, which was brought on mostly from thinking about Terrence. She would get over him one day, she understood, but meeting and loving him had been like reaching the end of her rainbow and finding that special pot of gold. A pot of gold that was now sealed behind a glass door not allowing her access. Nevertheless, she had Samantha Johnson to thank for enlightening her. She would always be grateful, knowing that Terrence had used her for his own pleasure. He had no intentions of loving her and when he had smothered the words *I love you* against her lips in the flames of passion, he had lied.

She set the glass down and swallowed back the bitter tears that emerged and mingled with the spring water she had drank, deciding that she did not know what was more painful—hating him or loving him. Nevertheless, she could not afford to hate him. Her loathing would only bring more misery in her life—and she needed peace.

"Carol." Gregory walked in, slipping out of his black suit jacket and hanging it in the closet. His pecan-tan skin seemed flushed from the outside heat, however, his smile was pleasant. "How are you?" He sat on the edge of the desk and crossed one leg over his thigh.

"Gregory, you know that I'm not well," she said, stilling the trembling in her voice. "I need you to prove that I did not steal from the company. These people have my signature on grants and . . ." Her voice trailed.

"I know, and I'll do everything that I can, but it really doesn't look good," he said. "After I got your message, I looked into the problem, and it's not going to be easy."

"Don't you have handwriting experts working for you?"

"This is not a cut-and-dried case, Carol, and it's going to get expensive," Gregory said, quoting her a fee that was far more than that of the divorce he had handled for her years ago. "And that's just for me to get started," he added.

Carol crossed her legs, releasing her dream of owning her own business. The idea that she'd have to struggle from scratch played across her mind. Swinging behind that thought was the one that if she was found not guilty, she would never be able to work at another company doing what she loved, because she would have a record of being a potential thief. She snatched a tissue from the box, rose from the sofa, walked to the window, and took her checkbook from her purse. "I need for you to start as soon as possible," she said, writing the amount he had quoted and holding out the check to him.

Gregory Stetson crossed the floor, taking the check. "Good," he said after looking at the amount. "I'll get started on those handwriting experts right away."

"Thanks, Gregory." She glanced away, hoping that he hadn't noticed her tears.

"You're welcome." He gave her a reassuring smile. "We only need to prove that the signature is not yours." He sat back on the edge of the desk, stroking his thumb against the edge of the cherrywood, and she noticed that he looked worried.

"Do you think you're going to have a problem proving that I'm innocent?" she asked.

"Carol, this is not a divorce case, and the company believes that you signed those grants and loans."

"What do you believe, Gregory?" She moved across the room and stood before him.

"I believe you're innocent until proven guilty," he said.

If she could afford another lawyer that she believed would really fight for her for the price she was paying

Gregory, she would feel much better. Nevertheless Gregory Stetson would defend her better than a public defender. "Will I hear from you soon?" she asked, managing to control the trembling in her voice and maintain her poise.

"I'll keep you posted on when the depositions will take place," he said.

Managing a rigid smile, Carol moved toward the door. "I'll be expecting your call."

"Don't worry, Carol," Gregory said as she stepped out into the corridor and carefully pulled the door behind her, instead of slamming it as she felt like doing.

Fifteen minutes later, she arrived home. After dressing in a short sleeveless black flare linen lounger, she stuck her feet into a pair of two-inch black heels and twisted her hair into a makeshift bun, then headed to the living room.

She straightened the green plant sitting in the center of the glass cocktail table, and decided that later that night she would clean, since she couldn't afford the cleaning service until she was gainfully employed. *If you don't go to jail,* a quiet voice inside her whispered.

Carol armed herself with a box of Kleenex and the accusation papers that threatened to land her in jail, and sat down at the white baby grand. Softly, she began stroking the keys, and humming along to the tune of "Our Father's Prayer."

Gregory Stetson's business was good. He had several cases that he was working on, but as always when things were going great, he mused, someone had to interrupt the smooth flow. The investigator he needed to work Carol's case, to prove that she did not sign those grant applications, had decided several hours ago that he was quitting. Gregory paced to the telephone and dialed the firm that he had left to open his own business years ago, hoping that he could borrow an investigator. The sooner he proved that Carol was innocent, the better.

Gregory finished speaking to the secretary of the firm he had called, and was informed that her boss was on vacation, and she was not authorized to give the investigators an assignment. She suggested that he should meet with her boss next week. With that said, the secretary offered to set up an appointment for him.

Gregory Stetson accepted her offer impatiently and hung up.

Chapter Twenty-seven

Terrence pulled into Carol's driveway, leaving just enough room behind her sports car for him to walk between the vehicles. As he took long strides to her front door, green shrubbery and colorful flowers brushed against the leg of his black trousers.

Through the opened drapes at her living room window, he saw her playing the piano, so instead of ringing the doorbell, he knocked hard. Today, he planned to convince her of his love and hoped that she believed him.

He saw her rise from the piano bench, wearing a black wide tent dress. She moved slowly as if she was exhausted. Her hair was pulled away from her face in a twist, the same twist that she had worn and that he had unraveled the night they made love. When he could not see her through the window any longer, he moved a step back, knowing that she did not like surprises, and most likely would not open the door if she could not see his face.

Carol opened the door and he watched the surprise in her eyes, and the way she pressed her full red lips together before she spoke, as if she were suppressing a smile.

"Why are you here, Terrence?" Carol spoke after gathering her composure. She allowed herself a moment to admire his fresh haircut, and to inhale the scent of his manly cologne.

"Because we need to talk," he said.

"Come in," she said, wishing that she could turn him away and close her door, as well as her heart, to him. Instead of doing that, she moved aside, clearing the way for him to enter her home.

He towered over her, searching her face as if looking for signs that would tell him exactly why she had left Georgia without telling him that she was returning to New Jersey, Carol mused, as she lowered her gaze from his lips.

"We don't have anything talk about, Terrence."

"I think we have plenty to discuss," he said, resting his hands on his narrow hips while holding her with his eyes.

"I've already told you the reason that I left," she said.

"Did you receive my messages?" he asked her.

"Yes," she answered him, feeling as if he were giving her the third degree.

"Then why didn't you call me?" Terrence was relentless.

"Because we have reached the point where it doesn't make sense for us to continue our relationship." She began moving to the living room with him clipping her heels.

"I need a better reason than that," Terrence said, reaching out to touch her waist, when his fingers slipped and grazed the top of her hips.

She wished that he would not touch her. Doing so

only made her want to go against her will and promise to date him again. He was inside her house now because she wanted him with her, and yet she knew the only way to let him go was to tell him the truth. However, talking to him about his mother was not what she wanted to do, thinking that he would never believe that Samantha Johnson had warned her that he was romantically involved with Wanda Mincy.

"It's over, Terrence," she said, walking into the living room. She turned to him and covered his hands with hers.

"Why, Carol? What did I do to make you like this?"

Some information was better left undiscussed, especially when other members of the family were involved. Family was important to her. Her father had warned her about marrying Boris, but she'd been barely twenty years old. She and Terrence had been adults for years, and she saw no reason for his mother's prejudices, unless Samantha Johnson had been correct. "Listen." She managed a smile as she studied his handsome face. "I don't have the time for a relationship."

"I don't understand," he said.

"My father is not feeling well and he needs me," she said, hoping that he would understand.

Terrence tossed his head with disapproval. "I understand that you want to be with your father, but, honey . . ." His voice ebbed and he shook his head. "I don't agree, but I'll give you the time that you need." He backed his way to the door. "If you want to talk," he said, reaching inside his trouser pocket, taking out his wallet, and removing a personal card, "this is my home number." He took a pen from his shirt pocket and wrote his office number on the back of the card, then held the card out to her.

To keep him from observing the tears settling in her eyes, she cast her gaze down and took the card, slipping the information into her dress pocket, lifting her gaze enough to see him turn and walk out of her house.

When he was gone, she stood at the window in her living room, focusing on the park across the street, to keep from concentrating on her problems, and thinking how she had just officially broken up with the only man whom she'd loved in a long time. So she watched the lovers in the park, strolling hand in hand, stopping to exchange glances. But when a couple stopped to share a kiss, she could no longer torture herself, observing the affection that they shared. The tears that had settled in her eyes slowly ran down her face, and she sank to the floor, crying aloud for the love she could never have and the man whom she had dismissed from her life as if their love affair had been nothing more than a summer fling.

Nevertheless, her reasons for breaking up with Terrence were deeper than Wanda Mincy. She believed that if Terrence knew that she was in trouble, he would offer to help her. She would gladly accept if she could afford his services, but she also believed that if he learned that she could not pay, Terrence would probably work for free. She wouldn't accept an offer from him because she believed in paying for services and she never took handouts from anyone.

When she felt drained, as if there were no more tears, she went to her room and slept.

Chapter Twenty-eight

One week had passed and several times Terrence stopped working and lifted the receiver to call Carol. He finally dialed her cellular number, in case she was visiting her father. He hung up before the telephone rang. He missed her; however, he was willing to give her the time she needed.

When they were in Georgia, she had told him about her family, and he realized that they were close-knit people. He understood that she would want to spend as much time with her father as possible. So why did he feel that there was another reason that she wanted to break up with him other than her believing that he was in love with Wanda?

He let the question slide across his mind for what seemed like the third time that week, and leaned back, resting his legs on the top of his desk. As he stared at the plaques and photographs on the wall, and the expensive art that he loved, he began to worry. Maybe she had rekindled a relationship with an old boyfriend, he mused. Or maybe she never loved him as much as he loved her. She was so special to him, so sweet, and determined. He locked his fingers behind his head and allowed the questions that had no convincing answers to glide across his mind as he remembered the hot passion that she had ignited in him. Had she used him for her physical pleasure? He didn't know. Terrence glanced at his watch, noticing the time. He pushed away from the desk and picked up his attaché case. Maybe if he went out for dinner and a couple of drinks, he would forget Carol for at least one evening.

The Café was filled tonight, but Terrence considered that it was Friday, as he sat at the bar sipping Courvoisier and observing the crowd seated in the dining room. The conversations at the bar mingled with the low sound of romantic music and laughter that rang out among the customers.

When he wanted to be alone and not around people he knew, he usually chose the Café to wind down and take his mind off his problems. However, tonight he had another reason for stopping by the Café. Last weekend while he was out for the evening, he thought he had seen Carol. He had followed the woman out into the parking lot. When she'd turned around, he'd realized that he had been mistaken.

"Mr. Johnson, are you having dinner with us tonight?" The waitress cut into his thoughts, and he was glad because the next thought that was standing at the edge of his mind was another thought about Carol. "Not right now," he said, taking another sip from his drink, feeling the smooth cognac wet his throat.

"Would you like for me to hold a table for you?" she asked, and waited for him to answer her.

"No," Terrence said, noticing that Gregory Stetson was headed toward the bar. Gregory had graduated law school a couple of years before him and had worked with the Johnson law firm, but had left shortly after Terrence had joined his family's business.

"What's going on, man?" Gregory slid onto a stool beside him.

"Nothing much," Terrence said.

"You're just the guy that I need to talk to," Gregory said when the bartender stopped in front of him.

"Scotch, Counselor?"

Gregory nodded and turned back to Terrence. "I hope you can help me. That way I won't have to go to your old man."

"I don't know. It depends on what you need," Terrence replied.

Gregory slipped out of his suit jacket and handed the coat to a passing waitress, then cupped his hand around the short glass. "I need an investigator who's also an expert with handwriting," he said, lifting the glass close to his mouth. "I know you guys have a couple of good people over there." He tasted the drink. "I have a client that has been accused of signing some important documents."

"How soon do you need her?" Terrence asked.

"Monday morning will be great, but I can wait until Tuesday," Gregory replied, setting his drink down.

"I'll see what I can do," Terrence said, running through a mental list, deciding on Kim, whom he thought was available.

"Thanks, man," Gregory said.

Terrence lifted his drink and took another sip, draining his glass. "It shouldn't take long for you to find out who's forging your client's name. But you still owe me one."

"I've been knowing this woman for years. And I don't think she'd steal anything," Gregory said, and chuckled.

"You believe she's innocent?" Terrence asked when the bartender appeared before them.

"Would you like another drink?" he asked Terrence.

"I'll have a glass of seltzer," he said, and turned back to Gregory.

"A few years ago, I handled her divorce, and I'm telling you, after everything was settled, I wanted to ask out. But she was so upset with her ex-husband, I had a feeling that she thought all men were evil."

Terrence chuckled, and his thoughts went to Carol. He was beginning to think that Carol was thinking on those lines. "So what—is someone signing her name to her checks?"

"No, it worse than that. She's being accused of giving grants to people who don't qualify."

"And you think she's telling you the truth?" Terrence asked.

"Yeah. She took a long vacation and someone saw an opportunity to give their friends a monetary gift, I guess. But anyway, she came back from Georgia sooner than planned because her father was sick . . . and that's when she read the letter—" Gregory stopped. "As soon as I finish with her case, I'm asking her out." Gregory took a drink of Scotch. "What?" He looked over the rim at Terrence.

"Your seltzer." The bartender set the glass down, and Terrence nodded a thanks and turned back to Gregory, giving him his full attention.

"What is her name?"

"Her name is Carol. What difference does it make?" Gregory studied Terrence for a second. "Aw, man!" He slapped his hand against the back of his neck. "Come on, Terrence, man, don't tell me she's your . . . I'm sorry."

Terrence propped his elbow on the bar's counter, resting his chin on his fist. He knew that Carol was independent, stubborn, and proud, and he knew that she would refuse his help. But he had to help her.

Gregory's practice was not as large as the Johnsons' firm, but he wasn't cheap either. And he knew that she was saving for a business. He thought about that as he continued looking at Gregory who was out to get Carol for himself.

"Terrence, man, don't look at me like that. You make me think that you want to take your offer back because I was planning on asking Carol out."

"I'll take that debt that you owe me now," Terrence said. "Let me work with you." Terrence knew that Gregory was a good lawyer, but he wanted to supervise this case, because having Carol going to jail was not in his plans.

Gregory leaned back. "As long as I'm in charge."

"I gave you the investigator," Terrence said.

"Yeah, for a price," Gregory argued. "Besides, she already gave me a check."

"Hold on to the money," Terrence said.

"Are you paying for all of this?" Gregory eyed him carefully. When Terrence was quiet, he nodded. "All right, you're in."

"And, Greg, don't say anything to Carol about my assistance."

"Why didn't Carol go to you?"

Terrence took a drink of water and ignored the question. Gregory was planning on asking her out as soon as he finished the work and he wanted him to tell him why Carol hadn't come to him with her troubles. "So, how did your last case turn out?" Terrence asked, changing the subject because Gregory did not need to know anything more about Carol than he already knew.

"Aw, man, my clients were lying so bad, I thought the judge was going to put me in jail!"

Gregory Stetson's focus switched from Terrence to the entrance and Terrence followed the attorney's gaze, noticing that Carol and a fair-skinned woman with a short haircut had just walked in and were headed toward a table, escorted by the restaurant's greeter. Terrence couldn't help but notice how Carol's round hips swayed underneath the calf-length dark blue slender skirt, and how her hair fell across her shoulders. He slipped a glance in Gregory's direction and was glad that he was paying attention to his drink instead of to the women.

"Would you guys like to order dinner now?" the waitress asked Terrence and Gregory.

"Yes," Terrence said, and they ordered Reuben sandwiches.

While Terrence and Gregory waited for their food, they discussed their past works, with Gregory asking Terrence about his Georgia trial, and Terrence going into details. Finally, they discussed their favorite subject, which was sports, and in the meantime, Terrence did not miss stealing glances at Carol across the room. He wanted to go to her and tell her that everything was going to be all right. But he couldn't do that. If she found out that he had teamed up with Gregory, she would probably never speak to him again.

The waitress set their food on the counter and it was not long before Terrence was biting into his sandwich and casting Gregory a glance. Gregory would probably love knowing that Carol had broken up with him.

Chapter Twenty-nine

"Carol, who would do a dirty thing like that?" Jay asked, dunking a small cube of French bread into her cheese-and-crab dip. Jay Prescott knew that Carol was an honest person.

"I don't know," Carol said, wishing that her problems were over, but also realizing that she had to be patient. "So, how has your summer been going?" Carol asked, not wanting to discuss the case further because she would worry.

"So far, good." Jay chuckled and stuck the dip inside her mouth. "How did you enjoy Georgia?"

Jay mentioning Georgia brought Terrence to mind and it seemed that no subject was safe to discuss this evening. "It was nice," she said, and smiled because thinking of him still brought a smile to her lips.

"Okay, who did you meet—what's his name?" Jay let out a short laugh.

"I met Terrence Johnson once, when I was in Georgia

a long time ago," Carol said. "He was down this summer and we started going out."

Jay laughed. "Oh, it's about time. So, why isn't he handling your case?"

"I don't think I can afford him," Carol said, tasting the edge of a York finger sandwich, and savoring the cheese sauce and turkey ham between the crispy pastry. "Do we have to talk about Terrence?" Carol asked, not wanting to get into details right then. She was already feeling insecure with all of her confusion and problems. And Terrence happened to be one of her problems. She felt herself beginning to tense, and relaxed.

"Of course, I want details," Jay said, waiting patiently.

Carol knew it was only fair that she should tell Jay about her and Terrence's relationship; after all, Jay had confided in her when she and Trent Prescott were going through a bad time. She stalled for a short time, listening to a favorite song that reminded her of Terrence, while laughter and quiet conversation filled the room. "For a while, things were fine," Carol said.

"Until. . . ?" Jay asked in a spunky voice.

Carol focused her gaze on the salt and pepper shakers sitting in the center of the table. "Until his mother decided that I was not good enough for him, and she politely told me that Wanda Mincy was the woman he was going to marry."

"This is the man who wins all sorts of court cases, and he lets his mother choose his girlfriend?" Jay giggled.

"I guess, Jay. I don't know, and I doubt if I'll ever find out."

"I don't believe her," Jay said, dipping another cube of bread in the dip.

Carol finished the last York finger sandwich and took a sip of her pineapple cooler. Sometimes she was frightened that she would live her life alone forever. Nevertheless, she would rather have a life without anyone special to share, than have someone attempt to make her feel unworthy. "But, Jay, the bad part of all this is that I really do love him," Carol said, telling her girlfriend how Wanda had been at the boutique, and all the other details.

"Did you tell Terrence what his mother said?" Jay asked, and looked toward the bar. "Oh, he's here." Jay tossed her head toward the bar in Terrence's direction. Seeing Terrence's photograph in the newspaper and on television made him easy for her to recognize him.

Carol followed her glance and locked gazes with him, then noticed Gregory walking toward the entrance. She wondered whether Gregory had mentioned her problem to Terrence. She banished the thought, trusting that he took client-lawyer confidentiality seriously, unless he and Terrence were a team. A pang settled inside her and she calmed herself, knowing that she worried too much over nothing.

"I hope you ladies enjoy your dinner," the waiter said while he set their food on the table. "Swiss chicken cutlets for you." He smiled at Carol. "And honey-glazed game hen for you." He set Jay's food before her. "Would you ladies like another drink?"

"No, thanks," Carol and Jay said in unison, and waited until the waiter had left them before they continued their conversation.

"No, I didn't want to talk about his mother." Carol sliced the meat and put a piece in her mouth.

"I think I would've told him," Jay said.

Carol chewed slowly, feeling as if Terrence was staring at her, but she did not look. She had to forget about him. "Jay, I don't have time to think about Terrence and his mother and Wanda right now, because I have a much bigger problem," Carol reminded her girlfriend. "Enough about me. How have you and Trent been?" Carol asked.

"Carol, Granny is beside herself, and she is about to run me crazy—asking every month if I'm pregnant." Jay sipped the wine, then chuckled.

"Mrs. Lee's not getting any younger," Carol said, wiping her mouth. Suddenly her food was no longer delicious. The thought of never having her own child was disturbing enough to make her lose her appetite.

"I know, but Trent and I have planned to get pregnant next year, and not at Granny's request."

Carol chuckled. "I think I understand, because I can hardly wait to become a godmother."

"Well, I hope you're prepared, because Trent wants four children."

"You're having four children?" Carol looked up from her food.

"No, I'm having two children. Trent has a right to want." Jay's cellular telephone rang and she answered the call.

Carol could tell from bits and pieces of the conversation that Jay was talking to Trent, and from the sound of the conversation, Carol could tell that they were very much in love. Carol smothered a smile. She was happy for Jay.

Less than two minutes later, Jay hung up. "Trent says hello."

Carol continued to smile, thinking of how hard her girlfriend had had to fight her grandmother to marry the man she loved. Carol banished that thought, reminded of how much she loved Terrence and how he could have cared less for her. He wasn't even ashamed that he had used her for his physical needs. One week ago, he had walked away from her without looking back. If she was ever cleared from the trouble she was forced into, again she vowed to bury herself in her work and keep her mind free of affairs of the heart.

Chapter Thirty

Two weeks later, Terrence Johnson sat in his office, an hour after most of the lawyers had left for the day, and looked at the signatures that investigator Kimberly Wilson had gathered during the week from the company where Carol once worked. Not one signature matched those on the applications that Carol was supposed to have signed. The only thing that had bothered Terrence was that it had taken Kimberly Wilson so long to get inside of Carol's old job, since she had to apply for an application and get hired first. Gregory preferred that she disguise herself and slip around among the employees. Terrence preferred that she take the legitimate route. That way, she would not risk being discovered, which he doubted, but he wasn't taking a chance, since no one from his firm knew about this venture.

Terrence dropped the list, rose from the chair, and stretched. The last time he had seen Carol was the night he had run into Gregory at the Café. He had done everything possible to keep himself from going to her that evening and he had succeeded.

He was now about to retire to the adjoining room to his office, where he seemed to have taken up residence for the past few weeks, and stretch out on the day bed. When he was home, he did not rest well. He usually found himself awake in the early hours of the morning and wanting to call Carol or go to her. So to remedy that problem, he worked late, and when he was too exhausted to go home, he stayed at the Johnson firm.

The office door opened and Kimberly Wilson walked in wearing black tight pants, a tight waist-length top that revealed her silver navel jewel, and a pair of high heels that added three inches to her five feet two inches and made her appear lighter than her ninety-eight pounds. "Listen to what I found," she said, waving a handheld recorder, then dropping it on the desk.

"If this doesn't have anything to do with work, I don't want to listen," Terrence said. Kimberley often recorded her favorite music and shared it with him, encouraging him to purchase the CD since she knew that he loved music.

Kimberly hauled herself up on the edge of his desk. "You're gonna want to hear this," she said, and added, "Which made me think that I should quit my job over at the loan corporation and work here instead."

"I don't know," Terrence said, pushing the button and listening to the voices.

"Does that make sense to you?" Kimberly asked.

"Yes, but I don't want you to quit your job yet." He pointed at the tape. "I think it would be interesting to see what else you can find," he said, taking the small tape from the recorder and laying it on his desk. "We'll talk tomorrow."

Kim slid off the desk and was heading toward the door, when Reese walked in.

"All right, Kim," Reese said as she passed and gave him a playful punch on his stomach.

"Why are you still here?" Reese asked Terrence after Kim was out of the office.

"I don't think that's any of your business," Terrence said, picking up and putting the tape inside his trouser pocket.

"Are you sure about that?" Reese asked him. "Because you haven't stayed home but one night this week, and you're sleeping here and I would like to know if you're losing your mind."

"Who hired you to check on me?" Terrence asked.

"Come on, we're going out." Reese grabbed Terrence's suit jacket from the closet beside the door and threw it to him.

Terrence wanted to visit Carol tonight, but maybe going out with Reese was a better idea. He pulled on his jacket. "I'm ready."

Minutes later, Terrence was stretching his long legs in Reese's black two-seater sports car and within the next ten minutes they were riding passed Shanghai Gold's, when Terrence saw Carol and a man walking toward her car. He tilted his head in the direction where he had seen Carol. "Make that U-turn," Terrence said as they neared the sign.

"I thought you wanted to go out," Reese said, looking at him from the corner of his eye, but he wheeled around, heading back, thankful that the oncoming traffic had stopped at a traffic light farther back. "Now what?" Reese asked once they were in the parking lot.

"I'll see you later." Terrence got out, taking long strides toward Carol, until he was blocking her and the man's path.

Tonight was just as good as any night to mend the broken pieces of their relationship, and he hoped that he would be successful. He knew there had to be more to their fallout than the trouble from her job and one other problem he had suspected. But he needed her to verify his suspicions. Every fiber in his soul told him that he was right and he intended to know tonight what had happened while they'd been in Georgia.

"Excuse us," he said to the man who was talking to Carol. "I need to talk to her." He nodded toward Carol, keeping his gaze fixed on his opponent, as jealousy coiled inside him and raked his body like a hot pitchfork. He was a man who moved methodically. He did not approach until he felt that he had the evidence to prove his case. He had stayed awake too many nights attempting to connect the missing pieces. He had been patient, ignoring his desire to visit her. Once Terrence had believed that he and Carol could mend their differences. Now he was not certain as he watched her and the man talk in what appeared to have been a serious conversation. He held the man's gaze.

"Bretton, this Terrence Johnson." Carol introduced the men. "Terrence, this is Bretton—my brother."

"Hi," Bretton said, extending his hand. "Nice meeting you."

Terrence reached out and gave him a firm handshake. "Hi." Terrence nodded, noticing that Bretton had the same complexion as Carol and was about his height. He was wearing a serious expression and seemed protective of his sister, Terrence considered, as he sized him up.

"We'll talk soon, and don't forget our conversation," Bretton said to Carol, and kissed her cheek. Carol was a woman who kept her feet planted firmly on the ground, and Bretton did not want her to worry, but even he would have been distressed if he was being accused of a crime he did not commit.

"I'll keep your advice in mind," Carol said, watching her brother walk to his black truck. She turned to Terrence then. "Terrence, we don't have anything to talk about."

"Maybe you don't, but I do." He took the key from her and slipped his arm around her waist and began walking her around to the passenger side of the car.

"We agreed that the relationship was over," she said to him in a firm voice, then she stopped, and underneath the last rays of the sun she studied his face. He was relentless—and as determined as she was. Only, Terrence's determination was misplaced. He wanted what she could not give him—the strong passion they had once shared. But she was not free to love him.

"No, baby, I didn't agree to stop loving you," he said, his feelings of abandonment returning. He felt as if his world had been snatched out from underneath him. Added to those feelings, he felt as if he had no control over himself. She had abandoned him simply because she did not trust him, and he had Boris Myers to thank for ruining Carol's beliefs in love.

As she held Terrence's gaze, his eyes seemed to smolder, and Carol turned away. She was beginning to feel powerless, aching for his masculine touch as she watched his gaze move to her lips. However, her troubles ran deep and she understood his generosity, which meant that if he knew, he would probably want to help her. "Terrence, I'm going home."

"That's fine with me, because I'm going with you," he said, determined and unwilling to bend.

Carol sighed. Terrence in her house was not a good idea, especially since he did not have a car. She let that thought slip by, realizing that she would give in to her passion and break all of her promises. "I don't know what's so important that you think we have to talk. So, I'll go to your place," she said as his hand swept the small center of her back and she shivered. "I've told you everything . . ." she started, unable to control the warmth that slowly raced through her when he stopped her.

"No, you didn't tell me everything," he said. "I believe that something happened in Georgia, and I want to know if I'm right or not." He opened the car door and waited until she was comfortably seated inside the small two-seater before he rounded the front and sank down behind the wheel. "I'm right?" He asked.

Carol was not certain, but she wondered if Terrence knew that his mother had talked to her about him, telling her of his intentions to marry Wanda Mincy. If that was the case, she intended to hold on to her promise. She would not whine to Terrence about how his mother did not like her. "Terrence, let's go." Carol looked across the parking lot and to the water that looked like one wide sheet of silver silk spreading out from the side of the restaurant to refrain from looking at him. "You didn't answer my question," he said.

"I know," Carol replied.

"We're going to settle this problem and I don't care if it takes all night." He started the engine and turned the light switch. The panel of her tiny red car lit up.

Carol's heart fluttered, hoping whatever Terrence had to say to her or thought that he needed to know would not take all night. Because she had no intentions of spending another night with him. "I'm sure that in a matter of minutes we can solve whatever it is that's worrying you." She cast him a quick glance as they rode out of the parking lot and came to a smooth stop to wait to merge with traffic.

"We'll see," he said. Even if he'd have to grill her as if she were a hostile witness, he was going to verify the information that had been given to him.

Carol stole another glance at him in the shadows of the car, noticing how the streetlights flickered quickly against his face as the car moved at a speed she only drove in when she was in a rush. "Will you slow down?" she said.

Terrence raised up off the accelerator and shot her a cool glance. "If we don't come to an understanding after tonight, I won't interfere in your life again," he said, shifting gears. *At least not until I have gotten you out of the trouble you're in.*

"And if we do?" Carol wanted to know what was on his mind, other than him wanting her to think that he loved her as much as she loved him.

"We'll work on the problem, Carol."

When she had felt uncertain in a relationship, she had politely stated her feelings and her beliefs and never saw the man again. But Terrence was different. He was the most compelling man that she had ever encountered. And he was stubborn, determined, and seemed to want everything to go his way.

Maybe if she had taken Jay's suggestion to tell him about his mother, he wouldn't be driving her car this evening. She fiddled with Jay's suggestion as he wove through traffic, passing shopping mall strips, and liquor stores and tiny bars with red flashing neon signs, as they headed toward the suburbs.

"When I'm finished tonight, Carol, we'll have an understanding." He switched his gaze to her, and his eyes quickly traveled to her lips and back to the street, before he turned on the radio, filling the tiny car with soft soulful jazz.

Carol lost herself in the music, and began to think about the sticky situation she had found herself in. She understood that every mother loved her child; however, Terrence was a grown man. But listening to Samantha Johnson, anyone would have thought that he was a teenager, and that she was following a cultural tradition to choose his wife. Samantha was determined to steer Carol clear of her son by telling her the truth. As that thought swirled and faded, Carol snuggled back into the black soft leather and folded her arms across her chest. Even if Terrence was being honest about his feelings for her, and she took Jay's suggestion and told him what had been said to her, would he believe her? After all, blood was thicker than water and she would not want to be the reason for any tension between mother and son.

Half listening to the music and not paying much attention to the traffic, the lit buildings, and the crowded malls' parking lots, her thoughts pressed her, forcing her to remember the smug look on his mother's face. It seemed clear to Carol that the woman wanted to make her feel insignificant and worthless. Samantha Johnson's words had clawed at her confidence, scraping the surface, bringing back memories of when Boris had belittled and disrespected her. Over the years she had managed to renew her confidence, and she had no intentions of falling prey to the sharp tongue of Samantha Johnson.

"We're almost home." She heard Terrence speak to her, drawing her out of the thoughts she had been lost in.

As they circled the winding street that was lined with tall oaks rising up over white sidewalks and two-story homes that were set away from the street on perfectly manicured lawns, she turned to him, not wanting to think about her problems anymore. "Did you win the case?" she asked, watching his mustache lift with his smile.

"We won," he said, nodding his head while driving into a wide black driveway and stopping in front of the garage door.

The large two-story house was just as beautiful as the other homes they had passed, and seemed to be too much for one man, but Carol didn't say anything. She suspected that Terrence loved lots of space. She lifted her purse from her lap and got out, then watched him uncoil his long body from the small car, lifting himself to full height.

Once inside the foyer, she caught a glimpse of the baby grand through the mirror that faced the opened great room door. A huge shiny green tree rose from a wooden container, which looked like a brown barrel, standing in one corner of the foyer, towering behind the lime-green wing-backed chair. "What would you like to drink?" Terrence led the way inside the great room, with its huge stone flaxen fireplace, a circular bright blue sofa, and wide-screen television that sat in a case beside rows of books and thick albums that seemed to be filled with photographs.

"A glass of wine will be fine," she said, walking beside him as he crossed to the back of the room to the long well-stocked bar.

"Sorry, I don't have any chilled wine," he said, thinking that if he would've known he was taking spontaneous action to bring her home with him tonight, he would have chilled her favorite wine. "I have Scotch, Courvoisier . . ." He named off the drinks, while rounding the bar.

"Scotch and ginger ale," she ordered, and slid on the stool, while he dropped three cubes of ice in the glass and mixed the drink. He made the same for himself and walked around to join her.

"Carol, I understand that you left because of your father. I want you to tell me exactly what happened before you left."

"Nothing happened that you need to know," Carol said, sticking to her promise.

"Did you have a conversation with one of my family members?" he asked her.

"Yes, Terrence, Mrs. Johnson spoke to me." She took

a small straw from the container and stirred the drink while deciding to break her promise not to tell him how his mother wanted her out of his life.

"What did you talk about?" Terrence asked.

Carol looked at him through a slanted gaze. "She talked about you," Carol said. She could not keep the truth from him any longer. If he knew, maybe he would go away and stop pretending with her. Besides, she had nothing to lose. She watched the question in his eyes and decided to free herself from the burden that weighted her. She deserved a better man in her life, regardless of the magic Terrence had worked on her heart and soul. She would recover from the passion.

"What did she say?" He looked at her and waited for an answer.

"Your mother made herself clear that I was the wrong woman for you." She took a sip from the drink that Terrence had mixed perfectly. "Are you satisfied?" She watched his disturbed expression.

"What reasons did she give you?" Terrence questioned her.

"Apparently, you and Wanda are lovers," Carol said, glad that she was getting rid of at least one of the worries that was annoying to her.

"Carol, our mother has a habit of choosing the women in our lives," he said, leaning closer to her. "I love Mother a lot, but she's going through a wishful-thinking stage." He covered her hand and she couldn't resist the warmth that spread through her. "My brothers fell into her trap and both have lived to regret the choices they made." Terrence eyed Carol with an intense gaze. "I learned from watching their pain. If I don't marry you, I probably will never marry anyone," he said. "Do you believe me?"

"Terrence . . ." She stopped and glanced down at his hand covering hers. She could not ask him to wait for her without giving him a reason. But if she was convicted, she would lose him anyway. "Terrence, I can't have a relationship with you right now—the timing is not right," she said.

"I asked a question," he said, getting up, crossing the room, and returning with a small recorder. He took a miniature tape from his pocket and slipped it inside the recorder and pushed the button.

"Are you recording our conversation?" Carol asked him.

"Listen," he said.

Carol could not believe what she was hearing, as she listened to Wanda's voice, sounding as if she were having a telephone conversation. "No, girl, I didn't hook him yet. But I have his mother on my side." There was a pause in the tape before Wanda began speaking again. "Yes, Terrence was going out with a woman named Carol Grant," Wanda said then paused as if she was listening. "Mmm-hmm, but Mrs. Johnson told her how Terrence was using her for his entertainment, and that put a stop to that love affair."

"Where did you get that tape from?" Carol asked, recognizing the anger that swelled inside her, as she stared down into the Scotch.

"One of our employees left her recorder on by mistake and was in Wanda's office while she was talking on the telephone," Terrence said. "Now, are you satisfied?" He turned off the recorder, leaned over, and nuzzled his lips against the side of her neck. She shuddered from his kiss and the soft mustache hair that tickled her skin. At the same time, her body grew warm from the effects of his kiss. But if she followed her heart and her soul, she would only have herself to blame for the misery she would have allowed into her life.

She pulled away from Terrence. Kissing him was making her change her mind about not being intimate with him until she knew that she was free. Nevertheless, she was feeling much better, knowing the truth and realizing that she could trust Terrence, but still her problem would not allow her to continue their relationship.

"Terrence, I have to go," she said, reaching for her purse when he pulled her to him, molding her curves against his muscular body. She recognized his strong masculinity. "I love you, Terrence." She whispered the words against the side of his handsome face, and in return he locked her tightly in his arms. His mouth covered hers in a demanding kiss as he parted her soft full lips with the tip of his tongue. She became weak from the shimmering pleasure as his kiss caressed her. The doorbell rang, drawing them apart, and they stood clinging to one another until he slipped his hands down her back and over her hips, ignoring the sound of the ring, until neither of them could stand it any longer.

Terrence groaned. "Whoever that is better have a good excuse for being here," he said, releasing Carol from his embrace as he took long quick strides to the front of the house.

Carol decided that she should go; she hadn't intended on staying with Terrence anyway. Before he had stopped her tonight and insisted that she come with him, she had made plans to visit her father. She checked the time on her watch. If she left now, she could probably speak to him before he went to sleep. She moved toward the front of the house, hearing Terrence speaking in a loud voice. "Devon, what do you want?"

"I stopped by to see how you were," Devon said as Carol entered the foyer, seeing the six-foot fair-complexioned man standing in front of Terrence. "Oh," Devon said when he saw her.

Terrence turned around and reached for Carol's hand. "This is my brother Devon," he said in a firm, even voice. "Devon, this is Carol Grant."

"Good meeting you, Carol," Devon said, extending his hand to her, giving her a nice smile and switching Terrence a glance.

After the handshake, Carol turned to Terrence. "I'm leaving but I'll call you," she said, moving past Devon.

"Carol," Terrence called out to her. "All right, we'll talk."

Terrence turned to his oldest brother. "Devon, you'll upset a nightmare."

Devon chuckled. "Can I come in?"

"Yeah." Terrence moved aside so that he could join him in the great room.

"I haven't seen you since you were back from Georgia." Devon grinned. "But I should've called first," he said.

"That's okay," Terrence said. He was always glad to see his brother.

"What're you working on?" Devon asked. He had been back for a week, and between helping his sons choose items that they did not exactly need for school and going out in the evenings to a few clubs, he didn't know what everyone was doing at the office.

"I'm going to Washington tomorrow," Terrence said. "But I'll be back in time for the family meeting."

"I don't know if I can make that meeting," Devon said. "But if I go, I can't stay until the end."

"Why? Did you meet someone?" Terrence was curious. Devon usually missed a meeting if he had a date or made some other arrangements.

Devon grinned. "Why did I have to meet someone?"

"I'm asking." Terrence laughed. "You usually don't attend meetings on a Saturday evening if you have a date."

"I'll talk to you about it later," Devon said, and leaned against the bar. "I'll have whatever you're drinking."

"I have a few things to get straight with a few members," Terrence said as he made Devon's drink and set it on the counter. "Because I'm fed up!"

Chapter Thirty-one

By Friday morning, Carol was anxious and worried. Monday was her court date and she did not know how she was going to get through the weekend without having an anxiety attack. She had not seen Terrence since the evening she had gone to his house, but they'd had several late-night telephone conversations from his hotel room in Washington where he was tending to business. However, he promised her that he would be home by next week. He still had not told her if he was working on her case with Gregory or not, and every time she mentioned the case to him, he always changed the subject. And Gregory was not giving her the answer to the question, either. When she asked if Terrence was working with him, he gave her a surprised look as if he thought that she was implying that he could not do his job.

Carol grabbed her purse and sunglasses and headed out to her car, planning to visit her father before she took herself shopping. And if she was lucky, maybe Jay would take a lunch break and they could have lunch together.

As she drove to her father's house, she counted her blessings, thankful that week after she arrived from Georgia, he'd been well enough to be discharged from the hospital. At least she did not have to stay in jail until the trial, and because of her spotless reputation, and noncriminal background, she had not spent a day in jail.

Still grateful, she pulled into her father's driveway beside Mavis's car. Mavis had taken on private duty since she had returned home. According to Mavis, she could barely stand to look at her emergency room ex-husband, Andrew Morris, and had plans to return to work when he took his nine-month leave from the hospital. Carol considered Mavis's problem as she got out of the car. Her father's redbrick house looked as peaceful as ever, with its long windows and rich green hedges.

She stepped on the porch and let herself in. "Good morning," she said to her father, giving him a peck on the cheek. He looked strong and healthy again.

"Hi, Carol." Willie Grant spoke to her with a bright smile. "How are you doing?"

"I'm okay," she said to him. Mavis walked out of the kitchen, wearing a white uniform pantsuit and white shoes, and carrying a tray that held a glass of water and her uncle's pill. "Hi," Carol spoke to her.

"Hi," Mavis said. "I think Uncle Willie is back to normal," she chuckled, giving him the medicine to take.

"I do feel good," he said, preparing to take the pill.

"The doctor has given him a clean bill of health and released me from my duties," Mavis said, and took the tray holding the glass and the paper container that had held the pill into the kitchen with Carol following her.

"I'll be right back, Daddy," Carol said. "Take your

time," Willie said, and changed channels with the remote control.

"What's going on with you?" Carol asked Mavis once they were in the kitchen.

"Besides work—nothing," she said.

"You haven't seen Reese?"

"No, and I don't want to see him," Mavis said.

"Mavis, he can't be that bad," Carol said, thinking she had given herself a chance to trust and love Terrence.

Mavis filled a cup with coffee and gestured to the coffeemaker. "Freshly made," she said, and moved to the table while Carol poured the liquid into a cup and joined her. "You know Reese is not bad at all. But I'm afraid of him." Mavis blew on her coffee before she took a sip. "First, he's too cute, and I know all of the women are chasing him, second—he moves a little too fast for me," she said, and smiled. "And I do like him. But I can't get involved right now."

Carol understood Mavis's fears. She herself had just gotten over any apprehensions she'd had about her and Terrence. "How do you know? Have you talked to him since you've been back home?"

"No," Mavis said, "but a man like Reese usually has women chasing him. Just look at my ex-husband. He's a doctor, he looks good, and he has lots of money. Need I say more?" Mavis took another sip and settled back in her chair.

Carol understood because she'd had problems with Wanda chasing Terrence. "What time are you leaving here today?" Carol asked.

"I'm leaving around noon, because I have to pick Mother up from the airport. She wants to visit with Uncle Willie."

"I have to thank Aunt Christine for her support." Carol smiled.

"Tanika is back in town. She has found herself a job at a boutique near the mall," Mavis continued.

"Back?" Carol was surprised. " I didn't know she was here," Carol said.

"She came up shortly after I left Georgia," Mavis said, telling Carol how Tanika had run away from her jealous live-in lover.

Carol and Mavis talked for a while longer over their coffee and made a date to go out that night. When they were finished planning where they would go for the evening, Carol went to visit with her father for a while and then call Myers' Research Center to see if Jay was free for lunch and learned that she was out of town for the day. However, Jay was expected back in the office by five o'clock that evening. Carol left a message, asking if she would like to go out with her and Mavis that evening. Carol also understood that Jay was married and it might not have been possible for her girlfriend to get away for the evening on a spur of the moment notice. Instead of going to lunch, Carol went shopping to keep from worrying about her court date and all the things that could go wrong and land her in prison.

At six o'clock, Carol answered Jay's call. She agreed to meet her and Mavis at the club for an evening of fun.

Around eight-thirty that Friday evening, Carol arrived in a cab, meeting the women at one of their favorite places on the outskirts of town that catered to the thirty-and-over crowd.

The club was illuminated by dim lights, casting a warm glow over the room that was filled with well-dressed women and men who were sitting alone or with their lovers. Then there were other groups who seemed to have had the same idea as herself, Jay, and Mavis.

Carol ordered the first round of drinks and settled back. "All right, these are the table rules," she said.

"We will not discuss our problems, no matter how much we would love to," Carol stated, realizing that she was the only woman at the table who was in trouble.

"And Jay is not allowed to flirt, because she's a married woman," Mavis added, and the women laughed.

"You're right, Mavis," Jay said, and raised her glass in a toast. "Girls' night out," she said. The clinking sound of glasses lightly striking together mingled with the music, making a joyful sound among the women.

"Carol." She recognized the voice and hoped that she was not hearing who she thought was calling her name. She held on to her glass and looked up.

"Yes, Boris," Carol said, her eyes traveling over his dark suit, to his face that had not changed much with age. It seemed that he was more handsome at forty-five than he was when she had met him. However, she doubted that he had changed much over the years.

"Can I have this dance?" he asked, holding out his hand.

"No, thanks," Carol breathed. He was the last person she had expected to see tonight, but she was not surprised.

Boris pulled back the extra chair and lifted Carol's purse from the seat and handed it to her. "You ladies don't mind if I sit down?" He sat before anyone could answer him.

"Boris, I mind that you're sitting with us. This is our night out and we don't want an intrusion," Carol said to her ex-husband.

"So, now I'm an intrusion," Boris said snidely.

"Please!" Carol was almost beside herself, and tonight she did not mind being rude. "Everyone at this table is out to have a nice evening. So go away. We do not need you with us."

"Sounds like you women have some jealous men,"

Boris said, cutting his eye at Carol. "So, did you get married again?"

"Is there a bouncer around?" Mavis asked, looking at Jay.

"I don't think so, but I'll make the suggestion before we leave tonight," Jay said, her arched brows pleated as she looked at Boris.

"Okay, I'm going," he said. "But we need to talk soon," he said to Carol.

Carol had nothing to talk to Boris Myers about. Matter of fact, she had never wanted to see him again, and this was her first time seeing him in years.

"We have nothing to talk about, Boris," she said when she noticed Wanda moving slowly to a table and making eye contact with her.

"Can I have your phone number?" he asked as he rose from the chair.

"No, Boris. Good night," Carol said, glad that he was leaving her. She had just gotten over all the pain and distrust she had allowed him to cause in her life, and was finally able to love again.

"I wonder why old dead-beat husbands don't show up until you find a new love?" Mavis asked when Boris had left them.

"Girl, don't ask me," Jay said. "Because I intend to stay married to Trent forever."

Carol did not know, and she did not care. "Who knows," she said as she kept a close watch on Wanda.

Carol, Jay, and Mavis drank, laughed, and talked until after midnight. "Ladies, I hate to cut this night short, but I'm going home," Carol said, rising from her chair. "I'll talk to you ladies next week," she said.

"I'm going, too," Jay said as she and Mavis joined Carol.

Carol stepped outside into the cool September evening, and turned on her cellular and was calling a cab when a strong hand grabbed her arm, whirling her around. "Terrence, I thought. . ." She looked at him, not liking the way his dark eyes shimmered. "I didn't expect you until next week," she said, wondering how *he* could be upset with her and acting jealous when he was headed into the club at this time of the night.

"I have been home for a couple of hours," he said, walking her to his car. "When you didn't answer your telephone, I stopped by your place to see if you were all right." He stopped and opened the door to the Mercedes and waited until she was inside.

Wanda had been the only person that she'd seen and known in the club tonight who probably had not minded her own business and called Terrence. Carol felt her anger rise as Terrence slid in beside her. "And who was that guy you were with tonight?" he asked as they eased out of the parking lot.

Carol heard the suspicious edge in his voice. "So, you're having me watched?" she asked, turning to him and noticing that the hard line in his jaw matched his eyes.

"I'm asking the questions," Terrence said as they headed toward her house.

Carol didn't speak because she was angry, and when she was angry, she sometimes said things that she later regretted.

"So what—you're going into a coma on me now?" Terrence gave her a slanted glance.

"I was out with my friends," she said.

"And who else?" As always, Terrence was relentless with his questions.

"Terrence, the man you're talking about is Boris," she said, wanting to end the interrogation that was turning into an argument, when she noticed his hand tightened against the steering wheel. The quiet tension that had built between them seemed to thicken. She knew that he was angry and she wondered if whoever had called him was satisfied.

"You listen to me, baby," he finally said as he pulled into her driveway and cut the engine and the lights. "I'm not sharing you with Boris Myers. You got that?" He reached back and lifted an overnight bag from the backseat.

"I would like to know who had nothing better to do tonight except to mind other people's business." Carol opened the door at the same Terrence was getting out and they met at the hood of the car. "After everything that I have told you about Boris, you have the nerve to think that I would go out on a date with him?" Carol snapped the questions as she unlocked the door and stepped into the warm glow that filled the foyer. "Anyway, you and I are just friends. Therefore, you have no right to get upset with me regardless of whom I talk to."

"I don't want a friendship," Terrence said. "I want what we had before."

"We can't be lovers," Carol said. "Not now."

"Because of Myers?" Terrence snapped back.

"Will you stop talking to me about that man!"

"How am I supposed to know? You were married to him once," he replied with a tight-lipped smile as he stood at the edge of the stairs.

Carol did not want to fight with him. She wanted to welcome him home instead, but Terrence was being ridiculous. She brushed past him and headed up to her room with him moving behind her, brushing against her hips. And as angry as she was at him for sounding insecure, she couldn't deny the warmth that spread through her. She reached her bedroom and headed to the closet, discarding her clothes and taking a short black gown from the rack. When she returned and was on her way to the bathroom, she noticed that Terrence had changed into a pair of black pajama bottoms and was staring out of the bedroom window lost in deep thought.

The bathroom door opened as she was patting her face dry. Terrence leaned against the doorjamb, watching the short black silk gown that barely covered the top of her firm thighs. He could not help but remember Gregory's call to him, bringing him up to speed on what was going on with Carol's case. When he told Gregory that he was on his way to visit her, Gregory told him that he was at the club and had seen Carol with two other women, and he didn't leave out the information that Carol was with a man, and he thought the guy might have been her ex-husband. Terrence remembered how hot he had gotten as jealousy had settled inside him like hot coals.

Carol dropped the towel in the hamper and brushed past him. She wanted to stroke his wide bare chest, but she was angry at Terrence for listening to gossip. She got into bed and turned out the light, and ten minutes later, she heard the bathroom door close and soon felt Terrence's weight settled against her bed until he was lying beside her.

Carol could not stand the silence between them any longer. She turned to him and stroked his chest. "Will you stop being angry over nothing?" she said, tracing an imaginary line over his smooth skin, when he caught her wrist and drew her to him. Terrence raised up on his elbow. "Just for the record"—he leaned into her and touched her lips—"I'm not sharing you with any man," he said, smothering the words against her lips.

Carol slipped her arms around his neck, feeling as if her blood had suddenly overheated and crawled through her veins. "Terrence, you have nothing to worry about," she said when they drew out of their kiss, and before she covered his mouth hungrily again. Her heart pounded in her chest as his lips touched hers. And she began to feel tingly all over when he circled his strong arms around her waist, drawing her beneath him and rising and kissing every inch of her body, sending her into a heated frenzy.

Carol was sure she would never be the same again, but then she was not sure about anything, since most of her thinking was jumbled and delirious. She seemed to have been reeling and swirling, and she wanted to speak. But nothing she said to Terrence was making sense to her.

Terrence reached to the nightstand, taking the thin pack, and proceeded to protect them. When he had finished doing that, he took his time peeling away the short black gown. Carol rose to meet him, and they sank into their feverish private world that was only meant for—and belonged to—them.

Time seemed to stand still as they skidded along rocky paths, climbing and slipping, and grasping to stay in the throngs of passion. His hands brushed lightly against her hips, sending pure pleasure and fiery sensations through her. Terrence wrapped her in his arms and they experienced a rhythm and harmony as they reached the peak of pure pleasure, and swirled off their axis. And then, as if magic had struck, they found themselves slowly spinning again until they exploded and slid out of control to the real world.

They lay wrapped in an embrace, basking in the glow of sweet love, as Carol dozed. As she fought to stay awake, she could not stop herself from pondering the aftermath of their love and what was she going to do if she was found guilty and lost her freedom and Terrence all at the same time. "Terrence."

"Hmm," he groaned.

"I love you, but I'm in a lot of trouble and I don't think we should make love again until we know whether or not I'm going to jail." She waited for him to answer her, and when, after several seconds he was still quiet but breathing softly, she called him softly again.

"Baby, stop worrying, you're not going to jail."

"How do you know?" She pulled away from him and sat up in bed, planting her hands on her hips, and watched him turn over on his stomach. "Huh?"

"I know—I think," he said, moving in and out of sleep, until he was awake. He didn't want to say much or even agree with her, since he was not supposed to know that she was in trouble.

"What do you mean . . . you think you know?" Carol stared at him.

"I don't know." He buried his head in the pillow and then rose. "Baby, I don't want to talk about work tonight."

Carol braced her fists firmly on her hips and continued to stare at him. Then she lay back down. "Terrence."

He answered her with a soft snore.

Carol lay awake for a long time, wondering what Terrence was up to. Maybe nothing, she pondered, rising up on her elbows and watching him sleep. She could not imagine that he knew about her problem and did not mention the trouble that she was in. Carol straightened and rested her back against the headboard, watching the shadowy light from the streetlamp band a dim light against her cream walls as her questions continued to haunt her. Terrence had been away a lot since he'd returned from Georgia. He probably didn't know. With that thought in mind, she snuggled close to him and slept.

The next morning, she woke and he was gone. She read the note that was stuck to his pillow. "Baby, will you marry me? Love, Terrence."

* * *

Six-thirty Saturday evening, Terrence crossed his parents' wide driveway and ran up on the porch, letting himself inside with his key. The house was quiet as usual except for the low classical music piping through the speakers and the ringing telephone that sat on the foyer's table. He ignored the sounds and pushed open the door to the study where the majority of his family members were mingling and discussing some issue that did not interest him.

"It's about time you got here," Samantha said as she pressed her hand over the skirt of her slender black dress and took a seat at the long oval table. "Where is Devon?" She cast Terrence a disapproving glance as if he was his brother's keeper. "I couldn't tell you," Terrence said, nodding a hello to his father and Reese who were both dressed in dark suits, and checking his watch, before he noticed his aunt Martha entering the room from the back door.

"Terrence, how nice it is to see you," Martha said, her rosy cheeks rising with her smile.

Terrence moved around to the table and pulled out a chair for her. "When did you get here?" he asked, as he made certain that she was seated confortably at the table. "I've been here for about three hours." She patted his hand. "You know, I am going to be the center of this meeting tonight."

"Really?" Terrence's expression grew serious as the others gathered at the table and Devon walked in. He wondered who had done what now, other than his mother who had taken it upon herself to meddle in his personal affairs.

"Oh," his aunt said, "I don't think my problem is such a big deal . . . but you'll know soon enough."

"Now . . ." Samantha started to say, when the door

opened again and Wanda crossed the room and sat beside her. "My dear, you're early. We're not leaving until another hour."

Wanda smiled and cast Terrence a sensual glance.

"As I was saying," Samantha continued. "Aunt Martha is having an operation and will not be able to live in her home while she's recovering." That statement brought about several grumbles from the family members.

"What kind of surgery are you having aunt Martha?" Terrence asked.

"I'm having hip surgery dear," Martha said, giving him a nervous smile.

"How are you feeling now?" He asked with concern in a low voice.

Martha's smile faded. "I'm ..." she began, when Cornell's booming voice interrupted her.

"Why can't she have a nurse to care for her?" Cornell spoke up.

"Because, Cornell, her home is going to be under construction for a few months." Samantha explained to her husband.

"Excuse me, but I think I'll wait until the meeting is over and then you can tell me what you decided," Martha said in a sweet, quivering voice. Reese rose and helped the seventy-five-year-old woman out of the chair and to the entrance that led to the living room. When he returned, Samantha continued.

"I was trying to think where could she live until she recovered," Samantha looked around the room at all the faces.

"Mother, convalescence works," Devon said.

"No, that's not a good idea. She won't be happy," Samantha said.

"Then she can stay with you and Daddy," Terrence

said, getting an idea of where his mother could have been going with her decision.

"No," Samantha said. "I was thinking that she could live with one of you guys." Samantha cast a glance at Devon.

"No, that won't work. My sons are over once a month," Devon said quickly, eyeing his mother as she turned to Terrence.

"You have been so rude to me lately, I'm afraid to ask you anything," Samantha said.

"I love her, but she can't stay with me," Terrence replied.

"Reese?"

He was about to say no, when Martha pushed open the door. "Have you made a decision?"

"Reese?" Samantha looked at her son.

"All right," he said, dryly, and accepted his aunt's hug and kiss that left a red ring of lipstick on his cheek.

"It's settled. Aunt Martha will recover at Reese's house. Does anyone else have anything to discuss?"

"Yes." Terrence rose from his seat, and before he began, he assisted Martha to a chair, then turned to his mother. "Mother, I'm not being rude, but I have watched you control everyone's life."

"Now, Cornell, he's being rude. Just look at his face," Samantha said.

Cornell raised a finger to his wife, motioning her to be quiet.

"You have controlled everyone's life. You chose wives for my brothers but I'm here to tell you that you will not choose a wife for me." He cast a sharp glance at Wanda.

"Don't tell me that you're still pining over that woman who's on her way to jail."

"Not if I have anything to with it," Terrence said,

switching his gaze around the table, knowing that he had everyone's attention.

"She stole money from the company that she worked for and you have not given up on her yet?" Samantha said.

"How do you know?" Terrence asked.

Samantha shrugged. "Her troubles are in every newspaper and I believe she has done all that she has been accused of doing." She nodded at Wanda.

Terrence felt his anger rising and his face was hot. "Let me tell you this. I am going to marry Carol if she will have me."

"And disgrace this family?" Samantha snapped.

Terrence avoided her gaze for fear he would give her a disrespectful stare. "I love Carol, and if I can't marry her, for whatever reason," he said, casting a glance at Wanda, "I'm not marrying anybody."

"I wish I knew what that ridiculous woman said to you to make you disrespect me!" Samantha almost shouted her words at her son. "She's poor, she has no class and to prove that—she's a thief!"

"Samantha . . ." Cornell's voice ebbed.

"Yes, honey, I think Terrence is right," Martha said.

"He's not right." Samantha Johnson touched her finger to her rouged cheek. "Not one of my sons in his right mind would ever date—not to mention carry on a love affair—with Christine Hart's niece"—she looked at Terrence—"or her daughter." She glared at Terrence.

Terrence pushed his hands into his trouser pockets and looked out across the room, not seeing expensive and colorful art on the walls, or the fresh flowers that were delivered daily, or the shelves filled with law books. He had stirred up a ruckus and he knew it, but this was the only way he knew to get his point across. He was tired of tiptoeing around this issue. This was his life and he was going to love whoever he wanted to love.

"You know, Samantha, you were not always wealthy," Martha said, glancing around the room. "If Cornell would have married Christine Hart, you would not have had all of these things."

"Aunt Martha, this does not concern you," Samantha said as her sons switched their gazes from one to the other, and then all three looked at their father but stayed quiet.

"You knew that they were engaged when you moved down the street from Cornell."

"How dare you come into my home, after I have tried to help you, and this is how you thank me? You embarrassed me in front of my children." Samantha's voice shook with tears.

"Was just telling you the truth. I haven't seen those girls in a while, but the last time I spoke to Christine, they were well educated and living nicely."

"Aunt Martha . . ." Samantha spoke in a strained voice.

"Samantha, she's telling the truth," Cornell said.

"Oh, I see. Now you have turned against me!" Samantha said, crossing the room and snatching a tissue off a shelf and wiping her tears while Wanda went to comfort her.

Cornell pushed away from the table and stood. "Terrence, you have my blessings to marry anyone that makes you happy, son."

Terrence nodded and sat.

Cornell turned to Samantha. "I have watched you over the years. And because of the respect and love that our children have for you, Devon and Reese almost ruined their lives. You leave my sons alone!" With that said, Samantha ran from the room and Cornell slipped into his suit jacket and walked out, his sons clipping the backs of his heels.

Nine-thirty that Saturday night, Carol's doorbell rang. She left the sofa where she had been flipping through the pages of her crossword magazine looking for a good puzzle to work on, and opened the door for Terrence. Before she could get the door open wide enough to allow him entrance, he pushed the door open and gathered her to him, holding her as if she would escape him.

"What's wrong, Terrence?" she whispered. Because of his tight embrace she could hardly speak much louder.

He didn't answer, but instead gave her another tighter squeeze before he released her enough to touch her lips with his and slowly cover her mouth with a heartfelt kiss. When he finally rose up, she studied his handsome face. "What is wrong with you?" she asked, pushing him at arm's length.

"Are you going to marry me?" he asked, instead of answering her question.

He let her pull him inside the living room and push him down on the sofa. "You know that I'm in trouble, and don't tell me that you have not heard or read about the lie that my boss is accusing me of." She pushed at the shoulder of his suit jacket and he rose and wiggled out of one item of his clothes.

"I still want us to get married, and it would make me feel really good if you say yes and start planning the wedding."

Carol gave him a playful punch and sat down beside him. "I'll have to wait to see what is going to happen to me," she said to him and watched as he loosened his tie and unbuttoned the top button of his shirt. If he could not be her husband, he would live his life as a bachelor. "I—" He started, when his telephone rang. He reached for the jacket that was lying on the sofa's arm, took the telephone from the pocket, and answered the call. While he talked to Gregory, he watched Carol go to kitchen, and shortly afterward, she carried a tray filled with a bottle of wine and two glasses upstairs.

Terrence finished his call with Gregory and went up to join Carol on the sofa in her bedroom. He wished that he could tell her that Gregory had filed for a motion to have her case dismissed because of the information that the Johnson's firm investigators had found. But he could not disclose his information for fear that Carol would break up with him for assisting her without her paying a fee. "Now, I'll answer the question you asked me earlier," he said.

"Please tell me what was going on with you." Carol smiled and made herself more comfortable on the sofa, folding her legs beneath her.

"We had a family meeting tonight, and I let everyone know that I love you and that I'm prepared to marry you if you'll have me," he said.

Carol wondered how his mother had taken the news, but she didn't ask. "I'm still not free to give you an answer" was all that she said. Terrence seemed determined to have her accept his proposal, and until she knew whether or not Gregory had requested an order for dismissal, and the order had been accepted by the judge, she would not agree to marry Terrence.

"I guess I'll have to wait for you," he said, lifting the wine to his mouth.

"Terrence, I don't want to come between you and your family."

He set the glass down and leaned into her. "Nothing or no one will get in our way." He searched her face. "Do you understand me?"

She parted her lips to say yes, when he wrapped her in his arms and captured her with a light feathery kiss. His embrace and sweet kiss sent a trail of delightful shivers through her and she deepened the kiss, drinking the sweetness from his lips. Another shiver raced through her as his strong fingers worked on her spine, as if stroking and tapping the ivories on his baby grand. When she could stand no more of the fire he was building inside of her, she slipped off the sofa and led him to her bed.

The dim golden glow of the bedside lamp welcomed them, casting a warm glimmer over the white sofa, glass cocktail table, and the large plants that nestled in two corners of her room. While she slipped open his shirt buttons, he removed from his pocket a silver protective pack, dropped it on the bed, and unsnapped his trousers. She pushed the smooth silk shirt over his shoulders and feasted her eyes upon his wide, hard muscled chest, before he slipped the black lounger over her shoulders and peeled away the lace bra and matching panties. Without warning, Terrence lifted her into his arms and lay her upon the king-size bed, crouching over her, smothering a burning path of hot kisses between her breasts to the center of her stomach, and to the tops of her thighs.

Terrence Johnson ignited a fire that she knew would take more than their kisses to extinguish. Bliss quaked her and she wanted him more as he touched her heart and soul.

She touched his jaw with her lips, feeling the soft hair against her skin. Her heart pounded in her chest as wanton thoughts raced across her mind. He wasn't making it easy for her not to want him as he stroked tender strokes up and down her spine, making her want him more than she had ever wanted any man. Her breathing became uneven. She leaned away from him, cupping his chin in both her palms, and eased her lips to his, kissing him with such passion, she knew that she would marry him tonight, and if she had gone to jail, she would never miss a meeting to make with him. Carol rolled her head from one side to the other, shutting out the thought that threatened to ruin the passionate moment. She inched from beneath his crouched body and drew him to her, and to replace her thoughts, she kissed him hungrily. Carol realized that she was acting like a love-starved woman as she kissed every inch of his strong body, filling him with amorous sensations as soft laments slipped from his parted lips. She rose to search his face, aware that she had chosen a strong and powerful man, when he dragged her to him and turned her over, covering her with a caress that reached the center of her soul. She felt as she were spinning on an axis of pure unabashed love.

Terrence heard his breath catch in his throat, and she felt her body swirl as she received the burning pleasure of a world that belonged to them. As always, they climbed a rocky mountain to gratification, exploring and caressing, and slipping in and out of every magic pleasure point, until her blood inched through her veins like hot liquid. Her heart rose to meet the scorching iron searing her like smoldering fire, burning and singeing, until they reached their peaks and slid recklessly back into the real world. They clung together, rocking back and forth, basking in the golden glow of pure passion, sleeping and waking again, spiraling up a path of pleasure and careening away from reality. He filled her soul and she was aware that she could never let him go because he was like medicine to her once-distrustful soul. The delirious thought moved across her mind as she skidded in and out of floods of joyous electrifying passion.

In the warmth of drowsiness, she could not deny the

fact that she was completely satisfied with her choice to love him. She had to admit that he was special, as she savored the strong curves of his muscular body against her. How she had gotten so lucky was beyond her, but her luck had not come without a price, a cruel voice in her mind reminded her. She would not worry. She scooted closer to him, resting her hips against his hard flat stomach, and slept.

The next day she and Terrence went shopping at the sports store to buy her a pair of skates before they drove to the skating rink, a place that she hadn't gone to since she was a teenager. "Terrence, I don't know if I remember how to skate," she said as they entered the building and he paid the fee. "If I break a bone, I'm holding you responsible," she teased while they sat on the bench. She pulled on a pair of new black skates, while Terrence stuck in his feet into a pair of worn leather skates that looked as if he'd had them since he was a teenager.

"I'm a responsible man." He chuckled. "It's just like riding a bike, baby. Once you learn, you never forget."

Carol wasn't sure if this was true for her as she stood and held on to him for support for a short while. Finally, she felt her balance and they held hands, at first gliding slowly around the rink to the warm-up and practice music.

"Hey, Mr. Johnson. What's up, man?" A young man who looked to be around twenty called out to Terrence as he and the girl he was skating with whizzed passed them.

"You got it going on, man," Terrence called back.

"Don't tell me that this a habit?" Carol asked, wondering if Terrence skated often.

"That guy was in my Big Brothers club," he said as they glided around the rink, passing other young men and ladies who knew Terrence.

"Are you still a member?" Carol asked.

"I'm no longer an active member, but I make dona-
tions," he said. Then the music started again, and a
man's strong voice blared through the loudspeaker.
"Grab your partner!" Carol knew it was time for serious
skating when the music changed to a faster rhythm.

"I think I need to sit down," Carol said, as visions
of breaking something that she might need later that
evening came to mind.

"Hold my hand," Terrence said, reaching and covering her hand with his.

She felt her strength and was doing just fine, until
suddenly a young boy headed in her direction, going the
wrong way. She was going too fast to stop, but Terrence
reached out and caught her hand. "Easy, baby," he
said, as he caught his balance and drew her to him.
"We need to get out of here. There are too many kids,"
he said, as they rolled to the bench and sat down to
take off their skates. Carol agreed with him silently as
she removed the skates and admitted to herself that she
had enjoyed the short time she'd spent on the rink.

They stopped off at the restaurant down the street to
eat lunch, ordering Philly cheese steaks and ice-cold
drinks while they a good conversation. It was then that
she glanced over his shoulder and saw Wanda giving
her a heated stare. Carol looked away and went back
to listening to Terrence telling her how he had won the
case in Georgia.

"Who was the real killer?" Carol asked, and glanced
back at Wanda whose gaze burned into her.

"Some guy from another town," Terrence said.

"You didn't know that when you took the case, did
you?"

"No, but I didn't think that my client was guilty,
either, otherwise I wouldn't have taken the case." He
bit into his sandwich and chewed slowly. When he was

finished eating, he took a sip of the cola. "I still haven't taken my vacation, so when this is over with you, I think we need to go away."

"That's a wonderful idea, and it's also wonderful that you are so sure I'm going to be found not guilty."

Terrence was quiet now; he didn't want Carol to know that he had his hands in the middle of her defense and his team had all the information he and Gregory needed to have the case dismissed.

Carol and Terrence spent the rest of the day in the park, lying on a blanket after lunch. They didn't talk much, but watched the ducks swim and glide smoothly in the pond, and she couldn't help but think how the beautiful fowls made their movement look easy, which reminded her of her life now. Others saw her as being calm and cool but beneath the surface she was a bundle of raw nerves, afraid for her life because of an evilness.

Terrence rose up on his elbow, leaned over, and kissed her cheek, loving her more than he could imagine. She was definitely the woman for him and he had helped Gregory to do everything in his power to make sure that she was free. "Why don't we get married while I'm on vacation?" he suggested again.

She couldn't think about marriage today or tomorrow or next week, when she was being burdened with the problem of probably never seeing him again after the trial. Although she would love to be his wife, she couldn't promise him anything. "Can we wait before we discuss marriage again?"

Terrence suspected that Carol was worried, and again he wished he could tell her what pertinent information had been found that would free her, but his hands were tied. "All right," he said, lying back down. He could hardly wait until Gregory told Carol their plan, and he would anxiously await her day in court.

* * *

Two weeks later, Carol rushed into Gregory's office after receiving a call from him the day before. She could not imagine what he wanted. All he had told her was that if everything went as planned, the news would be good.

"How are you?" Gregory asked her when she walked in and sat without being invited to a chair.

"I'm okay. What is the news?" she inquired and composed herself, resisting the nerve to get her hopes up only to be let down and have her day ruined, so she sat still and barely breathed while she waited for him to speak.

Gregory rested his arms on the chair handles and rolled back, resting his head against the black leather back, and held her gaze. "Due to some evidence, we—I—found concerning your case, I filed for a motion to dismiss."

"What did you find? Do you know who . . ." Her voice faded and she didn't know whether to laugh or cry. Her world was beginning to seem brighter and she felt much better as she listened to Gregory explain to her if they waited to go to court, it would probably take several months. Since he had the valid proof, he saw no need to prolong, and all he needed was for the judge to accept the motion. "Oh my God!" she whispered, "thank you."

Gregory pushed himself closer to his desk and grinned. "Don't celebrate just yet." He pushed back and stood. "I will meet you at the courthouse Monday morning at nine o'clock—don't make us wait."

Carol reached for his hand and gave him a firm shake. She knew she could not celebrate, but she could not keep the good news to herself. She thanked Gregory again and hurried from his office to her car. As soon as she was behind the wheel, she called Terrence and he was in a meeting, so she left a message with his secretary. Her next call was to Jay, and of course Jay wanted to celebrate that evening, but Carol refused. She wanted to make sure that Gregory was successful before she drank champagne to her freedom. Carol decided that she would wait to tell her father. He was recuperating well from his bout with high blood pressure, but she thought it was best not to say anything to him until after she had gone to court. And if the news was as she expected, she would inform him, otherwise she would wait.

Eight-thirty that evening, Terrence called her. He sounded exhausted, but he was happy for her and assured her that he didn't think she had anything to worry about. He told her that he did not think that he would be back from his meeting in time to attend court with her, but he would see her later. Carol placed her lips close to the receiver and made a smacking sound and Terrence returned her kiss.

Monday morning, Carol thought she was going to have an anxiety attack while driving to the courthouse. She worried that her black suit was not too sexy. The skirt was calf-length and her jacket covered her hips, but maybe she should have worn a blouse that buttoned to the top of her neck, instead of being barely able to tie the blouse at the vee of her jacket.

By the time she reached the courthouse parking lot, her worries had partially subsided. She caught a glance of Gregory's car and hurried inside to meet him. He looked even more distinguished than ever, dressed in a black suit and light gray shirt.

"You're right on time," Gregory said when she hurried toward him. "Let's go inside," he said touching his palm to her elbow.

The courtroom was cold, chilling Carol's skin, and

she pulled her black jacket closer around her as she glanced over at Gregory, who seemed to be comfortable. Carol suspected that maybe she had a chill because she was nervous . . . and afraid of what might happen to her.

She turned and looked over her shoulder, seeing her aunt Christine, Mavis and Tanika, and Jay. She smiled and turned back to face the empty bench and waited for the judge, when Reese sat beside Gregory. She raised her hand and covered her mouth to keep from speaking. Nevertheless, she figured that her suspicions were right. If Reese was with Gregory, then Terrence had had his hands all over her case. She let out a sigh of relief, knowing that maybe her case would be dismissed after all.

"All rise!" the bailiff announced, bringing the soft murmurs to a halt as the judge took his seat behind the bench.

Court began and Gregory presented his findings to the judge, motioning for a dismissed case against her, and all Carol could do was sit and listen to the evidence and proof that were being presented. Wanda and her cousin Paul had set out to destroy her and have her go to prison—they both had forged her signature. It was then that Carol remembered having seen Wanda in Paul's office a few years ago.

Carol hugged Gregory when the hearing was over and thanked Reese before she went to join her relatives and friends in the hallway. With tears in her eyes, she gave them each a hug for their support and belief in her. "Okay, I've made lunch reservations at the Café," Jay said.

"But, Jay, how did know we would have anything to celebrate?" Carol asked her.

"When I saw Reese Johnson sit beside Gregory, I went outside and made a reservation."

Carol smiled and shook her head. She would wring Terrence's neck later, for lying in the bed pretending that he could not answer her questions when she asked him whether he was working with Gregory. But first she would love him.

An hour later, they finished their lunch and Carol thanked everyone for their support and went to visit her father, telling him the wonderful news. He was as happy for her as she was for herself. They talked for a long time and finally she went home.

She had not been inside her house five minutes when the telephone rang. "Hello?" she answered and listened to Terrence's soft warm chuckle.

"How does it feel to be free?"

"Terrence, why didn't you tell me that you helped Gregory?"

"Because if I'd told you, we probably wouldn't be having this conversation." He chuckled again. "Listen, I'm leaving my meeting tonight for St. Simons Island. Would you like to join me?"

"Yes," Carol said, smiling.

"You'll have your ticket tomorrow," he said. "Carol."

"Yes?"

"I love you," he said.

"I love you, too." She smiled, as tears smarted the brim of her eyes. "Terrence, thanks for helping me."

"You're welcome."

Terrence Johnson's St. Simons town house rose up over the ocean and had a perfect view of the island. Tiny white lights shimmered against the water like diamonds sitting on turquoise silk, and Terrence and Carol were in love and finally at peace.

"Terrence, do you still want me to be your wife?"

Carol straightened from her comfortable leaning position against the veranda.

He gathered her away from the black rails and into his arms, and his warm chuckle floated out to her. "Are you sure that you want me for your husband?"

"Yes," she whispered as he moved out of their embrace.

"I'll be right back," he said, heading inside.

She waited for him, enjoying the cool evening breeze and her newfound happiness.

"We need to take care of some unfinished business, baby," Terrence's voice cut into her thoughts and she turned to him. He brushed his lips against hers with a feathery kiss before taking the gold bracelet from his pocket and slipping it on her wrist. "I'd planned to give this bracelet to you while we were in Georgia but you were mad at me . . ." his voice trailed off and he smiled down at her.

"Thank you," she said, touching the bracelet, remembering the expensive jewel from Christine's boutique, and how angry and jealous she had been that evening, when she glanced at Terrence, noticing that he was reaching inside his pocket again.

"I thought I'd save the best for last," he said, reaching out for her hand. "Carol, will you marry me?" He brushed his lips against hers with a feathery kiss.

"Yes!" She whispered, admiring the beautiful diamond engagement ring that Terrence was slipping on her finger. Once the ring was on her finger, she circled her arms around his waist and hugged him tight.

He brushed his lips against hers with a feathery kiss.

"Yes!" She hugged him closer to her.

"If you don't have a particular date in mind, can we get married while we're here . . . ?" He spoke close to her lips.

"I would like a Christmas wedding," she said, touching her lips to his.

"Christmas," he agreed, smothering the word against her lips.